MONTANA MIDNIGHT

Also by David emil Henderson:

DEADLY DIVIDENDS

MONTANA MIDNIGHT

A Novel

BY DAVID EMIL HENDERSON

Pine Tree Arts
Penn Valley, CA USA

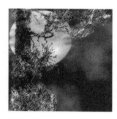

Pine Tree Arts, P.O. Box 129
Penn Valley, California 95946
www.pinetreearts.com
First Edition April 2011
(Revised with new cover, October 2011)

Pine Tree Arts is the creative division of
Pine Tree Press of Penn Valley, California, USA.

The characters, places, events, and all things in this book
are fictitious or used fictitiously. Any similarity to real
events, companies, places, or persons living or dead, is coincidental and not intended by the author.

Cover featuring Scott and Kristen Arnold, photographed
by Kevin Luoma at Blue Sky Cabins, Red Lodge, Montana.

Cover Moon image (altered): NASA

ISBN 978-0-615-47301-7

*This book is for Lance
and Kevin and Tammy*

and all our good times together in Montana

Spring 2011

MONTANA MIDNIGHT

Chapter 1: The Book Starts Here

DR. ROSCOE FULLER slogged through the snow on ancient wooden skis with leather bindings. These suited him.

Doc himself was a relic, well past eighty, his complexion coarsely woodgrained. He scorned the flashy fiberglass trappings that whished past him on these Montana slopes — young skiers, showing off like peacocks.

Wanting solitude, Doc traversed the hill until, finally, he was alone. The only sounds were creaking wood, his own hoarse breathing, and his thumping old heart. Here he stopped.

The air was dense with snow — not falling, but hanging against a vague but tremendous landscape. Among the visible details were midget treetops poking head-high above the snowdrifts. Because all the other mountains were thickly staked with tall timber, visitors often asked about these immature pines. Doc always said it was a long story and he didn't have time for it.

Doc shuffled forward, debating his route. He could take an easy slope called Miami Beach. On spring days, it was the choice of beginners and ski bunnies wearing cut-offs and halters.

Doc knuckled his nose and snorted.

Or, he could take the plunge, straight down Nathan's Trail. That connected with Powderhorn, then Grizzly Gulch. None of those were intended for old men on wooden skis with leather bindings. He wiped snow off his goggles and said, "Eh, the hell with it." He took Nathan's Trail.

From a distance, Doc's tumble looked like a human cannonball ricocheting from one mogul to another. The left ski broke away and went lancing over the snow toward the towers of Lift #2. The Ski Patrolman, believing this to be the worst wipeout he'd seen all season, launched himself down Nathan's Trail and skidded to a halt that slugged Doc with about eight pounds of flying snow.

"You meathead!" Doc roared, flinging snow off his face. "The hell's wrong with you!"

"Hey, sorry, man. You okay?"

"Crap." Doc gritted his teeth, realized that this goon with an insignia on his parka was the ski fraternity's angel of mercy. He chewed on his cold lips and tried to move his left leg. "Hell, it's broke. Don't just stand there like a dumb ape! Get me the hell down from here!"

The Ski Patrolman jerked out a Motorola handset and radioed for a sled. He said he had an old guy in bad shape, calling him names. Better get the county ambulance... and try finding Doc Fuller...

"Asshole!" Doc yelled. "*I'm* Doc Fuller!"

"Cheez, Doc. I'm sorry. With the goggles, I didn't recognize you... "

Doc ripped the goggles off. "Dang fool things — can't see worth a pounda shit."

The Ski Patrolman got busy, removing his own skis and staking them in an upright criss-cross. He said, "I've been trying to catch up with you for a week, Doc. About a project I'm working on."

Doc squinted at him. Despite the growing pain in his leg, he was curious. "Have I met you before?"

"No sir, not up close. But folks have pointed you out, and I called you on the phone a couple times."

"Oh, I see. Are you the fella who's been runnin' all over town with one of those laptop computers?"

"Uh, yes sir."

Doc waved a hand. "I try not to get within thirty feet of those damn things."

Confused, the Ski Patrolman raised his eyebrows and shifted his stance.

Doc said, "You know, they got all those gigabytes of RAM! Zillions of electrical thigamabobs flying around in there at the speed of light. And you put all that right down onto your lap! Ain't you afraid it'll make you sterile?"

The Ski Patrolman's expression was bemused. "Uh, no sir."

Doc said, "Never mind. Unnnhh! Listen, you got any morphine or some such? This fracture, it's killing me."

"Sure, Doc. I took the full EMT course." The Ski Patrolman shrugged off his pack, sorted through it and retrieved a syringe packet.

"EMT. Good Lord, gimme that." Doc snatched the kit, tore it apart with his teeth, assembled it, jammed the needle into his thigh. He said, "I hear you been asking everybody about the year Nineteen Seventy-four."

"Yes sir."

"I assume you mean the good old days."

"Uhh..."

"Let me ask you," Doc said. "What do you know about the 'Seventies? Were you born then?"

"I was," the Ski Patrolman said. "Right in the middle of the decade."

Doc was beginning to go slack from the morphine or whatever. Nodding, he said, "Did you ever hear of Watergate? Streakers? The Symbionese Liberation Army? The energy crisis? Did you know we had Daylight Savings Time in winter? Little kids stumbling their way to school in the dark? Our President flying commercial instead of Air Force One, just to save a little fuel?"

"I heard about Watergate," the Patrolman said. "The energy crisis — wasn't that from an Arab oil embargo?"

Taking a deep sigh, Doc slumped back onto the snow. "The talk was that the world was runnin' smack out of oil... none left by the time you grew up. All this comes shortly after Vietnam and National Guardsmen shooting college kids in Ohio... So next we get all this radical environmental business, young people gettin' violent over air and water and resources..."

For a moment it seemed as if Doc Fuller had lost consciousness. The Ski Patrolman stood and searched the up-slopes for signs of the rescue sled.

"A lotta families wanted to get out of the cities," Doc said suddenly. "Run to places like Montana to get their kids away from the drugs and disruptions. Well, 'Seventy-four was when the disruptions got here…"

"That's what I want to know about, sir." The Ski Patrolman hunched down. "My father was killed here, then, before I was born. In a manhunt. In a blizzard. My mom still doesn't know why. But people say you know — even about the politics, not just what was in the newspapers about the big ski project and the… disruptions. They say you know more than anybody, because everybody confided in you… So that's why I wanted to talk to you… uh, Sir?"

But Doc had conked out.

***

Dr. Roscoe Fuller didn't know the Ski Patrolman; didn't know any of the new bunches that started coming ever since the ski hill opened; didn't care to know. The one young man Doc Fuller had cared about was Nate Chambers.

Trying Nathan's Trail was like getting tangled with that fellow all over again — a man who, like his namesake trail, was carelessly groomed, shaggy on the edges, noted for all sorts of challenges.

For a man with Doc's memory, it wasn't so long ago when some men from afar had glanced at Jackpine, Montana, and decided this hardstrapped old town on the edge of the Rockies would be a proper location for a ski resort.

The subsequent turmoil had affected many lives only to a small extent, only a few lives to a great extent.

Among the few was Nathan Chambers, a young Vietnam war veteran with a pregnant wife, chosen to be mayor of Jackpine at the precise moment when the troubles had begun, when a Learjet had dropped from the blue and rattled the town out of its doldrums...

***

Doc opened his eyes.

They were sliding him into the ambulance, his leg in a splint. The Ski Patrolman was still there.

"Hangin' in there, Doc?"

"Oh sure. I'm perfectly comfy, thank you."

"Uh — say Doc. I've been meaning to ask. Those little trees, you know, up on the mountain where you were skiing... "

Doc scowled. "Young man, that's a story. I don't think I got time for it right now."

They slammed the rear doors and shifted the ambulance into gear, and Doc Fuller went back to dreamworld.

PART ONE
THE LEARJET

Tuesday, July 2, 1974, Approx. 4:35 P.M.

Chapter 2: Jackpine, Montana

THE LEARJET came like a blade, cutting long white contrails across the hard blue Montana sky.

On board, Hal Dexter became delirious watching the plane's shadow as it cavorted along evergreen slopes and across flower-strewn meadows. Necktie loosened, vest popped open, fingers sticking like nails into the armrests, he appeared much the same as when he crouched behind his desk at the Wisconsin Trust in Milwaukee — tense and seemingly on the verge of motion sickness.

Dexter jerked his attention to the other passenger and said, "Joseph — for God's sake, where the hell are we?"

His companion sucked a cigar and grinned. This was Joseph L. Bartz, senior partner of Bartz and Bates, Inc., an investment firm in Arlington Heights, Illinois. After three hours in flight, his ponderous body seemed squashed into the seat, his neck sinking into folds of flesh stacked from his yellow collar to his pink mouth. "I'd imagine," Bartz said, "we oughta be over the south-central part."

"The south-central part? Of *what?* Jupiter?"

"You know — *Montana.*"

"I *don't* know Montana. Everything looks just so *remote.*" Dexter crossed his legs and wagged a skinny ankle. He peered again through the porthole. Now that lunatic shadow was leaping from granite cliffs to slanted ledges, all crusted with summer ice. "For an hour, I saw nothing but grass and gullies. Now it's peaks and canyons. Not one road. Not one structure. Not a *utility pole* in hundreds of miles! Nobody *lives* down there, Joe. Nobody!"

"Well, hey, I took you the scenic route. It's *God's* Country. The *Big Sky* state. Sure, it's got mountains. You wouldn't stick a ski resort in some place like Kansas, would you?"

"No, but I'd hope to keep it on the same planet. Jesus, we need *some* amenities. Phones, plumbing... some electricity perhaps?"

The co-pilot instructed them to buckle-up; they were about to land.

Dexter stiffened. "*Land* he says?" His eyes swept the stupendous peaks and canyons. "Land *where?*"

Bartz, struggling with his seatbelt, made a grunt and said, "It's called Jackpine. It's got a population of fifteen hundred and an elevation of fifty-five hundred. It's got an airport with a four-thousand-foot paved runway. The airport sits on a bench of land — they call it a *bench*, it looks like a cutting board from up here. But it's okay. It's sufficient."

"Christ," said Hal Dexter, shriveling down. "I *hope* so."

***

Not far south of Jackpine, on a craggy slope in the Custer National Forest, a four-man volunteer rescue team was rope-handling a litter, lowering a young rock climber with bloodied face and shattered leg. The victim's companions and a gathering of deputies and forest rangers were waiting in a clearing at the foot of the slope, amid a cluster of four-wheel-drive vehicles parked randomly askew.

The shadow of the Learjet passed over them all in a dark

blink.

"The hell is that?" One volunteer on the slope hesitated, eyes scanning the sky. "That was like a jet! A small one, down low."

"I seen it," said the man behind him. "It was a corporate jet like you see on TV, and it was headin' straight for Jackpine. Had its wheels down, too. "

Looking for it, a third volunteer wasn't careful of his footing. Loose shale slid away beneath him, dropping him on his fanny. He yelped, and all hands grabbed as the heavy litter skidded downward, its injured passenger going frantic.

Only one of the volunteers managed to save the litter — and the life of its occupant. The man was tall and rangy-looking, with sweat beading his thick brows and stubbled cheeks. He took charge of the ropes from the rear, looped the coils around his hips and across his right shoulder. He spiked his boot heels into the slope and held on while the others regained their footing.

Nathan Chambers seethed over everyone's clumsiness but said nothing. He needed his oxygen to hold the litter.

Once up, the third volunteer thought again about the plane. "Say, why'd you suppose a fancy jet like that would come into old Jackpine? That airport, it's just for old beat-up crop dusters, like Pete Hawkins flies. Ain't that right?"

"Hell," said the second man. "The Forest Service has used that airport for those C-47s when they're fightin' fires."

"What's that got to do with this jet?"

"I'm just sayin'. *Anything* could manage to land at Jackpine, if it had to — for a bad enough reason."

"Well, it seems this is more special. It's like somethin' to make note of, like when we write down the dates of big storms. In fact, what *is* the date, exactly?"

"July the second of 'Seventy-four," someone said.

From behind them, the tall man spoke out with a tremble from doing all their work. "Dammit, I wish you guys would *haul freight*. It'll be 'Seventy-*five* before we get down from here... and I think the kid's fainted."

***

The Learjet bounced twice off the runway, reversed thrust, and shuddered to a halt just twenty feet short of toppling off the bench and, perhaps, smashing through the roof of the Jackpine hospital's wing for long-term geriatric patients.

In the sudden quiet aftermath, deliberately unsticking his fingers from the armrests, Hal Dexter said, "Sufficient?... This, Joseph, is what you call sufficient?"

The pilot, on the intercom, said, "Sorry, guys. Didn't see the cows on the runway until the last second."

"Cows?" Dexter said to Joseph. *"Cows?"*

Joe Bartz, busily brushing away the cigar ashes that had rained all over his lap and stomach, said: "Well, after all, Hal... at least we're not under attack by Indians."

***

The aircraft's hot tires clipped weeds poking through the runway and rolled to a stop near the hangars. After a minute, Hal Dexter was the first to clamber down. He found the thin air hard to breathe, the quiet unbelievable. He gazed at the ramshackle hangars and at the weathered lean-to that served for an airport office. A windsock hung straight down, symbolic of the lack of activity here.

Dexter turned as Joe Bartz waddled off the steps onto the asphalt. "Joe," Dexter said, "this place is a joke. I can't believe you're serious. Look at it! Do you expect to attract two thousand skiers a day — to *this?*"

"Like Brigham Young said, 'This is the place.' And Hal — the desert he was talking about is now Salt Lake City."

Dexter lifted both arms and dropped them. "From this, you'll be lucky to get Peoria."

Bartz sighed. He shaded his brow with a pudgy hand and searched westward. The airport bench above Jackpine was a good vantage point for viewing the misty ramparts of the Rockies. "There," he said, pointing. "Look for a camelback hump, to the left of those limestone palisades."

" ...Seriously?"

"Yes."

Dexter's lips were drawn tight as he squinted. The sun was brilliant and hot against his tender face. "That, uh, camelback hump," he grumbled. "Next, you'll tell me that's our fabulous ski mountain."

Bartz started walking, short arms flapping. "I grant you, Hal. From here, it's no Matterhorn. But take it from me, I've been on top, and it's grand." He spread his arms as wide as they could reach. "It's ten thousand feet high, broad enough for thirty chairlifts. And it has a view, like... you'd swear you were in heaven."

"A view? Of what?"

"Hal, listen to me." Bartz came over and patted Dexter's stiffened shoulder. "Right here, you see," Bartz said, "we're standing at six thousand feet, halfway up that mountain. The top is maybe eight miles away. So, you can't get a perspective. But from there" — he thrust a hand towards the top — "you can see all across the Great Plains. You can see at least a hundred miles."

Hal Dexter seemed not even mildly appeased. "If you told me we could see the Chicago skyline, that might have been slightly interesting. But a hundred miles of plains?" Dexter pumped at the air with both fists. "Good grief, Joseph! There's probably not even a cow-town in that hundred miles. Where the hell is Jackpine?"

"A few steps. Follow me."

Perplexed, Dexter trailed Bartz to the rim of the bench, looked down — and there it was.

"Well?" Bartz asked.

Dexter's eyes panned the narrow valley, evidently cut by a prehistoric glacier and deepened by a river which, now, was reduced to a creek roughly the width of the two-lane highway that paralleled it.

Along that highway and spreading six to eight blocks on each side were quaint wooden houses and false-front stores, a few gasoline stations, a grain elevator, bulk storage tanks, railroad freight station, cement plant, lumber yard, and some squarish stone buildings that might be the courthouse, school, and Masonic Lodge. The streets were quiet and lined with Chinese elms, mountain ash, and native pine trees. It all looked as peaceful as any place on earth.

"Well?" Bartz asked again.

"All right, it's charming," Dexter admitted.

"The city folk will love it!" Bartz insisted. "It's a bit run-down, maybe — falling apart since they shut down the coal mines in the 'Forties. But it'll come back. A boost from us, and it'll bounce back like Aspen, maybe even better."

"And all the citizens will be rich and happy, I suppose," Dexter muttered.

Shrugging, Bartz said, "Well, not everyone. This is an old town, and certain kinds of people don't want it to change. But don't fret about that. Most of them are eager for change. They're desperate for jobs and money."

Dexter looked around. "If that's the case, why are we still standing here? Where's the desperate man who's supposed to meet us? Where's the goddamned desperate car?"

Bartz had seen it approaching along the bench road in the distance, a station wagon trailing fine dust from its tires. He gave Dexter a gentle pat. "Patience, Hal. This isn't your rich and glittering insurance empire. This is *Montana*."

Chapter 3: Nathan Chambers

THE TRAIL-SCARRED green Jeep jerked around the corner onto Broadway and rumbled up against the curb. Overhead, an old faded sign dangled from rusty chains: W.W. Chambers Hardware And Ranch Supply Company.

Immediately, the driver cut the ignition and ordered the rattling engine to quit. "Whoa, you goddamned teakettle! Stop, you bastard piece of scrap metal!"

The engine died with a gasp, and Nathan Chambers, sweat-stained and dirt-mottled, pounced onto the pavement. Energetic strides took him to the door of his father's hardware store, which he unlocked and kicked wide open. "Hello! Anybody here?" He waited; heard nothing.

Back to the Jeep, water-blue eyes squinting in the sun, he reached for his straw hat when around the corner came a Forest Service pickup loaded with tired men in back and Dr. Roscoe Fuller riding shotgun. The rig held still long enough for Doc to climb down, dusting off his hands, thanking the others for help with the rescue. As the pickup pulled away, Doc came over and said, "Meant to thank you especially, Nate. Now how about it? Need help? Unloading?"

"You grab the climbing tools, Doc. I'll get the ropes." It was then that Chambers noticed he had smudged the white crown of his hat with fingers dirt-caked and bloodied from the climb. "Dammit all to hell, Doc. Look at that."

"Oh sure. It's what you get for helping somebody," Doc said. "Durn fool-ass kids. They had no business climbing that rock without a guide. Happens every summer, though." He started hauling ropes from the Jeep.

"I said *I'd* get those," Chambers insisted, reaching.

"Back off! You did enough." The ropes were heavy and Doc tottered under the weight, aiming his jaw at the remaining tools. "Don't stand there, Nate. Come on. Ass in gear."

"Christ Almighty, you are stubborn." Nathan plugged his hat over his thicket of hair and gathered the tools. He led Doc Fuller to the back storeroom, where they dumped their loads more or less where they belonged, on the floor. There was a fluorescent light and, under it, Doc's face looked like crinkled foil, creases in all directions. "Now then," Doc grunted. "I'm thirsty as a sailor. Let's go snort a few beers."

"It'll take me a minute," Nathan said. "Pops hasn't come back from Billings. I should check out the cash."

Doc shrugged. "Mind if I look at the trout flies?"

"Go right ahead."

While Doc browsed, Nathan punched open the cash drawer and sorted a meager collection of bills, checks, and IOUs. Listing them on a deposit slip didn't take half a minute. He slapped down the pen and gazed up. An amber glare hit the plate glass window from the boarded-up storefront across the way. With a sigh, he stuffed the money into a bank pouch and zipped it shut. To himself, he muttered, "It's sure promising to be a long winter around here."

"Indeed," said Doc, suddenly there. "Too bad you were closed half a day."

"Yeah, well... " Nathan tipped back his hat. "It's been like that anyway. The town's in a slump like I've never seen."

"You haven't lived long enough," Doc said. "I seen it go like this at other times. Boom or bust. Today, it's the fuel prices. Farmers can't afford to run their equipment. And your tourist trade is down, on top of it."

"I know it." Nathan switched off the lights. "Nowadays I look for fix-up chores around here. Just anything to keep from going crazy. Dad, he hardly comes to work — so we don't have to stand in here and stare at each other. Makes me wonder... if maybe I'm more burden than help to him."

"You had college, right?"

"Engineering degree, you bet. Worth dirt in Jackpine." Snatching the pouch, he went for the door, Doc following.

"What brought you back, after Vietnam?" Doc asked.

"Who knows, Doc?" Nathan paused and rubbed the gritty back of his neck. "I suppose the peace and quiet here — after all the damn noise over there."

Nathan slammed the door hard enough for the stubborn latch to catch and hold. His strength sent a shockwave up the storefront and swayed the old sign.

"Nothing else?" Doc persisted. "Holding you here?"

"Well, Mom and Dad, I suppose. Old pals like Russ Bancroft... "

"I mean, that engineering degree — you must've had something in mind."

Nathan Chambers had sad-looking eyes, heavily browed, but these were contradicted by a wide smile that cut through his sandstone cheeks like a chisel. "Well, if you must know, Doc... I was plain damned scared of moving to places like California, where you get drowned in people. If you know what I mean."

"I know the feeling. Around here, at least, you can feel kind of important."

"Important? Yeah, well." Nathan laid a fist on Doc's shoulder. "Here, maybe I could make a difference. If all us younger guys started drifting away, this old town would dry up. Then what?"

Doc nodded. "Come on. Let's you and me go have a quick one." He nudged Chambers toward the Olympia Beer sign a few doors down. "I got a proposition for you — maybe could make your day."

Chapter 4: Harold 'Hal' Dexter

MAYOR SHERMAN ARMSTRONG pulled the eyeglasses
down his sloping forehead and studied the little white card.

*

The Wisconsin Trust
Harold J. Dexter
Senior Vice President
Operations

*

The lettering was embossed in silver, and there was no
address or telephone number. *Thinks he's too important to be*
bothered, the mayor thought. He dropped the card on his
well-worn desktop and looked up. He saw a corporate
pipsqueak who reminded him of the little devils who used
to own the mines: narrow, smooth-shaven face; stern eyes
accustomed to decimal-point details; neatly trimmed hair
speckled with gray; expensive gold watch; starched white
cuffs. Then he shifted his gaze to the chunky fellow wearing
a cashmere blazer and a yellow shirt. "And who's this?"

"My project consultant," Dexter said. "Joseph Bartz, of
Bartz and Bates, in Chicago."

"Actually, Arlington Heights," Bartz said, extending a
hand.

The mayor traded limp handshakes without getting up. He waved at a pair of wooden chairs, the only other furnishings in the office above the fire station. "Sit down," he said.

Dexter dragged the chairs across the bumpy linoleum to the front of the desk. As he sat and carefully arranged himself, he glanced at the murky yellow walls. An American flag tacked up behind the mayor was the only sign of officialdom. A Burlington Northern railroad calendar fluttered in a light breeze from the open window.

"It's good of you to see us this late in the day," Dexter said, offering a friendly smile.

Armstrong eyed the two men mildly. "Got nothin' better to do," he said. "What in hell is The Wisconsin Trust?"

Dexter continued smiling. "Life insurance, mainly. But don't worry, sir. I'm not here to sell you a policy."

"At my age, I couldn't afford one. What *do* you want?"

Dexter pursed his thin lips. "Well, it's getting late; so I'll try to be brief. My company, The Wisconsin Trust — we've been tinkering with many, uh, diversified investments, frequently in partnership with other companies. We're into car rental agencies, for instance. And hotels and resorts. In fact, right at this moment, we're working with Mr. Bartz here" — he nodded at Bartz — "on what might be called a pet project. It's something that could put your little town back on its feet again."

The mayor leaned back, his swivel chair creaking, and wiped a thick hand across his nose. "Dear me. What sort of project?"

"Well... " Dexter restored his smile. "A winter ski resort, in fact." He waited to see how the mayor would react.

Armstrong said, "Is there such a thing as a *summer* ski resort?"

Dexter chuckled. "That's very good, Mr. Mayor." He shifted on the hard chair. "I presume you're aware of Wapiti Mountain? Eight miles up the North Fork creek?"

Armstrong's mind flashed back to days when he and his father had hunted elk on Wapiti's broad slopes. "I guess I'm aware of it," he said.

"Well, then. Maybe you know — almost the entire lower half of that mountain is privately owned. And we have acquired an option to buy it. It's a superior location for a ski resort."

"Oh, I see," the mayor responded. "Just the lower half, though."

"Well, no. Naturally, we intend to get a Forest Service permit to use the upper half — the public land."

The mayor grunted. "Uh-huh. Naturally. Um, if you don't mind my asking, why are you bringing this news to me?"

At this moment, Joseph Bartz hunkered forward on his chair. His face reminded Armstrong of a slice of white bread, flat and pitted, his closely cropped hair like a thin brown crust on top.

"Mr. Mayor," Bartz said. "We've come to you — well, basically, for your advice. And your support. You see, this whole project depends on Jackpine itself. This is a charming town. It's quaint. Skiers love that. But it's a matter, you see, of whether it would cooperate in serving as the base community. That's the crucial question. Do you know what I'm saying?"

Mayor Armstrong narrowed his eyes behind his spectacles as he listened to this. "What do you want from us?" he asked.

"Simply your cooperation and your support," Bartz said. "Hopefully, maybe even your enthusiasm. That sort of thing."

"Uh-huh." Armstrong again wiped his nose. "You don't want any money?"

It was Dexter who answered. "That's not why we're here. But if you're interested, I should mention that we have nothing against local participation. In fact, we see our project as just the beginning of a new period of prosperity for you."

"Well, I doubt that," Armstrong muttered.

Dexter folded his hands between his thighs. "Well, consider what's happening elsewhere. There's a global energy crisis, and you are literally surrounded by coal. In a weakening economy, you are within a few miles of the Free World's largest known supply of platinum — of *untouched* platinum. These resources will attract increasing interest, exploration, eventual development. That you can be sure of." Dexter nodded, encouragingly.

"Uh-huh," Armstrong said. "So where do you fellas fit into all that other business?"

"For now? We simply expect to be here, with you, when things begin to happen. *Encouraging* those things to happen — by attracting wealthy people here. Our ski project will do that, and then we can be your partners in a brighter future."

"Partners?" Armstrong asked lightly. "With little me?"

"With your entire community," Dexter said flatly. He began to doubt whether he was getting through. "Mayor Armstrong, I do hope you take us seriously."

The mayor brought his large hands down flat on the desk and leaned forward. His swivel chair snapped. "I always take these things seriously — all these damn schemes to exploit this town."

"Oh, really? *Schemes*, Mr. Armstrong? Obviously, you don't understand... "

"But I do!" Armstrong, eyes level with his hunched shoulders, stared directly back into Dexter's pupils. "We've had these ski proposals before, Mr. Dexter. Starting back in the 'Forties. There's lots of burnt fingers in this town. So don't expect no red-carpet welcome. Let me warn you, in fact. You go askin' these folks for money — well, you're liable to get tarred and feathered and booted to Wyoming."

Bartz reacted quickly: "Mayor Armstrong — let me be clear. We did not fly out here on a private jet to beg your poor citizens for donations. Whatever happened here in the past, it has nothing to do with us. Why, we've already spent a ton of money just on studies. And we're damn well prepared to spend a few million more just getting things off the ground. We've... "

"My *companion*," Dexter interrupted, "is impetuous, but he's stating facts. We have ample resources available to pursue this project. And we have held enough meetings with high-level Forest Service officials, in Washington, and getting their assurances, so that we're absolutely confident that *nothing* stands in our way, from a legal or policy standpoint."

"Then if you're so all-fired confident," Armstrong said, "go right ahead with your project. Who's to stop you?"

"No one will *stop* us, Mr. Mayor," said Dexter. "The point is, we had hoped to *cooperate* with the people who live here. And we had hoped for cooperation in return."

"You keep saying that," Armstrong said, "and I still don't know what you want. What *kind* of cooperation?"

"Well, for instance," Dexter said, "when it comes to getting the Forest Service permit for the upper mountain, there'll be public hearings, and... "

"Ah-ha," the mayor said. "You're afraid the town might raise a stink."

"Maybe," Dexter admitted. "Who can tell? There may be a few eccentrics around. People who'd stand in the way of Jackpine's prosperity, for their own selfish motives. Or for just no reason at all."

"I see. Yes." The mayor looked pensive for a moment. "Well, gents. This is all mildly interesting, I got to admit. But I just don't see that it should take up any more of my time." He pushed back his chair, ready to stand.

This took both visitors by surprise. "Mr. Mayor," Bartz said, perplexed, "we haven't... we've barely started to discuss this. You haven't seen any of the plans. Considering the importance to your community, and your responsibility, your influence, your... "

The mayor lifted his shoulders and laughed aloud.

Then, noting their expressions, he said, "I'm sorry, gents. Ah, me... Listen, Mr. Dexter and — ah, Bartz is it? Yeah. Well, I'm afraid my so-called influence, it's about as big as a gopher's nuts, to tell the truth. Besides, I'm quittin' tonight. In a few hours, Jackpine will have a new mayor."

Dexter and Bartz remained speechless as the mayor chuckled and swept a few items from his desk and pocketed them. "Excuse me now," he said. "I got to stop at the grocer's before supper, pick up my wife some cabbage."

"That's sweet," Dexter remarked. With a sideways glance at Bartz, he gathered up his briefcase. "Would you know," he said to the mayor, "who your replacement will be?"

"No idea," Armstrong said. He waited while Bartz struggled to his feet. "Although, you might stop at the Chambers store in the morning. If Chambers ain't the new mayor, he could steer you to whoever we stick with the job."

Bartz put out a moist hand. "Well... I'm sure the town is going to miss you," he said. "May I wish you happiness and success, in your future?"

"In my future," the mayor said, "I'll be dead. Thanks anyway."

Armstrong waited at the door until after the men had left. He heard them clattering down the stairs, muttering angrily to each other. Still curious, he stepped gingerly to the open window and peeked out. On the street, the men were climbing into a green Ford station wagon — with woodgrain vinyl paneling that was fading and peeling.

The mayor immediately stopped grinning. He knew that car, knew it too well. He certainly did not like seeing those two men ride away in it.

***

As the car proceeded along mainstreet, Dexter ignored this chance to inspect the town, and he stared at the back of the driver's head, an unkempt nob of thin gray hair. The hands on the steering wheel had begun trembling slightly, a delayed reaction to the news about the mayor's resignation.

"Well, I'm sorry about that — truly sorry," the driver said. "Sherman didn't tell me. He... often plays close to the vest."

"But you are *expected* to know these things," Dexter insisted. "That's what we pay you for."

"*Oh?* That... wasn't my understanding," the driver said.

Dexter was fuming. "Then, by God, let's *get* an understanding. That was a *humiliating* meeting back there. I felt like an unprofessional and uninformed nitwit, ridiculed by a small-town politician. I expect from now on that you will keep us informed about absolutely everything. We've got a *fortune* riding on this town, mister. If the mayor quits or his wife takes a crap, I want to know about it, down to the details of the color and odor. And damned quick!"

The driver said nothing.

"Is that clear?" Dexter demanded.

The driver slowed his car. He said, "What you're asking — it extends beyond our original agreement. It could lead to a conflict of interest. And that could put me in jail."

Dexter drummed his fingers on the armrest. "If that's a problem, I'm sure we could find someone else."

The car seemed to be drifting of its own momentum. Then the driver shook his head. He said, "No, I wouldn't suggest that. Perhaps... I might manage, somehow, to keep us all satisfied."

"You do that," Dexter said.

Chapter 5: Tavern Talk

INSIDE THE BAR, among dozens of Olympia Beer signs, it was dark and quiet except for the snick of a pool cue and the clunking of balls rolling into pockets. Nathan Chambers and Doc Fuller had bellied up to the bar and ordered Olys and, for awhile, had stood savoring the ice-cold brew in serious silence.

Now Doc hoisted a foot to the rail and located an elbow on the bar. He had closely spaced eyes which routinely probed for tiny clues to people's ailments. He focused them on Nathan and said, "Well, young fella. You found a wife in Jackpine. So, maybe sticking around wasn't an altogether bad idea."

"You're right there, Doc." Of all places, Jackpine, to meet a gorgeous female like Valerie Ensign. His mind sorted images of her abundant chestnut hair, her sleek shape and confident hazel eyes.

"You wouldn't figure, looking at her," Doc said, "that she'd be the daughter of that frazzled old army colonel."

Nathan nodded over his beer. Arnold and Geneva Ensign had transplanted their daughter fourteen times during the colonel's military career, to some of the world's most forsaken places, and a few of the most desirable. And then they retired on a ranch near Jackpine.

"However they did it," Nathan said, "her folks gave her the right stuff."

"You can say that again." Doc hoisted his glass in toast. "In all the right places, too. She feel comfortable here? Settled finally?"

"I guess. You have to remember, though — the last place she lived was near San Francisco, Doc. Green there year-round. Temperature always mild. She wore high-fashion clothes. Had friends living in places like Hillsborough, with views overlooking the bay. You know what kind of place that is? Hillsborough?"

"Where Patty Hearst was kidnapped?"

"That's it. It's rich as cream, Doc. Rich as cream."

Nathan cocked back his head and glugged down the rest of his beer. He said, "Her first winter in Montana. Valerie helped her dad pull a calf from a cow, one trapped in deep snow, in a ditch. They used block and tackle, and chains on the critter's feet. Messy business... Well. That cow died there. Died under their hands, making God-awful sounds. And then they kept the calf by the kitchen stove. They bottle-fed that maverick, cleaned up after it, 'til they found another cow that would accept it."

"Far cry from 'Frisco," Doc said. He motioned to the barstools, and the two of them sat. Nathan swiveled to face Doc and continued the conversation.

"There were nights out there when the power went off. And the wind shook the house like an earthquake. And it drove smoke down the chimney and into the parlor. One morning, they woke up and found all the trees in their yard had split and fallen, from the weight of ice and snow. All through this, Valerie... she just pitched in. She was afraid to leave her folks during their first year of retirement."

Nathan grinned suddenly. "Retirement, hell! They had bought this three hundred and twenty acres with irrigation, and they ran eighty head of Black Angus. The worst kind of cattle for being ornery. And old Arnold — hell, he's not old, just looks it. Well, he hadn't been on a ranch since he was eighteen. Geneva, not since she was twenty. Valerie, never. The neighbors were... well, you know that kind of contempt they have for greenhorns who make a go of it. They were downright thunderstruck when the Ensigns hung in there... and made it pay."

"Then you come along," Doc said.

"I sure did. Now Valerie's stuck here. She can't go back to California... or anywhere else." He licked the rim of his glass. "Anyway, I think — maybe both of us think — well, we ought to raise our family up here. Kids need to grow up where there's some room. And close to nature, I guess."

"And away from drugs," Doc noted.

"That, too."

Then Doc held up two fingers for another round. "How many you plan to have?" he asked, his voice professionally curious.

"Beers?"

"No, kids."

Nathan hesitated a beat before answering. "Depends on how the first one goes. Valerie tells me, Doc — you're not altogether confident."

"Hell, Nate. Don't you two get me wrong on that." Doc began pouring his second, a long golden stream tumbling into the glass. "She's not built for child-bearing, not like those women with wide hips. So there could be difficulties. But that don't necessarily mean she can't have a couple. She's slender but strong. Like a ballerina."

Nathan pictured her long legs. More like a showgirl, he thought. "You can't hardly tell she's pregnant, she's so slim."

"Well, that'll change," Doc said.

Behind them, someone smacked a cue against the rim of the pool table and cursed loudly.

Doc ignored this, changing the subject. "Here's my idea. You ought to join with me on some property I own, down by the creek." He aimed a thumb in the general direction. "I'm planning to subdivide it. Maybe put a par three course along there. Professional men from Billings, they're looking for property like that for weekend cabins. It's a damn good investment, Nate."

Nathan polished off his second beer. "I'm sure it is, Doc. Doubt very much if I'm in a position, though."

"Force yourself. Hell, Nate. In order to live in Jackpine and make enough money for a family, a man's got to develop property. There are damn few alternatives."

Nathan scratched an eyebrow, swiveled to face Doc directly. "You watch the news last night?"

Squirming on his stool, Doc said, "About as much as I could stand. I saw where the House Judiciary Committee decided to handle Nixon's impeachment hearings behind closed doors — those bastards. They want our votes but they don't want us to know what in hell they're doing!... So, okay... Down in Argentina, old Juan Peron kicks the bucket, and his wife just takes over as their new president. Maybe that's what we oughta do, put Pat Nixon in charge. And then here's our President limping around at the Black Sea, eulogizing Russians who died in World War Two — as if we Americans had only sat on the sidelines. Meanwhile, up in Moscow, the Soviets are arresting dissidents to keep 'em out of camera range when Nixon gets there... Damn. I just wanted to puke."

Nathan said, "That's one hell of a summary, Doc. But I wanted to ask, did you see about the doctor shortage?"

Doc frowned for several seconds. "I don't recall. Was it on NBC? I switched off, you know, just after Moscow."

A nod. Nathan said, "Just before Chancellor says good night, they visit a small town in Illinois which can't hang onto its doctors. So this town puts on a four-day festival to raise money for a new medical center — hoping that'll help."

"Hmm." Another frown. "Well, good for them."

"I mean, Doc... what's it gonna take to keep you here? And maybe get you some help. This town is one hell of a lot poorer than that town in Illinois."

Doc thought about this. He said, "Just don't let anything spoil the fishing. In fact... I'll tell you what." He raised a finger and his eyes brightened. "You know that deep pool in the creek by the old bridge? Where the Forest Service road crosses the North Fork? The trout are hitting like crazy in there, past couple of days. You should pack a supper. Take the wife up there for a few hours. Like now, before sunset."

Nathan smiled. He could almost hear the soft rush of the creek running fast over the boulders; almost feel the throbbing pull of a lunker rainbow. "Hot damn, Doc, that is one hell of an idea."

"Tell Valerie I prescribe it. For both of you."

"You send the bill, Doc. I'll be glad to pay it."

"You already have." Doc stood. "I like talking to you, Nate. You're just the kind of transfusion we need for this old town." He handed Chambers the bank pouch. "Don't forget this, Nate. I think you mighta earned it."

***

There was no breeze on the sidewalk. The sun was still high. Nathan thought about Doc Fuller's suggestion, about the cold water and crisp air along the North Fork. He became cheerful crossing the quiet street, right arm swinging the pouch, thin legs scissoring and skipping...

The Jackpine patrol car halted directly in front of him, and Police Chief Burleigh Driscoll stuck out his thick head. "Nate! Hold up a minute."

Nathan Chambers raised his hands. "I give up, Chief. Don't shoot."

The chief wasn't amused. He said, "We need you at city hall tonight. Eight sharp. Mayor's orders."

"What, again?" Nathan dropped his arms. "Now what?"

Chief Driscoll darted his stony eyes up and down the street, turned to Nathan and grunted. "The old man is callin' it quits," he said. His voice fell to a harsh whisper. His heavy shoulders lifted and settled. "Looks like you aldermen will hafta pick this town a new mayor."

"Well, dammit." Nathan swung a fist, chewed his lips, pushed back his hat. He said, "Christ Almighty, Burr. Sherman Armstrong was mayor when I was a high school punk.

How come he picks *tonight* to resign? Doesn't he know we got the *Rodeo* coming the day after tomorrow? That's a bearcat, Burr. We need every man we can get!"

"You're tellin' me? Look..." Driscoll squeezed his left shoulder partway through the door window. "We all knew this was comin'. Sherman spent his life bossin' the miner's union. Then the town. So... he got old finally. Been complainin' of his health. I can't blame him if he can't take it no more."

Nathan sagged, arms propped against the car. "I know it. It's been a wearisome day, that's all."

"You comin' then?"

"I'll be there. I won't like it a whole lot, but I'll be there."

"Fine and dandy. Now I got to track down two more of you city fathers yet. See you at eight."

The blue car jumped away with a rubber chirp, almost taking the bank pouch out of Nathan's hand.

Nathan stood a moment in the middle of the street, waved a car past, then dragged himself to the deposit box.

Chapter 6: Mayor Sherman Armstrong

MAYOR ARMSTRONG wasted no words with his resignation: "I'm old, tired, and fed up. I quit."

Then, looking around the conference table, he realized the glum faces hadn't awakened to the fact that he was through. He banged the table with his gavel. "It's your move, boys. Don't somebody want this stinkin' job?"

Kermit Czarnowsky — city council president, eldest and highest in seniority among the six aldermen — knew that he was entitled to first refusal. "No thanks, Sherman," he said. "With my health bein' what it is and all... " He flopped his hands on the table and shook his grayed head.

All down the line, aldermen took turns making excuses until Armstrong stopped them with a raised finger. "Good enough. You older fellas aren't right for this job anyway. You'd be no better than me." He looked at them, added: "I'm speaking just as a private citizen and taxpayer, of course."

The ex-mayor stood and leaned against the wall next to the American flag, his hands thrust deeply into the pockets of his baggy trousers. He pursed his lips. All waited for him to begin one of his three-minute lectures to "the boys".

"What this town needs is young blood," he said abruptly. "We're comin' to the end of lazy times. As they say, the handwritin' is on the wall." He paused. Alderman Roy Yancey, who reminded Armstrong of a Disney bear, was glancing around, stupidly, at the walls. Armstrong restrained himself from cuffing Yancey on his ears.

"What I mean is... you can actually smell the changes coming. We used to think, after the mines closed, we'd end up a ghost town. But the new Interstate, all those camper buses headin' to Yellowstone — they kept us alive... barely.

"Now you look around, you see movie stars buying up ranches. People can sell their expensive California properties, buy cheap up here, and retire on the difference. I sold my wife's old homestead to a California couple for nearly eighty thousand, and he thought that was so cheap he didn't even ask for an appraisal."

Armstrong took off his eyeglasses and wiped the lenses with a large handkerchief. "Just today," he said, "I had some gents come see me about building a ski resort. Nothin' much will come of it, I don't think. But it shows how they're thinking out there. Maybe sooner than we think, we're gonna wake up and find a bunch of ski bums in our bunks."

He inspected the eyeglasses, put them back into his pocket. "Well. Changes can happen too fast for an old man. That's why we need younger leadership, somebody who can cope with these things." He stuffed his big hands into his pockets and gazed at the old ceiling with its sagging asbestos tiles. "Let me tell you fellas a story:

"I always thought Jackpine was a solid name for this town — hell of a lot better than what they first called it,

Coalville, back when I was just learnin' how to piss standing up. It reminds me of the tree it's named after.

"A jackpine, the tree, it's one scrawny damn thing, all twisted, no good for lumber. If it's got any practical use, I guess it's just to hold the soil in place.

"But it's a damned pretty tree in its own way. And long ago I wanted to have one, in my backyard. Don't ask me why. Anyway, I tried digging it out of a slope in the Beartooths. But that tree clung so tight, its roots tangled in rocks and roots from other trees, I couldn't get no dirt with it. But that damned forsaken tree, it grew in little bits of sand and down into little cracks in boulders."

Armstrong's face suddenly brightened, and he eased himself away from the wall to lean over the table. He made a thick fist and waved it. "Hell, I figured. If that tree — by golly — if it could survive in nothin' but rocks and sand, it sure's hell ought to grow into a monster in my backyard, where I could give it good rich soil. So I hurried it home. I pruned its roots, made a nice big hole for it, put in lots of loamy soil and some fertilizer. I watered it gently, for days and weeks.

"For a month it looked good." He sighed. "A month. Then it died." His disappointment was still evident after all these years.

"Of course, you fellas know that's what always happens when you try to transplant a jackpine. I tried — I don't know, five or six other times, wanting to give 'em a better home. They always died from the shock."

He rapped his knuckles on the table. "And it's the same with this town. Same damned thing!"

Roy Yancey piped up, "I know! Boy, you just can't transplant them damn old trees. Die every time."

Armstrong gave him a patient look. He removed his eyeglasses from his shirt pocket, put them on, sat down, surveyed the other aldermen. "The point is, we need to preserve what we got, somehow." He banged his fist on the table. "And still, we got to be prepared to accept changes! Got me?"

"You bet!" said Roy Yancey. "That's why we need young blood. Wake up these old folks and get the show on the road! Right?"

Armstrong grimaced. "You're partly right, Roy. But don't get ideas. You're too dumb to be mayor." He fixed his eyes on Nathan Chambers. "How about you, Nate? What do you think about all this?"

Chambers shifted uneasily in his seat. He noted that Yancey wasn't offended by Armstrong's insult; the idiot was used to it. "Hell, I don't know."

Armstrong was patient. "Don't be shy. You're a reasonably bright young fella. Tell us what you think."

"Aw hell, Sherman... "

"I'm serious, Nate."

"Well, for Christ's sake," Nathan said. "I don't think any of us can tell about the future or have any control over it. Sure, we want new business in this town. We need it to live. And if we don't find a way to get it, we might as well board up everything and move out. And I got to tell you, if those guys that talked to you about a ski resort — if they're the guys who came on that Learjet today — I don't know that

I'd just brush 'em off. No sir. That idea excites me a powerful lot."

Kermit Czarnowsky seemed to awaken from a trance.
"Oh hell, Nate. How many times have we heard that before?
I say Jackpine's just going along even keel, always will. When
you're my age, you'll still be selling irrigation boots and barb
wire to the same farms and ranches. That's all there is."

The mayor said, "Forget that old buzzard, Nate. If
somebody started building a ski resort in Jackpine, what
would you do? If you were mayor, that is."

"Hell, Sherman, I don't want to be mayor."

"Sure you do. But skip that. Answer the question." Armstrong stood, walked around the table, placed his strong
hand on the younger man's shoulder. He forced Nathan to
look at him. "Well?"

"You're putting me on the spot, Sherman." Nathan
squirmed a little under the weight of the big hand. "I guess
I'd have to get on their backs, find out what they were doing, try to steer 'em in the right direction for this town. I'd
let 'em know we welcome new business, but we won't accept
the loss of what we've got. We don't want strangers taking
over, buying up property, raising taxes, crowding us out. It'd
be that kind of thing — keeping the town peaceful, keeping
our own citizens mostly in command. If we could manage
that."

"Damn right!" Yancey said. "No parking meters, either.
Or traffic lights. And you tell 'em they gotta pay for any new
sewer and water, Nate!"

Czarnowsky said, "You fellas want to have your cake and
eat it, too. Sherman, I may be an old buzzard, but I ain't

blind yet. You leave the town in the hands of these babes-in-the-woods, and all hell will bust loose. They're talkin' pipe dreams, and you know what that'll get us — high taxes before you know it, and the folks that built this town will be driven out."

The other aldermen — Christoferson, Dietermann, and Fox — hadn't spoken since declining their own unlikely services as mayor. Vincent Fox had wanted Yancey to get the job, simply because he'd have control over Yancey. Adolph Dietermann had assumed his friend Czarnowsky would get it automatically, and he resented Armstrong's break from tradition. Nels Christoferson, a man with six children and the patience one acquires in that predicament, decided finally that the talk was getting out of hand. "Shoot, I move that we appoint Nathan Chambers as acting mayor," he said. "It's only a year until the next council election. We can have a special ballot for mayor then, and let the people decide."

"No way," said Vincent Fox, working a wad of gum in his mouth. "The man we pick stays mayor for the rest of Sherman's term. It's the law."

"Then I still nominate Nathan Chambers," Christoferson said. "I don't care if it's until doomsday."

"Probably will be," Czarnowsky muttered.

From long habit, they all looked at Sherman Armstrong.

The ex-mayor merely shrugged, his expression totally neutral. "Hey, I got no say. The decision is strictly up to you fellas."

Chapter 7:

Woodrow 'Woody' Chambers

A MORNING RAIN SHOWER had gusted swiftly over Jackpine on July third. It left the pavement glistening and the cool air smelling of distant pine needles. Sunlight poured through holes in the shredded clouds and sparkled against the wet glass on the Chambers hardware store.

Woodrow Chambers was shorter than his son but thicker in the arms and chest. He glanced up from his tack catalogs as the front door opened and set the overhead bell tinkling. Down the center aisle approached a businessman in gray pinstripe, followed by a much heavier man in a cashmere blazer. Both looked out of place in the hardware store — out of place anywhere in Jackpine, where men wore suits and ties only to weddings and funerals, and not necessarily then.

The thin man spoke first. "Mr. Chambers?"

"That's me." Woodrow straightened up.

"Hal Dexter. And my associate, Joe Bartz. We flew in here yesterday, from Chicago."

Woodrow was surprised and suspicious. "You the fellas on that Learjet?"

"Yes. Yes, we're the ones, all right."

"Well, you don't say." Woodrow looked carefully at them both.

Dexter handed over a card. "I'm with The Wisconsin Trust. In Milwaukee. Mr. Bartz represents a group of our investors. In Chicago."

"I see," said Woodrow, not seeing.

"Do you have a place where we could sit and talk?" Dexter asked.

Woodrow shrugged. "About what?"

"About some plans. Some rather major plans. For your town." Dexter leaned closer. "I know you've got a business to run. But I guarantee it will be worth your while to hear us out."

Woodrow cocked his large jaw to one side and scratched at the thatch of white hair behind his ear. He looked from Dexter to Bartz and back, puffed his cheeks. "Now look here," he said. "I got no time for this — unless you want to tell me first what it's all about. Plans for the town, you say?"

Smiling, Dexter said, "I understand your suspicions, Mr. Mayor. But we can hardly talk here, over the counter... being interrupted by customers. And our time is short. How about... "

"Excuse me," Woodrow said. "Did you say 'mayor'?"

"Why yes," Dexter said, a thin furrow forming on his smooth forehead. "Haven't you been appointed mayor? We were told... "

"No, no. You've got the wrong Chambers. You want my son. Nathan."

The fat man's eyes rolled toward the ceiling. His hands flapped against his sides.

"It happens all the time," Woodrow said, smiling.

"Amusing, I suppose," Dexter said, looking not amused. "Where could we find your son, Mr. Chambers?"

"Well, that's hard telling." Woodrow rocked on his heels, folded his thick arms across his chest. "He said something about going over to the city garage. But that was an hour ago. Then he needed to stop at the Exxon station. Might still be there. Now... for sure he'll be back later this morning, to meet with the councilmen in the back room. But you won't be able to see him then, I don't think. Hmmm. Maybe if you gents give me an idea what you need to see him about, I could pass it along. And see if he wants to call you."

Dexter stared at him. Really stared. "Mr. Chambers, I have to be in Chicago tonight and Milwaukee in the morning. It's a long flight. And we'll lose an hour in the time change. Is there a possibility, any chance at all, that you could locate him? Now? While we wait?"

Woodrow put both hands on the counter and leaned forward. The motion amplified his bulk. He said, simply, "Nope."

Dexter lifted a palm, dropped it. Bartz sighed.

"I never saw you gentlemen before," Woodrow said. "I don't know what you want with my son. I don't know what kind of idea you've got concerning the town. But — if you want to leave a note or a number, maybe Nathan will get back to you." He smiled.

"All right," Dexter said. "You have my business card. Tell your son we're in room fourteen at the Parkway Motor Court."

"Oh, the Parkway," Woodrow said. "That's a nice place."

"Not hardly," Dexter said.

The two men turned and walked briskly down the aisle, banged the door as they went out but failed to push the latch closed.

Woodrow followed, tugged the door shut, watched their backs going down the sidewalk. The fastest pedestrians in town.

"Damn carpetbaggers," he said.

Chapter 8:

Police Chief Burleigh 'Burr' Driscoll

THE GROUP had gathered in the back of the Chambers hardware store. Like any bunch of men in any small town, they generally mixed business with personal anecdotes and slapped knees when they laughed. They poked fingers at one another, hooked thumbs in belts or suspenders, chewed cigars or tobacco. They scratched themselves in odd places, looked grizzled, sloppy, totally at ease.

Among them were Nathan Chambers and Police Chief Burleigh Driscoll, both sitting and rocking on nail kegs. On crates and against the shelving were Fire Chief Spud Berlinsky, medium-built and bald as a potato; City Attorney Webster Forsythe, wrinkled and lean, wearing a rumpled business suit and drawing on a pipe; and the five aldermen — jolly Roy Yancey and squint-eyed Vincent Fox, both from the First Ward; purple-nosed Kermit Czarnowsky and lanky Nels Christoferson, Second Ward; and beefy Adolph Dietermann, in suspenders, from Nathan's Third Ward. They hadn't yet found an alderman to fill Nathan's slot.

"We don't expect nothing more than the routine business of throwin' drunks in jail," Chief Driscoll said.

Outside, the mainstreet was filling up with tourists and cowboys arriving for the next day's rodeo. Pennants dangled from wires strung across the street. Rodeo posters had been taped to shop windows, and recorded Sousa marches blared from loudspeakers hung on lampposts. The music drifted into the stockroom through an open alley door.

"By approximately three A.M.," the chief went on, "me and the sheriff will shut down any bars that're still open. Spud will release the firemen — then all you fellas can go home." He raised a palm. "Of course, you never can tell."

Alderman Fox tossed nails back and forth in his hands. "Say, Burr," he asked the chief. "What about the rumors? I hear a bunch of longhairs are planning to go streaking down Broadway."

The chief sighed. "Don't worry none about that, Vince."

"Well, what *if?*" Fox persisted.

The chief hunched forward. "My boys got orders. Anybody tries anything dumb like that, we'll kick their butts in jail faster'n you can spit to the sidewalk."

"What's *streaking?*" asked Roy Yancey.

"Don't you read the papers?" Fox said. "They've been at it all over the country — running naked down the streets."

"Oh, you mean them hippies?" Yancey grinned. "Yeah, I seen 'em on TV. They never show any naked girls, though."

Dietermann snorted and pulled at his suspenders. "You ask me, it's the same bunch that was protesting over Vietnam. They got nothing better to do."

"Hey!" exclaimed Yancey, rolling large brown eyes. "You suppose any *girls* might streak here? Hey, Burr, don't arrest 'em too soon. I wanna get a look first!"

Fox tossed a nail at the grinning Yancey, and boisterous laughter filled the stockroom until Chambers interrupted.

"Roy might not have a bad idea there. Might be better if we don't take the streakers too seriously."

They looked at the mayor with uncertain smiles.

"You kidding, Nate?" Fox asked. "What happens if one of 'em goes shootin' past Tillie Culhane?"

"Oh boy!" Yancey guffawed, his beer belly bouncing. "Old Tillie! Holy smokes! Would she be pushed outa shape! Man, she'd round up the Salvation Army — bang them nudie bastards on the heads with her tambourine. *Jesus!*"

"I mean it," Chambers said. He leaned his elbows on his knees and spread his palms. "What's so harmful about streaking? You don't hear of anyone getting busted for it in other cities. So?"

The grins faded. The expressions became puzzled.

Driscoll slapped his tree-stump thighs. "Well, god-damn, now I heard everything! Nate, this ain't no other city!"

"How's it any different?"

"How? I'll tell you how." The chief jabbed a thumb at the silver shield on his chest. "Speakin' as a professional officer sworn to uphold the law, I say we can't allow no bunch of hoodlums to turn our ordinances into a joke just because they get away with it in some other places. This town is a law-and-order town, Nate. Our citizens demand it."

"Hear-hear," Dietermann said.

"Even... " Chambers said, "at risk of setting off a riot?"

"Riot? Who the hell said anything about a *riot?*" Driscoll's face became intense, his voice louder. "You're talking about a couple of punks poking their assholes in our faces, and you wanna just turn the other cheek? You listen here! You seen how them damn hippies and motorcycle gangs, how they tore apart whole towns in California. Let 'em bust one law, Nate, just *one law* while you look away, and pretty soon they're wrecking your stores and houses!"

"Easy, Chief... "

"No, *you* just rest easy! *We* know how to handle crowds and all the punks that come with 'em. Hell, we been doing it every damned Fourth of July for twenty-three years. And this year we got Mace, and the sheriff's men will have electric cattle prods, and... "

"Mace? *Cattle prods?* Jesus, Burr — you're gonna *inflame* those characters!" A redness glimmered through the tan on Nathan's face and neck. "That's exactly the kind of horseshit I don't want. There's no need for kids getting knocked silly for just having some stupid *fun*, for Christ's sake!"

"Listen, sonny." Driscoll set his jaw like an iron anvil and poked a thick finger at Nathan's face. "You just leave the police work to me. You got your own job to worry about."

Chambers didn't move. He stared into the chief's eyes.

"Uh-oh," Yancey muttered. "The talk's gettin' kinda thick in here."

When Chambers spoke, his voice was quiet but hard. "Sometimes you get a little carried away, Burr. But you get one thing understood. *My job* is being in charge of you. Your orders come direct from me, and I don't give any goddamned hoot in hell if you like it or not. You got that?"

An awkward silence enveloped the stockroom. Even the band music outside had hit a lull between record changes.

It was Yancey who broke the stillness. "Oh boy," he said, his hand wiping his flat forehead. "Whoever thought we picked us a fireball mayor last night?"

There were nervous chuckles, but the chief didn't hear them. He said, "Okay, Nate, I got your number. If that's the way you're gonna play it, then it's your responsibility. No matter what. I just hope you're around when things start poppin'."

And then he slid his eyes away.

"I don't get it," Czarnowsky said. "If some streakers show up, you're just gonna leave 'em be?"

"Whatever the man says," Driscoll said.

"Look, guys," Chambers said. "You know goddamn well. The crowd on the street tomorrow night, they won't be here to attend church. No streakers are going to offend them, But try jumping out with Mace and cattle prods, after all the crap that's been hitting this country... *then* we got trouble."

"Like I said," the chief grumbled, slowly standing. "The man's the boss, and I can't argue with that." He jerked his cap forward and went out the back door.

"Well," Fox said. "I'm sorry I asked the question."

The group split up quickly then, leaving the store from front and back.

City Attorney Webster Forsythe, lingering behind, touched Nathan's arm as they strolled toward the front. "Welcome to your new job, Nate," he said. "I hope you realize, though — Burr was right on the edge of quitting you."

Chambers turned. "And I was on the edge of firing him, Web."

Forsythe's eyes widened. "On the day before the rodeo? Well, that wouldn't have been wise."

Forsythe was a slow-talking, hunch-shouldered man with sagging flesh under his eyes. He was the only man in town who wore a suit daily, usually the same suit, crumpled over his frail body. He also was a good listener, known for his confidentiality.

They stopped at a counter near the front door.

"Web," Chambers said. "You come right ahead and tell me if I'm wrong. But the way I learned it, the United States Constitution says our government is run by civilians."

Forsythe smiled, started knocking the dottle out of his pipe into an ashtray on the counter. "Something like that," he said.

"So what's worse? Some beer drinkers baring their butts? Or hard-nosed cop who thinks he can run a police state?"

Forsythe's scraggly brows lifted in surprise. "A police state? Golly, Nate. Don't let anybody else hear you talk like that. They'll think we've got a flaming liberal for a mayor." He smiled, removed a tobacco pouch from his jacket, began refilling the pipe.

"No joke," Chambers said. "I'm having trouble with Burr, and he's been chief of police a long time. He and Sherman, they got along fine — a couple of oldtimers who helped heave this town together out of rock and sagebrush."

"That's right," Forsythe said.

"Man like that, he's respected. By the whole town."

"Exactly."

"And deserves it."

"Of course."

"Now I come along, green as grass."

"Well... sort of."

"And I go and chew his ass. Right in front of the whole city council. In front of you. In front of Spud Berlinksy."

Nathan sighed. "Does it even matter if I'm right?"

Forsythe raised his bony fingers to Nathan's shoulder. "Yes. Yes it does, Nate. It matters, and you're perfectly correct to insist on civilian authority. Certainly on policy decisions."

"But you, Web. Even you think I'm too damned eager."

"Eager?" Forsythe shook his head. "My guess would've been six months before you'd have the nerve to go head-to-head against Burleigh Driscoll. Doing it on your first day as mayor... that does seem a little eager."

"Shit."

"But never mind. There were people who thought Harry Truman went overboard when he fired General MacArthur. You just stick to your guns, Nate. You're on the right track."

"I sure's hell hope so."

"You just nipped a military junta in the bud and saved Jackpine for Democracy. You even caught a few old farts by surprise, including me. That's not a bad start." He gave a kind wink that deepened all his wrinkles. "In fact, it's damned good."

***

Nathan Chambers watched the attorney leave, a narrow body of debris adrift in a tide of holiday pedestrians. Then he turned and saw his father standing behind a counter, leaning on his forearms.

"Sounded like some commotion back there," Woodrow said.

Woody Chambers was built like a boxer, with the same crewcut he had worn in the Pacific during World War II. Now white, the crewcut made a sharp clean contrast to the weathered skin that pouched his face. Nathan watched, and the face glinted like brass. His father was, as usual, amused.

"It's not so damned funny," Nathan said. "Being mayor is horseshit."

"Oh well," Woodrow said. "First day's always the toughest."

"Don't bet on it." Nathan looked out the window, saw Patrolman Buck Chism going around with posters proclaiming Jackpine's "open container" ordinance, intended to prevent people from drinking their booze on the streets and sidewalks, all in a feeble attempt to maintain order. "Tomorrow," he said. "That's the day I'd prefer to skip altogether."

Chapter 9: Valerie Ensign Chambers

AT ONE FORTY-FIVE, Doc Fuller had about finished his examination when Valerie Ensign Chambers said, "Roscoe, it's okay, isn't it, for me to have sex with my husband?"

"Oh hell yes," Doc said.

Valerie sat up, swung her legs off the table. "For how long? I mean, when would my pregnancy start to interfere?"

Doc thought about it, scratching his jaw. He said, "You go right ahead, long as you both feel comfortable. Or until I tell you different. How's that?"

Valerie gave him a restrained smile. It produced dimples on her cheeks. "It's just that... I'm enjoying it now."

"Fine," Doc said. "Nothing wrong with that."

"I mean, it was good before. But now it's better."

"How so?" Doc asked, not really interested, but keeping the conversation alive while he stashed his instruments.

Valerie gave the question some thought while buttoning her blouse. She said, "Well, Nathan's more gentle while I'm in this condition... " She laughed. "And naturally, I don't have to worry anymore about getting pregnant."

Doc said, "That worried you before? I figured you both wanted this critter."

"Of course. But I'm a little afraid. It was my mother. She had a terrible time when I was born. That's why I'm an only child. It affected her whole relationship with my father. She's strong-willed — *intent*, you could say, about keeping him at bay." Valerie sighed. "It isn't the kind of relationship I'd want with Nathan. I... well, you know."

"No," Doc said. "I don't know."

"I love him." Valerie's eyes sparkled, brilliant hazel against her suntanned complexion. "I had never met anyone like him. He's strong, but not pushy. He's easy-going, peace-loving, modest. Quite the opposite of my former... acquaintances."

"But?"

"When he proposed, I was a pushover. I said yes without thinking of the impacts. And I wasn't expecting pregnancy... Not yet. Not here."

"Not here?"

Valerie shrugged, gazed out a window. "I was hoping we'd explore various options before settling down to a family. Nathan has terrific potential. He has an engineering degree and dedication, and there are companies almost anywhere that would be glad to get him. And I had a degree, too, and some career ideas of my own. But now... " Her voice trailed off.

"You talk about this, with Nate?"

"Oh no. I couldn't."

"Why the hell not? He's your husband!"

Closing her eyes briefly, Valerie nodded. Her expression was both whimsical and a little sad. "But — I think he'd be crushed. Nathan thinks Montana is the greatest place to raise kids and he's probably right. If I start talking about some metropolitan area... You know what? He'd tear himself apart trying to find ways to make me happy. I don't want to give him that burden. Not after Vietnam. Certainly not after they appointed him mayor. And this talk about a ski resort... I just don't know. Maybe I should just shut up."

Doc looked up sharply. "Excuse me. Did you mention a ski resort? Here?"

"A ski resort, yes. I guess it's not public knowledge yet, but some strangers are here looking at the possibilities. Nathan told me this when he came home for lunch. He's probably on his way to meet with them now."

"You don't say," Doc mumbled.

"Maybe I shouldn't have. I'm new at this, being a mayor's wife."

"Hell," Doc said. "Word gets around anyhow."

"But... do me a favor?"

"Hmm?"

"Don't spread it around, not yet. Wait until Nathan announces it."

Doc wagged his head, didn't respond.

"Roscoe, please?"

"Oh sure. My lips are sealed. Hell. I don't talk about what's said in my examining room."

"Thank you."

"A ski resort, though. Now that is damned interesting." He hurriedly dispatched the remaining instruments to their proper drawers and cubbyholes. "In any case, you need to talk to Nate. Tell that fella what you told me. Remember, a pregnancy isn't something a woman carries alone. Your life's just as important as your husband's. If you two don't take that into account, you'll never be happy."

Valerie nodded. "Roscoe, you're so kind."

"Kind, hell. I'm just old. Makes you mellow."

"Mellow is nice."

"No... mellow is yellow. Older I get, the more scared I am," Doc said.

Valerie gave him a skeptical smile. She said, "Roscoe, what in the world do you have to be scared about?"

"A whole damn parade of things. And you bring me more. A ski resort in Jackpine, by God. A woman afraid of her pregnancy and not telling her husband." He produced a stern gaze.

"I will talk to him. I promise," Valerie said.

"You do that. That'll solve one of my concerns."

"I can't do anything about the ski resort," she said.

"Well, me neither, I guess." Doc shook his head. "Doubt anyone else can, for that matter." His expression turned sour. "You have a nice day, Mrs. Chambers."

***

Walking home, Valerie wondered why Roscoe had addressed her so stiffly as "Mrs. Chambers" when he normally called her Valerie or Val. Had her mention of the ski project ruined his day? If so, why?

Valerie usually enjoyed the exercise of walking between Doc Fuller's office and home. Often she jogged the route.

Today she trudged it.

Chapter 10: Temptations

NATHAN CHAMBERS was admitted into a motel room with orange bedspreads and chairs, pale yellow walls, green shag carpeting. A large Mediterranean dresser was ornately carved in walnut. Above it, suspended on a brass chain, was a cut-glass lamp globe the size of a basketball.

In the midst of this flamboyance stood a man in executive gray with sharp eyes probing Nathan top to bottom. "Mr. Chambers? Mr. *Nathan* Chambers? And, I hope to God, *Mayor* Chambers?"

Chambers nodded, extended a hand. "All three, I guess."

Hal Dexter visibly relaxed. He introduced himself and Bartz, who waddled to a tray of ice and plastic cups and beverages, which Chambers declined.

Dexter said, "We've had less trouble meeting governors and senators, Mayor Chambers. Have a chair. We've fallen behind schedule and need to plunge right into this, if you don't mind."

"Suits me." Chambers took one of the orange chairs. "Got some obligations waiting for me, too." He crossed his legs and hung his hat on the toe of his boot.

Dexter zipped open a briefcase and began feeding documents to Chambers, rapidly summarizing the content. "I'm sure you've been alerted to this by your former mayor," Dexter assumed. "These copies are yours. Keep and study them."

Chambers thumbed his nose and started flipping pages while he listened. He noticed figures on annual snowfalls along "the Beartooth Face." There were projections of skier-days starting with a chairlift capacity of a thousand per hour the first year and mounting to six thousand by 1977, nine thousand by 1980. There were topographic maps showing locations of proposed ski runs, lift towers, water storage tanks, utility lines, lodges.

The report mentioned major earthwork, installing culverts and blasting stumps and rocks with dynamite. Some boulders were bigger than cars; they'd have to be blown to chips. Nathan could feel the town rocking from the blasts.

Dexter said, "That's just raw data, Mr. Chambers. May I call you Nathan? It is comprehensive, Nathan, but raw. It's being incorporated into a master plan. Let me show you." He unfolded a large-scale drawing and spread it onto one of the queen-size beds. It half covered the bed. "The Master Plan, Stage One."

Chambers went to the bed. Plopping his hat on the back of his head, he bent over and stared. In various colors, the North Fork Canyon was transformed into a mass of roads and structures. Black lines indicated where chairlifts would span the canyon's slopes, with most concentrated on Wapiti Mountain to the west. Broad white bands represented the ski runs, winding randomly down the slopes.

Chambers whistled. "And all this... it's 'Stage One'?"

Beside him, Bartz said, "I see it's excited your interest."

"Hey... not so fast." Chambers hitched his shoulders. "Even if I do get a bit excited, that's just one opinion. I don't speak for the whole town."

"Maybe not," Dexter said. "But from what I've heard, you are considered a progressive figure in this community. True?"

"Look," Chambers said. "I *have* favored a ski area for this town — nothing this big — but I did try talking to people, like the bankers in Billings. Got nothing but politeness and coffee. Then I got Chet Huntley to agree to see me over at Big Sky, the ski village he helped put together. But he died in March, you know, before I could get there. It was in all the news. Now you bring *this*. How long have you been *working* on this? "

Bartz, his face smug, said, "It's been just under two years."

Chambers turned sharply. "Two *years*? How in hell did you manage *that*? Without anybody knowing?"

"Oh, a few people knew," Joseph Bartz interjected.

"Who?"

Dexter said quickly, "You'll probably learn directly from them. Meanwhile, I'm pleased to sense some enthusiasm here. If you could spread that around, ask your town council to endorse this project, guide your fellow citizens along... "

"Not sure I can do that." Chambers tugged an ear. "I can't hardly get over it. You did all this work for two years and almost nobody knows about it. In a town like Jackpine, that good a secret is about as rare as a pet grizzly bear." He peered again at the large drawing. "This label, it says 'Eagle Peak Ski Complex'. Where'd that come from?"

"Yes," Dexter said. "We plan to use the name Eagle Peak instead of Wapiti Mountain. We feel no one would know the meaning of Wapiti... "

"It's an elk," Chambers said.

"Well, yes, but nobody knows that. Nobody knows how to pronounce it. That makes it difficult to promote. Eagle is much better. People associate that with the soaring feeling they get from skiing. We've done motivational research on this, Nathan. Don't worry about it. Now, if there's anything you think you'll need from us — *anything* at all — let's hear it. We want to get this rolling."

"I just need time," Chambers said. "It's a lot to cram down the gullet."

"Yes. Well, we don't have much time. The Forest Service has scheduled a public hearing for October. Meanwhile, we've got to finish the master plan. And the environmental impact statement. We need to be ready for any opposition. It's vital that the process shows maximum public support."

"A tall order," Chambers said. He prowled the carpet. "What happens if maybe half the folks don't swallow this? It's one monster of a plan."

Bartz took Chambers by an arm. He smelled of cigar smoke. "That's where you come in. Convince them it's for the best. They'll listen. You're their mayor."

"An *appointed* mayor," Chambers said. "The people here are downright independent. You don't tell 'em what to think." He slid away from Bartz, turned to Dexter. "A project this size... What'll it mean to the town's economy and population, and all that jazz?"

"All good things." Dexter sat back and crossed his legs. His narrow foot in a black loafer wagged side to side. "Hundreds of new jobs at the resort complex alone. Then will come a need for more and better overnight accommodations. With more taste and class," he added, a wave of his hand dismissing this room.

Chambers asked, "Don't you think this place is decent?"

"It's shabby." Dexter leaned forward. "You must realize — *all* you people must come to realize — that skiers, certainly those we plan to attract, are people with money and position. They spend a thousand bucks for a ski outfit for one or two trips. Then it goes to the rummage. And they think nothing of it."

"No wonder the country's in trouble," Chambers muttered.

Dexter went on, "You can see we'll need better establishments. For food and drink and specialty shops. Boutiques. That will attract investment dollars. In one decade this town could surpass Aspen or Vail. It really could. You're closer to the Midwest cities, less than an hour from direct flights that land in Billings. Combined with shorter lift lines, that means double the ski time, and that's the whole ballgame...

"Listen, play your cards right, and this town will come alive. You'll grow prosperous. You'll be able to afford better schools for your children, a better hospital for your sick, better doctors, better care for your elderly. And from what

I've seen, you have a hell of a lot of elderly on your hands."
He looked at his watch. "Any questions?"

"That big drawing. That for me to keep?"

"Absolutely," Bartz said, gathering the drawing and pre-
senting it. "This — and anything *else* you need."

Dexter stood. "It depends on you, Nathan. From this
point forward, the lid is off. Spread the word, build support.
Don't miss this chance to do a great service for your town."

Bartz added, "We're betting our cards on you. Likewise,
you'll do *yourself* a favor by coming aboard. There's room for
alert people to *profit*. Understand?"

Chambers looked at the man. He took the stack of materials without comment. He touched the brim of his hat.
"You guys gonna keep in touch?"

"We'll be back before you know it," Dexter said. "Back
with an army."

Bartz put a hand on Nathan to guide him out the door.

***

Chambers dumped the reports onto the passenger seat
and sat thinking. When he revved the Jeep's engine, he
thought he heard the metallic knocking again. The Exxon
mechanic hadn't found anything. Even so, Chambers kept
hearing that occasional knocking — or thought he heard it.

It had been like that in the motel. Nothing he could
pinpoint. But he had heard a pinging in there, too — or
thought he did.

It was too much to grasp. He whipped the Jeep onto
Broadway, tires blasting gutter cinders behind him. And he
worried that sooner or later the damned engine was going to
blow itself clear to North Dakota.

Chapter 11:

Game Warden Russell 'Russ' Bancroft

THEY SAT like neglected relics of another age — two squat Stearman biplanes converted for crop spraying; a high-winged Cessna with its cowling removed; a red Piper hunched down on flattened tires.

Past them, alive and blinking with lights, the sleek Lear-jet taxied daintily, executed a smart pivot onto the runway, and crouched as its engines screamed and its wings vibrated. Then the pilot released the brakes and the dart zoomed.

Hal Dexter and Joseph Bartz were silent as the thrust pinned them to their seats. The jarring of earth abruptly gave way to the smoothness of lift-off, and the *thizzz-clunk* of the retracting landing gear signaled they were clear of Jackpine.

Bartz stuffed a fat cigar into his pink mouth and struck a blue flame from a gold-cased lighter. "So, what'd I say, Hal? They're ripe as September peaches. Didn't I say that?"

"They're not so ripe in my book, Joe. Two of those people wouldn't give us the time of day. The new mayor is confused and suspicious… "

"So?" Bartz puffed up a gray cloud that made Dexter wince and claw at the ventilator control. Bartz said, "Confused, sure. Suspicious... maybe. But not antagonistic, Hal. It's like you have a horse for sale and they want to examine the teeth. They're like that. But they want your horse. And don't forget our little friend the mole, the way he jumped when you jerked his strings." Bartz stuck the cigar back into his mouth, pleased with himself. He patted his round stomach with both hands.

"Our friend the mole?" Dexter shifted his weight. "Joe, I'm not half as smug as you about this affair. How can I report to Mr. Spears with confidence? For God's sakes, you know Spears."

Bartz lost his contentment at mention of that name. Ernest Lucius Spears was no ordinary business tycoon.

He was a warlord.

"Joseph," Dexter said, "tell the pilot to make a few passes around this area. I'd like to get a bigger look at it before we leave."

A few minutes later, Dexter pointed to a thin ribbon leading north out of Jackpine, where the valley sloped down and broadened. He asked, "Where does that highway go?"

Bartz peered through the porthole. "Oh, that. That highway goes down to Billings. Sixty, seventy miles. That's Montana's largest city, Hal. Eighty thousand people, a couple of colleges — and a lot of skiers."

Dexter nodded. "And the other way?"

"The other way... you won't believe this, Hal. That crazy highway, it climbs a series of switchbacks, goes right over the top of the Beartooth Plateau. Up eleven thousand feet, then it dumps into Yellowstone National Park."

"And how far is that?"

"Up, down, and around — again, about sixty miles."

"Oh?" Dexter was interested in this. "Yellowstone? Now you're talkin', Joe! You mean, our skiers could scoot over there? See Old Faithful and all that crap if they wanted to?"

Bartz wagged his head. "Afraid not. Not in winter. They close the road October to June. Too much snow... "

Dexter looked bewildered. "If it's only sixty miles, couldn't we manage to have it plowed? I mean, Jesus Christ, it's *Yellowstone*, for God's sakes! It's just the sort of attraction we need, to get a new resort off and running!"

"No, no, you don't understand." Bartz winced. "It gets *unearthly* up there in wintertime. Snowdrifts get thirty feet high. I kid you not. Even in May, when the Park Service starts chopping through, it takes weeks to clear one lousy lane. Sometimes they blast the drifts with dynamite."

"Are you serious?"

"Hey. I checked all this out. In winter, Hal, that plateau becomes the worst goddamn place in the universe. Ice-cold, wind like razor blades. People have been killed by the blizzards. Not even the goats can stand it."

The description made Hal Dexter shiver, just thinking about it.

"You want to fly over it?" Bartz inquired.

"Hell, no," Dexter said.

***

The mule deer, a doe, kept jerking its head puppet-fashion as it chewed a bunch of native wheatgrass and warily eyed the human figure across the creek.

Russell Bancroft squatted on the bank of the North Fork and tipped back the wide-brimmed gray hat of a Montana game warden. He had seen the deer from the road and picked his way down for a closer look. He had expected to count more deer, but he found just the one nervous doe.

As Bancroft listened to the gurgling water, he recalled a time, not many years ago, when he would have counted at least thirty deer along this stretch. But the swelling of civilization kept driving back the wildlife, deeper into the remnants of wilderness.

Nowadays, he reflected, most of the deer he saw were dead carcasses along the highways.

He gazed into the crystal pools near the streambank and watched for the quicksilver flash of trout. Instead, he saw the glint of a beer can. He reached into the icy current and felt almost ashamed at invading the bright water with oily human hands.

Placing the can on soft earth, he leaned back and nestled his elbows into a cushion of pine needles. He felt sparkling reflections against his closed eyelids, smelled the piney air, sensed the shivering coat on the doe across the creek.

Then came a howl of unearthly noise.

The deer, on springs, made great slow-motion bounds into deeper timber. The creek made less fury. Aspen leaves fluttered, and pine needles hummed like tuning forks.

The wind-howl overhead echoed sharply off the canyon slopes as Bancroft peered skyward. The Learjet was a flash above the treetops, but he recognized it — the same plane that had landed yesterday in Jackpine.

Ignoring the plane, he turned his attention back to the creek. The swelling and falling water moved swiftly as before, but the scene wasn't the same. More than the deer was gone.

The howling over the trees returned, louder and lower. Bancroft turned from the creek and scrambled up the slope to the roadway for a better look. He was panting when he stopped on the gravel and leaned against the sky blue International. On its door next to his hip was the emblem of the Montana Fish and Game Department — a grizzly bear, extinct almost everywhere except Montana.

The plane was nowhere, but its echoes were rebounding off the canyon's upper limestone and granite formations. Then he saw it, a silvery speck against the great greenish-black masses of the forested mountainsides.

Bancroft reached into the truck for his radio mike, thumbed the talk button, spoke. He listened to the crackling of the loudspeaker, tried again. It was useless; he was too deep in the canyon for his signal to escape. He tried once more, then jammed the mike into its cradle.

He leaned against the truck, watched with arms crossed as the singing, shimmering plane made two more swoops through the canyon, then suddenly winged up and away. The silence filtered back and the creek resumed its gurgling.

He was immensely annoyed for being unable to send a message out of the canyon.

He had hoped to have the Fish and Game office in Billings relay his report to the Federal Aviation Administration at Logan Field — have them order the plane out of the canyon before it might crash and set the whole forest afire.

Leaving of its own accord wasn't satisfying enough, not for Russell Bancroft. He had wanted the bastards cited, nailed to a cross, expelled forever from this sacred place.

He went down to the streambank one more time and collected the beer can before leaving.

Chapter 12: Benjamin 'Ben' Bayliss

SNOW had dusted the distant peaks and rain had fallen on the forests in the night. But the July Fourth morning broke out brilliant, hot. The sun was a white torch, shriveling the morning shadows, etching the old town's rustic details.

The day's disturbances began with the popping of cherry bombs ignited by youngsters who happily ignored the fireworks ban imposed by the last session of the Montana Legislature. Later, the wind became gusty, snapping the mainstreet flags and whipping Valerie's linen skirt as she strolled with Nathan along the crowded sidewalk. Friendly citizens, out for the annual parade, offered congratulations to the new mayor and tipped their hats to his pretty wife.

Nathan and Valerie acknowledged the congratulations until they grew tired of them; checked briefly into the hardware store where Woodrow Chambers kept pace with a scattering of travelers buying picnic supplies; finally selected a spot at the curb to stand among the expectant gathering.

"Look at the people!" Valerie chimed, clinging to Nathan's arm. "Where'd they all *come* from?"

"The rodeo's our big annual whoop," Nathan said. "They come from all over. A lot come up from Yellowstone, tourists wanting to see real cowboys."

Valerie held wind-ruffled hair away from her eyes and surveyed the colorful assembly; the many cars with out-of-state plates; the squadrons of motorcycles from Billings and beyond parked in shiny chrome formations along the curbs; the children, prancing onto the street, being ordered back by bustling parade deputies.

"Unbelievable," she said. "All the news about an energy crisis, California people waiting hours in gas lines, I didn't expect to see *anybody* here."

Nathan wrapped an arm over her shoulder. "Maybe we're the last place they could still find gas."

Valerie opened her shoulder bag and removed a camera. It was a Leicaflex, a gift her father had bought in Germany some years ago. In her hands, it became an efficient instrument for capturing artful images of the West — oldtimer portraits, buck-and-pole fences wandering through sagebrush. She hoped someday to have a collection for a book — a book, she mused, for San Francisco coffee tables. In the eyes of her former friends, it might actually justify her extended visit to Montana.

She attached a long-focus lens and began scanning the crowd through her viewfinder. A small girl in a ten-gallon hat and oversized cowboy boots caught her eye. *Click-snap.* The girl displayed a series of impatient expressions, restless poses. *Click-snap, click-snap, click-snap...*

Shifting the camera, she caught an approaching figure staring back into her lens. The man waved, quickening his pace, stopped in front of her as she lowered the camera.

Benjamin Bayliss was one of Jackpine's fixtures. Among the citizenry, he was not so much welcome as necessary, like a razor blade or toilet. He was the editor of the Jackpine *Spectator*.

"Morning, Ben," Nathan said to him.

"Morning, Mrs. Chambers," Ben said to Valerie.

Bayliss had an all-black Nikkormat dangling around his neck like a cowbell. He focused his attention on Valerie's expensive Leicaflex. "Fine camera you've got there, Mrs. Chambers. Mind if I take a look?"

"Sure." She held it out to him.

Bayliss clutched it, examined the precision lens, peered through the viewfinder, swiveled the lens barrel in all directions. He took his time with it.

Watching him, Valerie couldn't help frowning. There was something about the man that gave her the jitters.

To those who paid attention to his weekly newspaper, Benjamin Bayliss was mainly a fellow who wrote and behaved like a pompous jackass and substantially resembled one. He had oversized teeth and ears, brown hair that splayed over his forehead like a whisk broom, a long carrot-shaped nose stuck flat to his face, and a tendency to release bursts of laughter punctuated with nasal snorts. He also was a staunchly liberal democrat, persistently critical of the city's slow-motion government. Once or twice he had given Nathan Chambers an editorial hind-kick, and by the shifty glance he now aimed at the new mayor, it became evident he was about to do it again.

He handed the camera back to Valerie. "Nice equipment you've got," he said. "Don't let somebody bump or grab it, in this crowd."

She gave him a cold smile, turned away with enough contempt that he was aware of it, resumed her through-the-lens crowd searching.

"Nate," Bayliss said quickly. "I'm meaning to ask you. About that meeting yesterday —" He jerked a ballpoint from his shirt pocket, flipped open a spiral notebook. "The one in back of your store?"

"What about it?"

"Seems to me it was held without public notice. Seems to me it was *illegal*. What do *you* say?"

Chambers had known this was coming. He said, "Bull."

Band music signaled the beginning of the parade. Ignoring it, Bayliss cocked an eyebrow. "Maybe you don't know about the state's open-meetings law. Maybe for your benefit as the new mayor... maybe I should quote the law directly: *'The people of this state do not wish to abdicate their sovereignty to those elected to serve them,'* etcetera. I've told Sherman Armstrong at least a hundred times. I print the law in the *Spectator* three or four times a year. But maybe you don't know it, huh? Maybe you missed it, huh?"

"I know the goddamn law, Ben."

"'God-damn law'... I see... "

Chambers shot him an exasperated glance. "The law requires open government and I'm all for it. But the meeting yesterday was a legal exception. About the rodeo and how we'd handle the crowds. That's all. Police security."

Bayliss grinned. "I got to write this down." He jotted a note. *"'Police security'*, oh sure. In little old Jackpine... only on the surface a quiet community. Underneath, a hotbed of subversive activity. Were the G-men there? The CIA? Or maybe you're right, I shouldn't know. They could come and stuff me in a rubber bag, hide me away in a sanitarium in Louisiana... "

"Have your fun. We hold that same meeting every year."

"Exactly. A long history of crime. And you're *condoning* it?" Bayliss kept writing. "Other than, *heh-heh*, police security, what else did you politicians discuss in that smoke-filled back room? How about a replacement for your old post in the Third Ward?"

"Never mentioned it. It's on the agenda for the next meeting. A regular *open* meeting. So, Ben, cut the crap."

Chambers turned and watched over the heads of the crowd as the American flag approached at the front of the parade, its staff held high on horseback by the president of the Jackpine Rodeo Association, Melvin Barclay.

Behind Melvin, strung out for several blocks, were the high school band; the baton twirlers from Hardin; hordes of local children on gaily decorated bikes and tricycles; teams of pack mules entered by outfitters and guides; a Forest Service pickup exhibiting Smokey the Bear...

"You aldermen get together," Bayliss persisted, "and I know what happens. Maybe you *intend* to discuss only police business or personnel discipline, or some such other confidential stuff. But next thing I know, you all show up at a regular council meeting, and your minds are all made up. You approve this, deny that, change ordinances, and the public has no idea what you're *doing!* They don't hear your *deliberations!* You ask me, Nate — *that's* what's crap."

Chambers puffed his cheeks, let a compressed wisp of breath escape from tightened lips...

"Okay, Ben. Tell you what." He watched the passing of the American Legion float, built on a flatbed truck, staffed by elderly women in frontier dresses and elderly men in World War I uniforms.

"You get yourself a coffee mug and a bottle of No-Doz," Chambers said, "...and you hike over to our next so-called executive session. You listen all you want. You can hear us go 'round and 'round about every damn little detail, listen to Otto drone on and on about his goddamn federal forms, or Spud telling how this kind of fire nozzle is better than the kind we got. I'd be pleased as *Punch* to have you share our misery, you sonofabitch. And you write it all in your damn newspaper, too. Maybe it's about time people found out just how goddamn *boring* it is."

Bayliss nodded but said nothing for a moment. He lifted his camera to snap the Elks Club float, an elaborate depiction of George Washington crossing a crepe-paper Delaware. Next came the riders competing for Best-Dressed Cowboy and Best-Dressed Cowgirl, wearing jeweled hats and fringed shirts, perched on silver-adorned Mexican saddles, aboard high-stepping Appaloosa or Palomino stallions. When the police car went by, with Burleigh Driscoll cramped sternly behind the wheel, light bar flashing, Bayliss gave Chambers a curious glance.

"Could I stay through everything? Even the personnel disputes?"

"What personnel disputes?"

"Like yesterday in the smoke-filled room. I hear you and the chief got into one whale of a donnybrook."

"Jesus." Chambers flipped a hand. "Well, there you are. If you're going to hear it all anyway, you might as well be there. At least get the story straight, maybe."

"What *is* the story?" Bayliss lifted a pen.

"No comment."

For a long time, the parade offered riders on horseback, two blocks of them, clopping along the pavement, ending finally with the city's old streetsweeper bringing up the rear. Its sprinklers and brushes busily wetted down and smeared flat the many mounds of dung dumped by the horses.

"Well, good!" Bayliss flapped his notebook shut, nodding at the sweeper. "Maybe it's the last time I'll have to endure *that*, at least."

"What's that?"

"Watching you fellas shine up the shit."

He nodded at Valerie.

Strolled casually away.

Chapter 13: Rodeo!

SPREAD ACROSS a sun-baked bench of land adjacent to the airport, the Jackpine rodeo grounds collected a swarm of cars, pickups, horse trailers, and motorcycles. Inside the arena, spectators made sunshades out of program booklets, handkerchiefs, cardboard beer cartons, whatever they could find. In the rising heat, most of them drank cold beer. Lots of beer.

The Grand Entry brought a column of riders cantering into the arena in pairs, splitting into two concentric circles of galloping horses, then lining up abreast in front of the grandstand for the National Anthem. Among these riders were officials of the Jackpine Rodeo Association, the 1974 rodeo queen, the stock producer and his staff, and famous rodeo clown Mickey Bagnell, who later in the day would perform in the barrels during the bullriding event.

The crowd thundered its approval, then settled down as the announcer named the horse and rider coming out of Gate Four to begin the first section of bareback riding.

Nathan Chambers watched all this from under the grandstand, where he and two dozen fellow Rotarians each year operated a food and beverage concession to raise funds for local projects. For the next three hours, they would dispense a truckload of fast food to a crowd estimated at more than two thousand.

The rodeo association had outdone itself this year, despite the sour economy and energy crisis. After months of enlisting sponsors, the association had scraped up a $9,000 purse, largest in the rodeo's 23-year history. Combined with entry fees, it was enough to attract nearly two hundred top riders, competing for dollars and points they hoped would carry them to the National Finals.

In order to attend this and similar events on the same day in Cody, Wyoming; in Red Lodge and Livingston, Montana; and in towns throughout the Rockies, the cowboys landed chartered planes on the adjacent runway, hopped the fence to ride, then took off for the next town.

Harley Wyatt was not among the stars who arrived in a chartered Beechcraft. Instead, he had driven all night along Montana's lonely highways in a dinged-up Ford pickup with a Coors six-pack for company.

Arriving late, Harley had to settle for riding slack, well after the main performance. Meanwhile, he smoked his last pack of Winstons, wandered around the stockpens, spat into the dust, perspired in the heat, thirsted for more beer, and wished his entry fee hadn't eaten so much of his billfold.

Several times, Harley drifted toward the Rotary Club stand, smelled the burgers sizzling on a grease-spitting grill, and each time he backed off.

He contented himself with listening to the rodeo sounds. The announcer's voice crackled on the loudspeakers; the band performed toots and drumrolls to the antics of the clowns. The crowd erupted in a roar each time some wiry cowboy clung to his tailspinning stallion a few seconds past the horn; or whenever a horse flung its rider against the barricades with a whump of flesh against wood; or when a clown plunged into his steel barrel at the instant when a charging Brahma sent the barrel twirling through the dust.

With the second section of bullriding underway, the crowd at the food stand rushed back into the arena, and Harley no longer could keep his distance. He strolled to the counter, saw most of the Rotarians were facing out the rear of the booth, peeking between the grandstand seats at the bullriding action...

...Except the tall man with dark eyebrows working at the grill.

Harley noticed this fellow had more determination than skill as he pegged at the sizzling meat with his spatula, got his arm spattered with hot grease, leaped back and roared "Gawd-dammit!" And poked the spatula for another try.

"You do that about the way I ride."

Nathan Chambers turned and stared at Harley Wyatt. He wiped his hands with his stained apron. "Nobody could be bad as me. Not in this whole wide world."

"You mustn't do that for a livin'," Harley guessed. "Looks to me like you're tryin' to destroy the entire beef surplus."

Chambers slumped. "It happened during the ladies' barrel race. That's when the whole crowd comes flying down here like they're running from skunks. I had burger patts stacked ten-high on the grill. Juices flowing over the sides, catching fire... Smoke was getting me in the eyes." He let out a sigh. "Then they started the bullriding, and everybody was just all of a sudden gone. Now I got sixteen leftovers, all burning up to cinders."

"Well... Maybe I'll take one," Harley said, pulling out his billfold. What he saw inside the leather changed his mind. "On second thought, maybe just a Hershey bar."

Chambers studied the cowboy for a moment. Then he stacked three patts on a bun, slipped the works into a paper wrapper, handed it over the counter. "I'd be grateful if you'd eat the damn things while they're still chewable. Save my conscience from thinking about the poor dumb steer that gave its life for this."

"Well... "

"There's no charge, mister."

Harley's eyes brightened. "Well, shucks," he said. "I'm like you. One thing I can't stand, it's watchin' beef go to waste. Especially after I work so damn hard to raise it." He grabbed the hamburger, chomped at the bun.

Watching him eat, munching and licking, Chambers said, "I'd be extra pleased if you'd kindly dispose of the rest."

Harley nodded his head. "Well, sure, why not? Where I come from, we hurt steers worse than this and they get well afterwards."

Chambers brought more buns stacked with meat and watched with interest as Harley made them disappear. "You ridden yet?" he asked.

"Nope." Harley licked his fingers. "I'm on slack. Probably catch my ride near sundown."

Chambers waited as Harley put a fist to his chest and burped.

"Too much salt," Chambers acknowledged. "It helps sell the beer. Maybe you'd go for a beer. We got Oly and Bud."

Harley was tempted. He thought it over. He really wanted to save his last two dollars for hard liquor. "Water," he said. "You got plain water?"

Chambers went for a cup. When he returned and placed the water on the counter, there was a silver dollar there. "What's this?"

"For the Rotary," Harley said.

The silver dollar had come from his boot.

Chambers said, "Good luck — on your ride. Okay?"

Harley, head back to guzzle water, raised a thumb. He set down the Styrofoam cup, licked his lips once more, said, "I appreciate that, mister. The luck, I sure could use it. It's been a raccoon's age since I drew a halfway decent horse."

***

But Harley Wyatt did not get a decent horse. In the orange light of sundown, with no one left in the arena but the officials and a few drunken diehards, he shot through the gate on Old Whirlie and went for one of the dizziest rides of his life. Spinning like a centrifuge, his body was thrown out of control. His right hand whipped everywhere and barely brushed the saddle horn; but the judges caught the fault and disqualified him.

Even so, just for spite, Harley stuck to Old Whirlie like a blister, and the pickup men — riding circles around the violence — were unable to cut in to help the cowboy off. The horse got itself dizzy and tumbled over, thrashing and kicking, grinding its rider into the dirt. When Harley managed to get untangled, and staggered to his feet, he heard a roar like the crowd that no longer was there. He had spots in his eyes, ached all over, and his ribs — barely mended since his last ride — were again pinching his guts.

Unsteady on his bowed legs, his sweaty dust-coated shirt sticking to his chest, Harley wobbled out of the arena and across the deserted parking area, clambered into his pickup, started the engine, and drove aimlessly away.

He had nowhere to go — except to find himself a badly needed drink. With his last two dollars.

***

There were others like Harley; other losers who dragged themselves in the dark and neon from one hot and crowded Jackpine bar to another. Bloodied and belligerent, they mingled on mainstreet with the few winners, the many fans, the hard drinkers, hoping to be included when a spender appeared and ordered a set-up all around.

Harley eventually found himself staring into a shot of bourbon, hunched over the mahogany bar in the Night Rider Saloon, when a bearded biker slammed the bar alongside him, slapped down a tattered hundred-dollar bill, bellowed an order at the bartender.

The cowboy squinted sideways at the biker's grease-stained hand, the money it held, the studded leather vest, the ratty T-shirt, the cobra tattoo, the scraggly beard. And then, because his curiosity got the best of him, he asked:

"Now where'n hell did a sonofabitch like you get ahold of so much money?"

The biker glanced left, right, not believing the cowboy was speaking directly to him. "You talking to me, fella?"

"Sure am." Harley pivoted on the stool. "If I ain't dreamin', that's a whole hundred-dollar bill in your paw.

Don't say it. Lemme guess. They give it to you over at the welfare department."

The biker's gaze turned rock hard. "None of your god-damn business, cowboy."

Harley slowly pushed back the barstool and stood up. The top of his hat came about level with the biker's eyes. "Ya know," he said, "I oughta take offense to that kinda smartass backtalk. But I'm just here to be sociable. I figured I got a share in that hundred dollars, on account of me pay-ing the income taxes which supports that damn welfare of-fice. Seems to me, it would only be fair for a fella like you to show your gratitude and buy me a drink. It seems to me."

The biker grabbed the front of Harley's shirt. "Listen good, dungfoot. Bug off. Get your stupid ass outa here be-fore I get mad and yank your face off."

"Now you're gettin' excited," Harley said, not even re-motely intimidated. He had spent part of the evening wres-tling a 1,500-pound bucking horse to the ground, and he wasn't about to be put off by a mere 250-pound man. He planned a punch that would begin at his right ankle, up through his thigh, his back, his shoulder, along his arm to his fist, all in one perfect motion, exploding with full power against the biker's temple. He said, "So just forget about buyin' me a drink. Hell, that's all right by me. I already thought of a better idea. Let me buy you one."

Harley snatched up his bourbon with his left hand and tossed it in the biker's eyes. And with his whole right side, he delivered his punch.

Within seconds, chairs had scraped and boots had clat-tered across the pine floor, and enough cowboys had grabbed the biker to thwart his efforts to strike back. Struggling, shaking his head from Harley's blow, the biker cursed while Harley casually looked him over. "I'll be damned," Harley said to the others. "He ought to have been out like a light. Must be he ain't got nothin' inside his head except cee-ment." He pondered briefly. "And look at all this hair. Damned if it ain't just like a horse's tail." He tugged at the hair, suddenly jerked it, and sent the biker backwards to the floor with two cowboys helping to take him down.

The bartender, wiping glasses and trying to appear nonchalant, peered over the bar. "Whatcha doin' there, boys?"

Harley straightened up, gave the bartender a puzzled frown. "This here greaseball," he said. "I just don't know what's got into him. He's all hoppin' mad, and I was only just purchasin' him a drink, purely outa kindness of the heart. He's kinda down and out, don't cha know."

"See whatcha mean," the bartender said. "Looks like he's plumb flat on his back."

"Ya know," Harley went on, "I get this charitable feelin' comes over me. Kinda makes we want to help a poor sonofabitch like this... Like, take a look at his hair, for instance. You could sweep the floor with it. Why hell, I bet he ain't had no haircut in... what wouldja say, fellas? A year, or two?"

While the biker kicked and snarled, one of the cowboys holding him suggested, "Christ Almighty, Harley. If you're so all bent outa shape to help the bastard, why don't *you* cut his hair?"

"Say. Now why'n hell didn't *I* think of it?"

The struggle immediately intensified as the biker reacted. Two more cowboys joined the cluster, lifting him onto a barstool. "Whoa! This fool idiot's gonna hurt himself. Somebody get a rope to hold'm down."

"Hey-hey," the bartender said. "Ain't you gents had enough calf ropin' for one day?"

"It ain't no calf," Harley snapped, locking an arm around the biker's neck. "It's a goddamn stubborn jackass. Now hold still, big fella. This ain't gonna hurt 'cha, not one little bit."

The bartender went back to wiping glasses. The Night Rider Saloon had been the site of many impromptu clippings, usually at the expense of hapless hippies who wandered in, unaware of this cowboy custom; but frequently cowboys snipped one another in winter months when hippies were scarce. And this time, as far as the bartender was concerned, the biker had it coming. He had entered a cowboy bar, flashed big money, and insulted a luckless rodeo rider.

Using sheep shears kept on hand for such occasions, Harley went to work on the biker who sat in silent anger, wrapped in rope, nostrils flaring, hands balled into fists.

"Now, I believe that's much better," Harley said, slapping clippings off the biker's shoulders, stepping back to admire. "You go show your momma, though. And if she ain't altogether satisfied, you could always hustle back here and we'll trim a little more off. Always better to take off a little too little than a little too much, I always say."

The biker — chopped nearly bald above the ears — slid off the barstool. Fiercely brushing ropes aside, he hissed, "You dung-scuffers are gonna pay for this."

"Hey now," Harley said, grinning. "Nobody owes nothin'. It's all for *free*." He stuffed the hundred-dollar bill down the front of the biker's shirt. "Hold this in your bosom for when you don't find such a charitable feller as me."

The saloon rang with laughter as the biker stomped out.

***

Outside, mainstreet trembled under the pressure of an expanding crowd. Hordes of young men and women flowed from the saloons onto the sidewalks, carrying beer and liquor with them, clambering onto the hoods of parked cars. Empty cans piled up in the gutters, where weaving cowboys stumbled over them while dodging hornblasts and headlights from an endless procession of vehicles.

Erwin Wooster, Jackpine's most notorious drinker, for once blended in as he sat on a curbstone, trying to free his left foot from a sewer grate. He finally jerked his foot out of his shoe, grumbled as the shoe landed with a hollow splash in the stormwater. He hobbled away with his toes protruding from a ragged sock.

Above the neon, student-age men and women appeared on rooftops, dangling legs over the parapets. Some of them sprinkled beer onto pedestrians, enticing a few hotheads into climbing awnings in vain efforts to strike back. An arm of one awning broke loose, dumping the climber.

The sight of all this was awesome to Nathan Chambers, who couldn't remember a year when the July Fourth celebration had been so uncontrollable. He toured the sidewalks with Fire Chief Spud Berlinsky, and together they did what little they could to minimize the damage.

"It's like a damned rock concert," Chambers marveled. He surmised the energy crisis had caused this, provoking young people into a final fling before their world came unglued.

Berlinsky worried most about the people on the roofs. He told Chambers the buildings were old, the roofs weakened by years of heavy snow, the mortar crumbling in the parapets. "We ought to send some men up there," he suggested. "Chase off those goons."

Before Chambers could reply, a nearby woman screamed. "*Wahoo!* Lookit there! A *streaker!*"

Where she pointed, a naked youth jogged along with the stream of traffic. His flabby white skin and dark blotches of body hair were stark in the headlights, almost fluorescent green under the mercury vapor streetlights. Horns blasted, male voices boomed from car windows.

The excited woman began jumping, breasts bouncing under a tight T-shirt. "*Go* for it!" she shouted. "*Let 'er rip!*"

The runner, waving, was followed by two more naked figures, their bearded heads bobbing above the cartops. From behind them came the trilling of a police whistle.

The streakers pumped past in a greenish-white blur. Moments later they were back, pink now under the red glow of a Kentucky Fried Chicken sign.

Berlinsky touched Nathan's elbow and pointed. Burleigh Driscoll, red-faced and huffing, his gray uniform stained with sweat, emerged from the crowd and planted his big feet squarely in the path of the three runners.

For just a second, the first runner broke stride. Then he cut to his right, trying to dodge past the chief. The second runner collided with him, and together they fell against Driscoll. All three went down like bowling pins.

"Aw damn," Chambers said. "There she blows."

Sitting on his buttocks, legs pinned beneath the two streakers, the chief yelled and flailed his arms at the third one. "Hold it there, you asshole! *Chism!* Grab that other punk!"

From between parked cars, Patrolman Buck Chism made a sudden dash, his holstered Smith & Wesson flapping against his thigh, his police cap flying off behind him. Chism threw himself at the running figure, caught him at the knees, and both men hit the pavement with a thudding skid.

Deadly silence.

Then hoots and catcalls erupted as the men got up.

Patrolman Chism helped the runner to his feet. "You okay?" he asked. "You okay?"

"I'm okay, I'm okay," the runner grunted, wincing. "But holy Christ, man, you didn't have to *tackle* me!"

The hooting mob spilled onto the street, circling the officers. Driscoll tried to bull his way out, bellowing, *"Break it up, break it up!"* while hauling a streaker at the end of a pair of handcuffs.

It was at this moment when Harley Wyatt came out of the Night Rider Saloon, curious about the commotion. Immediately, he was jumped by three husky bikers. They bounced against the saloon window and rattled it, catching the attention of the cowboys inside.

Harley's reinforcements came through the saloon door in a drunken heap. Fists began swinging. Blood splattered onto a white silk cowboy shirt worth eighty dollars. There was a flashing of tire chains, a sharp crack of fist clipping jaw. Window glass shattered into pellet-sized fragments, hailing down onto hat brims and sidewalk.

The melee caught the attention of two volunteer firemen standing at the curb. They raised their cans of Mace.

The rooftop spectators, howling with glee, showered the scene with beer cans and bottles. The Mace began panicking those within sight or smell of it.

Two more store windows crashed to the sidewalk. A block away, a fire engine set off its siren and sat in the stalled traffic, its beacon flashing blood-red light streaks across the mob.

A team of firefighters in tan rubber coats and black hip boots jumped down from the truck and unraveled a canvas firehose. Prematurely, someone turned open the valves and sent water surging through the hose. It whipped in all directions before the firefighters could pin it down. A stream of water struck a cluster of people on the sidewalk and knocked them over. Fancy hair-do's instantly resembled seaweed. One woman's thin blouse was blasted away.

In the midst of this, Chambers sent Berlinsky to halt the water and gas attacks, then caught up with Driscoll and grabbed the chief's arm. *"Let go of this kid!"* he yelled.

"You're crazy!" Driscoll shot back. "He assaulted me! And *look what he started!"*

"He ran into you by *accident!* And the damn riot started *across the street!* The kid had nothing to do with it!"

"Says *who!"*

"Says *me!"*

An empty can bounced off the chief's head.

"I'm telling you," Chambers shouted, "it's not worth it! Release the kid before things start getting really *ugly!*"

"All *right*! All *right!*" Purple veins bulged on the chief's scarlet face. "Get the hell going, you! Go get some clothes! Now!"

"I *can't*," the streaker whined. "I'm *handcuffed!*"

"Goddamn it to hell..." The chief searched his shirt for keys, then his pants. Finally he snapped open the cuffs. "Now beat it! Before I change my goddamn mind!"

"Yessir!" The youth backpedalled, turned, shot through the crowd like a greased hog. A cheer went up.

After another sweep, the firehose fell off to a trickle. Sheriff's deputies moved swiftly along the curbs, pushing back the remaining onlookers with nightsticks. "Back off the streets," they ordered. "Clear away — it's all over now."

Most of the crowd had thinned away into doorways, automobiles, sidestreets. Where fights had been stopped with Mace, deputies began sorting men apart, lifting fallen ones to their feet, sending those who needed medical attention to a parked ambulance.

In a few more minutes, the traffic resumed its motion, and Berlinsky started sending men to clear the roofs.

Chambers exhaled a long-held breath, propped a foot on a car bumper, looked at the sagging chief. "Close," he said.

The chief didn't answer. His eyes were bloodshot.

"Let's go and shut down the bars, call it a night," Chambers said.

"Right," Driscoll said. "And pray the town don't lynch us in the morning."

Chapter 14: Milwaukee, Wisconsin

THE NATIONAL HEADQUARTERS of The Wisconsin Trust was moored in palatial splendor upon a rolling lawn at Milwaukee's northwest outskirts.

Hal Dexter marched through the employee atrium where clerks and secretaries usually assembled for salad lunches in a garden setting. This Friday after the Fourth, the music and fountains were off, the tabletops barren.

Dexter entered an office suite with its doors open, receptionist absent. He heard Bob Taylor speaking and lightly tapped the door as he entered.

"Yeah — come in, Hal." The lanky man behind the crescent desk was leaning far astern in an executive swivel lounger, holding a phone to his ear. His free hand was across his flat chest, scratching the armpit of his golf shirt. "Well, maybe we can trade starting times with Jerry's group," he said. "A nine-thirty tee-off is the best I can do, Hank." He cocked his head at Dexter, rolled his eyes. "Yes, yes, I'll supply the scotch, you prick!" Taylor smashed the phone down and dropped his feet into the deep carpet.

"Good morning, Bob," Dexter said.

Taylor nodded and rocked in his chair.

"Sorry if I'm delaying your golf match," Dexter said.

"Business before pleasure; that's the rule around here." Taylor stopped rocking and settled his freckled forearms on the desk. "So anyway. Tell me about your great western adventure."

Dexter shrugged. "Hardly exciting. The best word I can think of is — rustic."

"Rustic? That's it?"

"Well... Perhaps I expected too much," Dexter said. "After hearing those sparkling descriptions from Joe Bartz... "

"Bartz is a turd."

"Yes," Dexter said.

Taylor scratched at a reddish brow, peeked at his Rolex, then squinted at Dexter. He said, "Well, let's keep this tight — the details can wait. Give me the highlights, then your bottom-line assessment. Can we do that?"

"Fine."

Dexter opened his notebook and gave a terse report of his contacts in Jackpine, ending with the mayor. After a reflective pause, he commented: "Um, I think he'll need some softening-up, along with certain others." Another thought, then: "It may not work, and it may not be worth the trouble. But if you want to keep things humming out there, we'll probably need to grease a few wheels."

"Okay... How much grease?"

"Well, not a whole lot. I don't think it's worth a whole lot."

Taylor sniffed and swiveled, reached for a hefty stack of printouts. He dumped them in front of Dexter. "These are the latest spreadsheets. Have you studied the investment stream lately? My God, Hal, there's enough grease in there to overhaul a battleship. Let us not become too timid when it comes to lubrication. Apply liberally, wherever there's even a tiny squeak."

"Bob... "

"Yeah, what?"

"Must we?"

Taylor's light brown eyes, ordinarily docile, became wary. "What's that supposed to mean?"

"It means," Dexter said, stiffening, "that I think we ought to take another look at what we're doing out there. Bob, a project of this size needs something I didn't find. It needs a location that's convenient to the masses, or some natural attraction to bring crowds from afar — something unique. And I'm sorry, but we don't have that. Not that I could see."

Taylor's inverted reflection scowled from the glass desktop. "You turkey. Do you realize that Mr. Spears picked that location himself? *Himself?*"

"Of course, Bob. I know that."

"For Christ's sake! You were sent out there to do some local PR work, not to second-guess Spears and the board of directors. Look, that man wants to build a winter Disneyland. If it doesn't have a natural Matterhorn, he'll manufacture your goddamned Matterhorn."

"At horrible expense. As I see it."

"Hal, read my lips. We are not going to defy Ernest Lucius Spears. The board agreed to this project. Two years ago! So did I."

"Two years ago... Bob, two years ago, we weren't anticipating an Arab oil embargo. The winter sports were growing by leaps and bounds then. Two years ago, environmental restrictions were virtually non-existent."

"You don't have to remind me that times have changed, pal." Taylor waved his arms and sprang to his feet, began prowling the deep carpet. Framed on the wall was a formal portrait of a handsome woman and two redheaded boys. He poked at it. "Last Christmas, I took Michael and Jeffrey to Aspen. We were waiting two hours in lift lines. Two hours, by God, and you can't tell me there isn't a demand for more ski slopes." He jammed his hands into his pockets and rattled some coins and keys.

"But how long will that demand continue?" Dexter asked. "Bob, the economy is trembling now and getting worse. Look at your spreadsheets for either discrete or continuous compounding of interest. How can we predict our internal rate of return? With interest rates still climbing, with the falling GNP and rising unemployment, with New York on the edge of bankruptcy and a predicted hundred million federal deficit... "

"That's beside the point!" Taylor plunged back into his chair and chopped the air with his right hand. "Harold, look. I could argue that you've just listed all the reasons for charging ahead. The costs won't ever get any cheaper than right now. But that's totally irrelevant. It's purely academic."

Hal Dexter nodded and slumped back in his chair.

Taylor shoved aside the printouts and spoke softly. "Okay, maybe Spears doesn't exactly own this shop. But he holds all the crucial keys. And if he *ever* suspects that you're even *slightly* disloyal... Woe is you. Woe is us."

Dexter, face reddened, said nothing.

"Harold, don't scare me like that," Taylor said.

"You're right, Bob. It's only the stockholders' money. Let's have some fun."

Taylor grimaced, pressed a fist against his chest and burped. "God, I'm nervous these days. Hal, the ladder to the top in this outfit is tall and spindly. I'm only a few rungs from where I can have the power to do some good. But up here, I can't stand any tornadoes. I can't stand a breeze. So please listen to me, Hal. Listen well."

Dexter remained silent, motionless.

"Don't get Spears on the warpath, buddy." Taylor pointed a throbbing finger. "You do, and I swear to God I'll blow your fucking brains out."

Dexter sighed and picked up his notebook. He got to his feet and answered quietly, before turning to the doorway:

"In this outfit, Bob, there are no brains."

Chapter 15: The Jackpine City Council

EVERY CHAIR was taken in Jackpine City Hall, and more citizens stood along the walls. The room had become a pot of human stew, simmering under a layer of tobacco smoke and smelling like bad meat and old leather.

City Clerk Otto Cuculich, a chickenlike man with small round eyeglasses pinned to his beak, watched the crowd as it stirred along the edges, ready to boil. Cuculich was a twenty-year veteran of protest meetings but seldom had seen a crowd this hostile. He tapped a pencil against his soft palm and sat up straight, anxious to display his neutrality. He meant to show that he was only the *recorder* of these proceedings, not part of the brew.

Down the table, Vincent Fox worked his gum like a wad of road tar in his mouth. A shiny drop of sweat clung to the tip of Kermit Czarnowsky's nose. Cuculich had silently counted the roll and noted with satisfaction that all officers were present, except the mayor. He glanced down at the empty chair and wondered how much courage it would take for Nathan Chambers to come and occupy it.

Then with the clock ticking to the hour of eight, the crowd split and Chambers came through. He kicked back the chair with his boot, plunked down some folders, and silenced the crowd's mutterings with a whack of his gavel.

"Pledge of Allegiance," he said. Chairs scraped as all good citizens stood hastily and joined the recital.

Before everyone was resettled, Chambers called for approval of the minutes. Cuculich rummaged up his notes and started reading in his cracked voice, which frequently made him sound nervous even when he wasn't. He concentrated on getting each item just right, to avoid any additions or corrections: "— Motion made by Alderman Dietermann to defer the question of the state gasoline tax refunds to the Streets and Alleys Committee. Seconded by Alderman Christoferson and approved by six ayes and no nays... "

The table rattled, and Cuculich looked around to see that it was Roy Yancey, squirming and pretending to be interested and alert. Chambers, however, was ignoring the minutes, pulling out sheets from the folders he had brought. The citizens were droning among themselves. Fire Chief Berlinsky was staring at the air.

Cuculich read the remainder of the minutes to Roy Yancey.

Next, Chambers called for approval to draw warrants for paying the bills against the city. Yancey's motion started an argument when he referred to the warrants "*in* their respective *amounts*" while Dietermann insisted the proper wording was "*from* their respective *accounts*."

Fox snapped, "I second the goddamn motion," and the vote was taken. Cuculich wrote down, automatically, six ayes and no nays.

When Chambers proceeded to reports of officers, Cuculich began wondering why the mayor wasn't bypassing these routines to let the citizens speak. The heat was becoming intense. Cuculich knew these people, their temperaments and their roots. He knew that Jackpine, like many mining towns, had been settled by hardboned immigrants: by Yugoslavians who had come to blast the rock; English and Irish who became bankers and politicians; Scottish and Italians who opened the merchant trade; Finnish, Germans, Austrians, and Russians who broke sod and planted sugar beets and barley; Scandinavians who raised livestock.

They all had endured decades of ethnic turmoil. But, in time, they had banded together in common need to survive hard winters, floods, droughts, the Great Depression, two world wars, and mine disasters — including one, in 1947, that killed forty-three of their fathers, sons, husbands, and brothers.

Ultimately, with shared struggles and limited choices, mixed marriages were inevitable and brought Catholics and Protestants into the same households. And there were unifying causes such as building the high school and hospital.

Now they had another common cause — punishing the city fathers for the "July Fourth Fiasco." In olden days, some councilmen might have had support among their kinsmen.

Not tonight.

Tonight, while the mayor steadfastly held to the agenda, perhaps to underline the council's authority, these people were getting ready to fry him in pig fat.

Cuculich felt sweat trickle down his spine.

Suddenly, he became aware of a silence. Then he heard the mayor say: "We'll now hear statements from citizens."

Immediately they were in Pandemonium. Hands waved, voices yapped and screeched, all demanding recognition.

Chambers twirled the gavel, then pointed its handle at a swarthy man with a stomach like a medicine ball. "Ivan Bezdicek," he said. "You first."

While the crowd moaned and sat back, Bezdicek squared up his posture and hitched up his pants. He was owner of the Night Rider Saloon and said he was representing the Jackpine Bar Owners Association with twelve dues-paying members, each and every one of whom was both a taxpayer and contributor to Jackpine civic organizations and youth groups.

"And I'm speaking for all of us," he declared, "when I say we're more than a *little* upset about that riot we had rodeo night. Most of us, we lost money the first time in twenty years on the rodeo. We had smashed windows which our insurance don't cover. And that plate glass is damned expensive. We had to shut down early! And right now, some of us got petitions posted at our bars. We want a recall of this here mayor or the council or anyone else who's responsible for lettin' the situation get outa hand like that. And we got a pretty good bunch of signatures already."

"Ivan," Chambers said. "It was your saloon where the first fight broke out — where it all started."

"Well... I don't know nothin' about that. All I know is that the windows was smashed for three blocks, and beer cans on the street the next morning was like a mirror, blinding your eyes in the sun. But *inside* my place, there wasn't so much as a spilled beer or broken shot glass. I run a quiet place, Mr. Mayor."

Chambers smacked his knuckles against the table. "Dallas Carpenter is next. Sit down, Ivan."

Dallas stood. She was a tough-minded bartender with red wavy hair, tall in cowboy boots and jeans, heavy chest filling a man's shirt.

"What I wanna know, is what's goin' on when our police and councilmen can't handle a rodeo crowd quiet-like any-more. In all my years tendin' bar on rodeo nights — and we had some rowdy ones before — I never seen where the fire-hoses had to come out. Who the *hell* screwed up?"

Before Chambers could reply, a ghostly woman stood up like a black candle in a long dress, her gnarled hands clutch-ing an equally gnarled cane. "Mister Mayor!" she snapped.

This was Tillie Culhane, Jackpine's contingent of the Salvation Army for nearly forty years. Contrary to Roy Yancey's premonition, she hadn't encountered any streakers on rodeo night, but she had spent the evening in her dark-ened parlor, Bible in one hand, cross in the other, praying for deliverance.

Now Miss Culhane's eyes bored holes through the to-bacco smoke while she barked off a tirade against the morals of anyone who would tolerate nakedness in public. "Sodom and Gomorrah!" she shouted. "That's what this town is com-ing to! Lord, save us!"

As she raved on, Chambers crossed his forearms on the table and watched the others settle into catatonic trances.

"And as for *you*, Nate Chambers," she lashed, startling him to attention, "who made *you* the mayor? *I* didn't vote for ya. *Nobody* did! My late husband Elmo, he was president of this council before you was born, and back then they didn't put up with all this wicked foolishness!" She hoisted the cane, and for an instant Chambers thought she was going to club him with it. "Those who *abide* wickedness are doomed to *perish* in it!" And with that, she smacked her cane against the floor and dropped onto her chair like a collapsed marionette.

While everyone remained speechless, Chambers casually fished out a sheet of paper and stood. "Well, now I know what it feels like to be Richard Nixon."

The remark produced chuckles from an audience suffering from an overdose of Tillie Culhane.

Chambers continued: "Ivan, there's no need to include the councilmen on your recall petition. The responsibility is mine."

There were some murmurings, which Chambers ignored.

"I'll tell you what bothered me about dealing with the kind of crowd we had on rodeo night...

"First, we've got only a few officers with any kind of police training. The rest — the volunteer firemen, the councilmen, myself — we have no experience in crowd control.

"I'm not talking about arresting some drunken cowboys, like in past years. Back in the old days, cowboys would come and raise some hell. But they showed respect for lawmen and they stayed in bounds, more or less. This new bunch of kids — the kind you saw running naked and climbing the roofs — they're from all over. And they're different."

"You can say that again," Vincent Fox muttered.

"I'll say it again. They're different. They've been through the war protests. You all heard about Kent State. These kids can't trust authority, so they don't respect it. And they sure's hell won't be intimidated by it."

Nathan saw a general raising of heads and continued:

"Suppose we sent a few half-trained officers charging into that bunch, armed with cattle prods. Suppose some of our volunteers went after 'em with ax handles. You think those kids would turn into wimps and run? Hell no, they wouldn't. We'd be up to our eyeballs in a bloody street fight with people getting hurt. And I'm telling you, if one of them got crippled, or worse, the lawsuit would just about bust this town. Believe me, we got off cheap on the broken windows."

"But you can't coddle troublemakers, Nate," Dallas Carpenter said. "I don't hold with that."

"You're right, Dallas. But we don't have any other kind of response that works. We can't shoot 'em. Whatever they look like, they're just American kids."

Dietermann said, "So what're you sayin', Nate? We gotta board up the windows and *hide* every year?"

The crowd started murmuring again, and Nathan knocked the table with his knuckles and continued. "I phoned up to Helena. They referred me to the Department of Corrections — the state prison at Deer Lodge. The assistant warden, he teaches crowd control. He gives classes for the Highway Patrol, the prison guards, and I don't know who else. He said he could come and teach us, if we pay his expenses. That's about a hundred and fifty bucks."

There was more talk, a few affirmative nods. Chief Driscoll, hunched with elbows on knees, looked skeptical. Attorney Web Forsythe, pipe in mouth and legs crossed, looked thoughtful.

"It's up to you folks," Nathan said. "You can circulate that petition. Or you could help us out."

"Help in what way, Nate?" Dallas asked.

"Manpower," Nathan said. "Or womanpower. This expert said we need about two dozen extra men or women on the line. In order to back down a crowd with minimum violence, we need a strong show of force. He recommended a police auxiliary — all volunteers, trained and equipped. We also need some cash donations. For helmets and badges, some basic gear."

"Well, I can write a check," Dallas said, "but I'll leave the rough stuff to you men."

Chambers looked directly at Ivan Bezdicek. "You think the Jackpine Bar Owners Association could chip in? It's a civic cause — one with direct benefit for each and every one of your charitable members."

Bezdicek shrugged, coughed, adjusted his posture on his chair. "Well, I don't speak for the whole association... " He stopped. "Well, when it comes to their money, I don't. But I can kick in a hundred from my own pocket. Most of the others, I'm sure... they would, too."

"Twelve hundred dollars should be almost enough," Chambers said.

Hands went up. Chambers pointed to Jonas Barclay, Melvin's eldest son, who ranched near Red Rock Creek. "Say," Jonas said. "This here police auxiliary — would it be like a regular outfit, uniforms and all? Or just like a posse?"

"I was told we should have a regular force that looks professional. Shirts would be uniform, anyway. Plus, we'd have badges and helmets, maybe belts for nightsticks."

"You got some paper, I could sign up?" Jonas asked.

Chambers slid the sheet to the front of the table. "The line forms to the right," he said.

***

It was a starry night, cooled down finally, and Chambers took surges of fresh air into his lungs.

"Nice going, Nate," said a familiar voice behind him.

Chambers turned. "Bayliss. What the hell you still doing here? The excitement ended two hours ago."

"Not really." The newspaper publisher looked up at the stars. "You saved the best for last."

Chambers stuffed his fingers into his jean pockets and rocked on his heels. "You mean about the ski development."

"Glad you remembered to mention it. After your fun with the police auxiliary business... God, what a wild notion that was! After that, you went into hours of committee reports, old business, old-old business... the endless and still unresolved discussion on naming a replacement for your Third Ward vacancy... "

"Goddamn boring. I warned you about that."

"You notice, by the way, that Otto still records six ayes, with five aldermen? Anyway, everybody was long gone. Picked up their hats, stomped out their cigarettes, and moved out. Except me. So then you decide to hold an executive session on personalities. Smart, Nate. Smart."

"I don't know anything about smart," Chambers said. "We thought it would save us from another meeting. We let you stay."

"Then finally," Bayliss said, an accusatory tone in his voice, "*finally* — you mention this humongous ski project is set to begin construction in a *year*. Banner *headline* stuff! And you spring this *afterwards* — after everybody's gone home, and I'm half asleep." Bayliss shook his head.

"Well hell, Ben. I was just following the agenda. New business always comes last."

"Oh sure. Meanwhile, what happened to that other bombshell? Slip your mind?"

Chambers glanced at his watch. "Ben, it's almost midnight. Stop playing games."

"I'm not the one playing games."

"Then what the hell are you talking about? What other bombshell?"

Bayliss showed large teeth in the darkness, a crude form of a smile. "You know what I mean... the coal. The *coal!*"

"Ben, gimme a break?"

"I know about it. I dig deep in county records. Always have, always will. And there I find it. Old coal rights being bought up, left and right, thousands of acres. All spread among three different buyers — but all in one month. Obviously, some kind of consortium."

"That," Chambers said, "is news to me."

Bayliss let out a long breath. "Then read about it Thursday." He started to strut away, hesitated, turned back. "By the way. That vigilante troop of yours. The *po-leece auxiliary?*"

"Shoot. What about it?"

"The way things are going, you're gonna need more than a private army to keep *you* in office."

The big teeth flashed. Then Bayliss was gone in darkness.

Chapter 16: The Jackpine *Spectator*

THE NEWSPAPER OFFICE held no sign of life when Nathan Chambers entered in the morning, a rolled-up *Spectator* clenched in his fist.

It was an old storefront building, crudely partitioned with hardboard panels, papered with yellowed clippings and cartoons. The publisher's desk, an ancient rolltop, was jammed into a corner under heaps of galley proofs and invoices. Two other desks, gray steel with rubber tops, showed grimy evidence of use by the women who worked part-time on subscriptions and classified ads.

Chambers ducked under oily flypaper coiling from the ceiling and barged through the swinging doors to the print-shop. A trouble light was shining into the open top of a computerized typesetting machine, and Benjamin Bayliss was leaning there on his elbows, staring glumly into the Compugraphic's innards.

Chambers shoved the newspaper under the trouble light. Three headlines dominated the front page:

Giant Ski Project Threatens Jackpine
Mayor Silent on Coal Mystery
Mayor Enlists Riot Troops

Bayliss straightened up slowly. "Nate. Glad you're here. Lookit this mess." He gestured into the machine. "Those itty-bitty wires and all those silicon chips. You're an engineer — maybe you can figure 'em out. Huh?"

Despite his pique, Chambers glanced into the unit. "Ben... "

"They sent me a so-called repair kit," Bayliss said. "Buncha chips with little prongs, like toy spiders, all in neat little compartments." Bayliss sighed. "When this contraption acts weird, I phone some technician on the West Coast. I describe the symptoms. He talks some foreign language, then tells me to pull out chip such-and-such. Plug in the replacement. Burp the goddamn thing once or twice..."

"Ben... "

"I tried it," Bayliss said. "Tried every kind of chip except a cowchip." He gave Chambers a mournful look. "All this shitty thing does is make beeps and print out garbage."

Chambers stared. "Sounds to me like you and that stupid machine got a whole lot in common!"

Bayliss smirked. He said, "That's pretty good. You're angry, obviously. Something I wrote?"

Chambers whipped open the paper to a page where he had underlined parts of Ben's editorial column:

*

"...The impacts of these startling developments are plain as black and white... The black is the coal dust that once again will clog our men's lungs and dirty our streets and streams... The white is a ski hill monstrosity which may bring tremendous benefit to out-of-state developers at the expense of our overburdened local taxpayers... "

*

Bayliss had listed various public works projects necessary to service such a large resort, then turned to social aspects:

*

"Do we want our quiet community overrun with playful Mid-west millionaires? Do we want our children employed as waiters, cooks, and servants to the rich — and exposed to pipelines of marijuana, cocaine, and heroin? Do we want sons and husbands crawling back into dark holes to risk Black Lung disease and repeats of the 1947 mine disaster? And whether we do or don't, do we even have a voice in these matters?

"Apparently not. Because these things are coming without warning and without public involvement...

"Projects of this magnitude do not spring to life overnight. They require extensive on-site planning and cooperation from local authorities. Meanwhile, our greenhorn mayor has been chasing rainbows ever since he returned from Vietnam, a hero of sorts, winning our misguided gratitude and our votes for two terms on the city council. And now, suddenly, he is the mayor. And now, quite suddenly, we have overwhelming ski and coal projects coming down our throats...

"But is it a rainbow you are bringing to Jackpine, Mr. Mayor? Or a dark muddle of black and white? And, we must wonder, who gets the pot of gold?"

*

Chambers flung the newspaper to the floor.

"Colorful writing," Bayliss said. "You gotta give it that."

"One color you left out," Chambers said. "For journalism, it's yellow as puke."

Bayliss looked genuinely surprised. "I got to write that down — quote of the week!"

Chambers pressed a finger against Bayliss's shirt. "I want a retraction, Ben."

"A what?"

"Retraction. Whatever the hell you call it — you know what I mean, you sonofabitch."

"Poor lad — another altruistic public servant victimized by the cruel press. How's about some coffee?" He reached for a scummy kettle on a hotplate. "This stuff comes out of the spout like a Tootsie Roll — best damn coffee in town."

"Ben, I had plenty of your poison for one day."

Bayliss dribbled some black brew into a stained cup, sipped, squinted at Chambers. "A retraction," he said. "Once in a blue moon, I may feel compelled to print a retraction — for an error of fact. That editorial, though, that's strictly opinion, clearly labeled as opinion. You're a public official and fair game. As a journalist, I do have an obligation to be your adversary. Nothing personal, though."

"Nothing personal? You stand there, accusing me of secrecy, hinting at outright graft and corruption. You say I might be guilty of conflict of interest — that I'm somehow in cahoots with these out-of-state developers. And that ain't *personal?*"

"Hey. If you disagree, Nate, you could submit an opposing view. I'd be tickled to publish it."

"I'd be tickled *pink* to watch you *rot!* You got no business coming to this town and trying to stir up a hornet's nest. Back when old Sam Ketchum owned this paper... "

"You didn't know how to read back then."

"That's beside the point. Dammit, the folks here liked the paper and they loved old Sam. They don't like this kind of mudslinging horseshit you pretend is news. They... "

"*Now* look who's getting personal!"

Bayliss became suddenly angry. His donkey mannerism turned into something grotesque, his eyes bulging and his teeth jutting as he snapped a finger at Chambers.

"*You* talk about Sam Ketchum as a great man and find me rotten by comparison. Are you aware of who is lying in state today — at this very moment — in the United States Supreme Court? Our former Chief Justice Earl Warren was a *great* man, and he didn't just write nice folksy opinions that wouldn't *offend* anybody. He stood for what he believed was *right*. So you tell me this, Mr. Mayor — how come you sat on those ski plans for *two weeks* before telling anyone? How come I had to learn about it at the end of a four-hour council meeting? How come all these plans have been in the works around here for *years* — and nobody knows a damn thing?

"... Except *this:* During those years, *you've* been talking up a ski project like some pitchman for snake oil. Now all of a sudden, it's a big *surprise* to you? Bull. No wonder you don't want news in a newspaper. You don't want anybody to know what'n hell you're *doing!*"

Chambers said, "I'm telling you I *didn't* know about the ski project until ten days ago!"

"*Somebody* had to know. And the *minute* you found out, you had a duty to make it public. Why didn't you? Was it graft? Was it corruption? Conflict of interest? Negligence? Had to be *one* of those."

They stared at each other.

In the silence, a dripping faucet made wet plunks behind the door of the toilet.

Chambers said, "You forgot one other possibility, Ben."

"Yeah?"

"Stupidity," Chambers said.

Bayliss cocked a brow.

"Hell," Chambers said, throwing his hands wide. "I plain didn't think about it. The ski project hardly seemed real. I had the rodeo coming at me. Then the riot, the recall petitions, the whole town in an uproar... Those things were *real.*"

Bayliss studied Chambers. He said, "Well, let's neither of us go off half-cocked. Maybe you're nothing worse than a bit naive. Maybe I'm cynical and in crappy moods too often." Bayliss waved a hand over the Compugraphic. "Like this machine. I'm sensitive to heat. It's been too hot lately."

"You're telling me."

"Nine years, I haven't missed a deadline," Bayliss said. "It becomes agony. Tuesday after Tuesday, I'm here all night sometimes — trying to finish up, put the paper to bed. I get this machine. It's supposed to save time, but I spend God knows how many hours pampering it. It cost me nine thousand, but hell, I can't squeeze one more dime out of my advertisers to help pay for it. If I raise the rates, they cut their space. I can't win. Half the customers, they don't pay. I go to collect, they complain their ad didn't pull. They don't know one damn thing about merchandising, but they blame me because their little two-inch ad in eight-point type didn't cause a stampede." Bayliss looked weary. "Listen, what the hell. Nobody's forcing me to do this. Right?"

Chambers said, "Sounds like you need a vacation."

Bayliss snorted. "If I took one, there'd be no newspaper."

"Take one anyway."

"Sure." Bayliss smiled wanly. "You'd love that."

"Sure would."

He nudged Chambers. "I'll go when you go. Otherwise, who'd keep an eye on you?"

"Ben... I got me a wife who does that."

***

Valerie was showering when the phone rang. She shoved aside the curtain, wrapped herself in a towel, scooted to the den. She picked up on the fifth ring. "Hello?"

"Valerie? This is Russell." Then, "Bancroft."

Valerie smiled. "Hello, Russell Bancroft." She couldn't help remembering his attentions when they'd first met. That was before she'd met Nathan.

"Nathan there?" Bancroft asked.

"'Fraid not." She loosened her grip on the towel; it began to slip slowly down her body. "He went to see Ben Bayliss — if you want to try catching him there."

"How long was that? When he left?"

The towel fell. Valerie stooped to recover it. She listened to his breath in her ear, then said, "Oh... twenty minutes."

"Well... " Bancroft hesitated, just breathing. "It's about the articles in the paper," he said finally. "Need to talk to him. But I have to head up to Greenwood Lake in a little bit. Then, it's to the high country for a few days. Uh... "

Valerie smiled sympathetically. "All I can do is tell him, Russ. I'm sure he'll try and catch you if he can."

"Yeah. Well, okay. That'll be fine. Thanks, Valerie."

Valerie cradled the phone slowly, letting it slide off the ends of her long fingers. She was acutely conscious of her moist body.

She and Russell Bancroft had almost... almost...

Hurrying to the bathroom, she dried her body, set her hair, smeared her face with lotion, then slipped on a pair of jeans, linen blouse, and sandals.

She spent the rest of the morning working up a sweat and getting grimy in the garden.

Chapter 17: The Views

DR. ROSCOE FULLER saw Nathan Chambers leaving the newspaper office and waited for him by the Jeep.

"Take that gal fishing yet?"

"Dammit, Doc — I forgot all about that!" Nathan squinted south over the glare of windshields, eyes searching for distance.

"Prescription's no good — unless you take it," Doc said.

"I know it." The street felt hot. Nathan said, "Maybe I could do it now — get the hell out of town."

"Don't let *me* hold you up," Doc said, motioning to the Jeep. There was something in the way he said it.

Nathan looked at the crackled face, the close-set eyes. The usual fire wasn't there. "Something wrong, Doc?"

"Hm?" Doc Fuller seemed distracted. "No... nothing. Funny thought struck me, is all."

Nathan waited.

"That idea I mentioned," Doc said. "My property down by the creek. It came to mind just now. Maybe you forgot, though."

"I didn't forget." Nathan could guess the rest. "Doc... "

"Comes to me clear as a bell — why you wouldn't take up my offer. My ideas for developing property." He wrinkled up his nose. "Small potatoes."

Nathan aimed a pair of fingers at the newspaper office. "That damned paper... Doc, it's just a misunderstanding. Don't believe everything you read."

"Now, now." Doc shrugged. "Big ski project like that — it's bound to get you caught up, one way or another. Listen here. Don't mind me. I'm too old these days." Doc worked his face into a fake smile. "The wife, the baby, you got every right — hell, the obligation. Chance comes, grab it."

"I'm telling you, Doc. This ski resort, I've got nothing in it. Nothing personal."

Doc flapped his arms. "I'm not saying you do. None of my damn business anyway. I'm only saying you'd be better off with them than me. What's a few cabins by the creek? These outside fellas, they're talkin' *condominiums.*"

Doc turned and was twelve paces up the sidewalk before Nathan had a chance to react. Then it was too late. He slumped.

He wished there was a rock; something he could pick up and throw.

***

Nathan stepped from the Jeep onto the rim of the East Bench. Below him, the town was settled out, north and south, all peaceful and relaxed. Sparse traffic moved silently along the streets, paced in rhythm with the shifting breezes.

Behind him, a horse romped among an endless sweep of wildflowers: Goldenrod, Larkspur, Sunflowers, Indian Paintbrush — an Oriental carpet spread from there to Canada. Chambers hunkered down, deep in waving blossoms, and chewed thoughtfully on a stem.

Across the valley, the hazy Beartooth Range sprawled in languid folds and mounds like figures of giants snoozing under thick green blankets. High up, traces of snow remained in shadowed pockets, and he could visualize skiers drifting down, powder plumes trailing high and bright.

Looking across the wondrous scene, Nathan felt like a character in a fairy tale; he just couldn't remember which one. He stood, took another glance, thought some more, adjusted his hat.

Then he vaulted into the Jeep and cranked up the engine, listening for the ping. His muscled forearms twirled the steering wheel around sharply, onto the road back down.

It was several more minutes of bouncing down the ruts before the identity struck him — the fairytale figure and its colorful domain.

Among the gorgeous wildflowers on the East Bench, overlooking a vast kingdom-like landscape, and having nowhere near the power everyone expected of him, Nathan Chambers felt very much like... the Wizard of Oz.

Chapter 18: Bancroft's Wilderness

CLOUDS LIKE STRINGY FOG were raking down the ridge and through the trees above the lake. A stiff breeze riffled the water, and Valerie shivered.

She fished from a timber footbridge over the inlet, letting the rushing stream carry her line onto the lake. Below her, Russell Bancroft was sitting on the bank beside Nathan. They looked like schoolboys, legs stretched out, hat brims down over their eyes, weed stems dangling from their lips.

The air smelled of pine and approaching drizzle. Valerie leaned over the rail. "I think we're going to get rained on, guys." She watched Nathan sniff the air and hold his palm out. He nodded. "Maybe a sprinkle. We won't melt."

Macho schoolboy response. Being cute.

***

"It's an environmental catastrophe," Bancroft stated. He had read the entire ski project file at the District Ranger Station.

Nathan stared at the dizzy currents in the creek. "Russ, it seems to me they're going miles out of their way to avoid damage to the environment."

"Avoiding obvious ruin, that's all." Bancroft glanced toward his old grey gelding, packed and saddled for a few days in the backcountry. The horse was grazing and dragging its reins, stumbling among the stones. "Their draft impact statement... " He hooked a thumb at the horse. "Reminds me of ol' Barney there. Half blind, skips over a lot of things."

"Such as?"

"Wildlife forage. That whole southeast face of Wapiti Mountain, it's critical winter range for the elk. That's how it got the name. Any big activity up there, like this ski development — it would drive off the herd." He paused. "We keep doing that — pushing the game farther back. A hard winter comes along, elk can't come down to their old range and they starve. The problem exists now. We're sometimes forced to issue elk permits twice a year, allowing hunters to thin the herds to fit the land — what's left of it."

Nathan enjoyed elk. He liked watching the bulls through binoculars, staking out perimeters around eighty or ninety of their cows on the open slopes in February each year. But he said, "Russ, this is just one ski resort."

"Wrong. It's this one plus the next. Plus other projects scattered along the Beartooth Face. Plus mineral exploration. Plus timber harvests on the other side. I swear, buddy — some days those trails in there get like a California freeway, all the activity in there. There's no more solitude for man nor beast. Hell, you don't know. You haven't been up there in a long time."

Bancroft tossed aside his chewed stem and picked another. He said, "It's the whole ecosystem I'm talking about, not just the elk. The elk are a yardstick. You can measure the quality of the total environment by their presence — or lack of presence."

Nathan was watching Valerie. The cool air rushing along with the creek ruffled her thick hair, raised goosebumps on her brown shoulders. Nathan considered bringing her jacket from the Jeep; the yellow tanktop she wore looked thin as gauze. "Val," he said. "You okay?"

"Not complaining... *yet*." Valerie struck a brave pose, chin raised, body canted against the bridge railing. From this angle, her pregnancy wasn't evident and she looked like a pin-up poster.

Bancroft was watching, too. "What's she fishing with?"

"Black Gnat."

"Doggone. No wonder she's not getting any action. Should try a Muddler Minnow size ten or twelve. Or maybe a Woolie Worm."

Nathan looked the other way.

"How come she's doing it like that?" Bancroft asked. "Her line's the wrong way, dragging in the current. The trout for sure will see the hoax. The way to fish the creek is standing down in the water in waders. Casting upstream."

"Can't have her in the creek," Nathan said. "It's too damn fast and slippery."

"You say that like she's made of glass."

"She's pregnant, Russ."

Bancroft raised his brows. "Speaking of water, that's another problem. Their plan describes a system of wells and storage tanks. Naturally, they realize streamflow can't service the whole development. And they don't want any litigation over water rights."

"So?"

"They don't mention, and nobody knows for sure, how the underground water might affect the surface flow. This is a critical point, and they disregard it." He pointed a stick toward the lake. "Look out there. The reeds are sticking up all across the water. Few years ago, they'd be submerged this time of year. For that matter, you and I wouldn't be sitting on this spot. We'd be up to our necks in fast water. You can see" — he pointed — "the old high water mark. Way back there."

"Maybe we had a few dry years," Nathan said. "Maybe part of the creek wandered off somewhere."

"Hell, I'll bet it's the summer cabins along the main fork. With all their wells. October, when they close up the cabins for winter, you'll see the stream rise again. Not from fresh rain, buddy. From less drain. You get a bunch of new wells drawing water for two thousand skiers, that would drop the water table. You bet. Then, would the streams go dry? What would happen to downstream water users? To the trout?"

A water ouzel flew out from under the bridge, and Valerie's line went zinging. For a moment, Nathan thought the bird had snagged the line, but it landed peacefully in a shallow backwash and began submerging for food.

"I've got one!" Valerie shouted.

Bancroft yelled, "Set the hook!"

The line fell limp. Valerie wound the reel, and there was no pull except for the current. "What happened?" she asked. "Did I lose it?"

"You didn't set the hook," Bancroft said.

"That's the fish's job," Valerie retorted, pouting.

Bancroft gave her a dour look. "Look here," he said. He hoisted Nathan's unused rod and flicked the tip smartly. "Like that. See?"

"Mind your own business," Valerie said. "I'm just a girl."

Bancroft seemed slightly offended. He glanced at Nathan. "Don't you teach her anything?"

Nathan smiled. "Can't. She's already been taught everything at college. A graduate from San Francisco State."

Valerie plunked down her rod and marched off the bridge, right up behind Nathan, and with both hands gripping his hat brim, she jammed it down over his ears.

"Hey!"

"Don't be such a smartass," she said.

Nathan appeared to be exerting mighty effort to lift his hat, his eyes wide with mock terror just under the brim. "I can't get it off! Look what you did!"

"You can't get *anything* off!" she shot back.

"The hell you mean? Got you pregnant, didn't I?"

"You?" Valerie cocked a shoulder. "Who knows?" Then she scooped handfuls of silt and dumped it on his hat. She sauntered back to the bridge.

"Sonofagun," Nathan said, removing his hat and knocking off the silt. "That lady... " He looked at Bancroft. "No wonder you pawned her off on me."

Valerie cocked her hips and raised a fist. "You want it next in the chops?"

Nathan hoisted his hands. "I give up! Please don't stomp on me!"

Bancroft was befuddled by all this. "You folks always carry on like that?"

Nathan shook his head. "Hell no. Only when we're together."

Bancroft sighed. "Well, I ain't got all day. Let's get to the subject of sewage and garbage."

"Must we?"

"The developers mention a two-stage treatment plant. For the volume of crap that two thousand skiers can dump per day, there's no way a two-stage plant will handle it. Not without polluting Hellroaring Creek. Does anybody care?"

Nathan said, "I care. I just don't know beans about sewage treatment."

"How about garbage? Are you willing to let 'em truck it to the city landfill? Doubling the load? They don't mention any alternative."

"I don't know, Russ."

"See? The Forest Service will decide the permits based only on forest impacts. The town impacts are your problem. And it will affect your parking, your hospital, your property values, your police and fire, your crime rate. Even your schools. It'll strain electrical generating capacity." Bancroft tossed his hands. "You'll have double the population in town. Not gradual. All at once. Like having the rodeo every day."

The thought was momentarily boggling. Nathan said, "Not *every* day. Just the ski season. Five or six months."

The thought was still boggling.

"And that's another problem," Bancroft said. "It's seasonal. Seasonal industries are the worst kind. You get a gang of imported workers half the year. The other half, you contend with stragglers. You get lots of transients. Nothing for them to do except make trouble."

Nathan had about enough. "Through yet?"

"What riles me most," Bancroft persisted, "is the total lack of objectivity in this whole business. You and your merchants will want this damn resort come hell or high water. You don't want to examine the negative issues. The Forest Service, they don't have any concern outside their own jurisdiction. And on the forest, they're prejudiced in favor of the resort."

"Prejudiced in *favor?* Come on. The ski resort means a lot more *work* for them."

"Exactly." Bancroft started counting fingers. "More work; more staff; more money; bigger budget; bigger bureaucracy. A little empire they can nurture. Exactly what government employees do best. Take it from me, I know."

Bancroft scratched at whiskers. Nathan shut his eyes and imagined bureaucracies.

"Also," Bancroft said, "it fits the Forest Service management philosophy. It's called multiple-use. It means *using* the forest, for the maximum benefit of *man.* Says it right in the book. For timber, mining, exploration, recreation and, dead last, wildlife. Provided the critters don't get in the way of the rest."

"You've got an ax to grind," Nathan observed.

"With who?"

"The Forest Service."

Bancroft shrugged. "Half our sovereign state is in some kind of federal custody. It causes some friction."

"Well, let's just think about Jackpine," Nathan said. "It needs a shot in the arm. It's stagnating. It's... "

"Bull. That's chamber of commerce talk. It's the same everywhere. They all say, 'We gotta grow!' Jackpine could hit fifty thousand population, you'd still hear the same thing. If there's no constant growth, there must be stagnation."

"Not the way I see it. I figure we need to grow enough, then we'll get stabilized and... "

"Stabilized? Nate, we *are* stabilized, with the same population more or less for twenty years. That's as stable as you can get. But in another breath, you're calling it stagnation. What's the difference?"

"There you go," Nathan grumbled. "You're bad as she is."

"Who?"

"Valerie."

"What?" Valerie asked.

"Never mind," Nathan said. He sighed. He said, "Suppose, for the fun of it, if I agreed with you and wanted to cut some fat off this project. How would I do that?"

"First," Bancroft said, shifting to face Nathan, "trimming a little fat is no damn good. This thing would grow right back up, like weeds. You need to stomp it cold. Knock it right the hell off the planet."

"For crying out loud, Russ... "

"There's only one way you *might* do that. The National Wilderness Act of Nineteen Sixty-four. Congress charged the Forest Service with finding areas that qualify for wilderness preservation. You need to get on their backs, Nate. Demand they do a wilderness study before they decide on any resort permit."

"Uh... "

"The way the Forest Service tinkers around, the study would take several years. By then, the developers would pull up stakes. They'd go raise hell somewhere else." Bancroft smacked his hands. "By damn, we might even get lucky. The whole area might be designated a national wilderness. Then no form of permanent structure could ever be built up there! No kind of motorized vehicles would be allowed! By God, Nate... that'd be damn fine."

"Question."

"Yeah?"

"Why me? Why doesn't the Forest Service do this on its own?"

"You're kidding," Bancroft said.

They watched the creek for a moment.

"Look," Bancroft said. "It's pristine as all hell, once you close the snowmobile trails and tear out the fisherman privies. It's about like the Bob Marshall area. That qualified."

"Fine. So go tell 'em. Why ask me, I ask again?"

Bancroft frowned. "I might just do that, if you won't. Trouble is... I'm under a department reprimand. I raised hell with the Forest Service last spring. That was over the condition of the trails. Everybody got upset. Memos to Helena, Washington... "

"Uh-huh."

"Seems I upset the cozy political truce between Fish and Game and the federal agencies, and they're after my balls."

Nathan said, "Now you're afraid of losing your job."

"Mostly the pension," Bancroft said. "Aside from that, I think you'd have more credibility with them. Local *mayor* and that crap."

Nathan cranked himself to his feet, dusted his jeans. Upstream, he saw a curtain of rain coming ahead of the mist.

"You're saying," Nathan muttered, "I should dump a project I've dreamed about for six years; so *you* don't have to risk jour job and pension."

Bancroft stared at him. "I'm proposing you save your *town*, not my *ass*. I'm suggesting you might save a whole wilderness for future generations. I'm saying you're in a helluva lot better position to approach it than me. I'm begging you, open your eyes before it's too late. That's all I'm saying."

"Aw, hell."

Turning, Nathan saw where the fog had layered across the lake. It silhouetted a rubber raft paddled by a woman with a small boy.

Bancroft had followed Nathan's gaze. He lunged to his feet, stared at the raft across the water. "Damn it!" he said.

Bancroft scooted across the boulders to the shore. Feet planted wide, hands on hips, he fired a whistle across the silent lake, then motioned violently with his arms.

"What is he doing?" Valerie asked.

"Beats the hell out of me," Nathan said.

The rafters started paddling toward the game warden.

Valerie said, "We ready to go? I'm chilled to the bone."

Nathan wrapped an arm around her. "I'm sorry," he said. "Let's clear out."

The woman beached her raft. The boy jumped out, sloshing barefoot in the shallows. Bancroft flipped open a booklet and started writing in it. Valerie started to reel in...

Her line snapped taut. "Oh wow!" Her rod quivered and bent into a steep arc.

The wind was stirring the pines; the water had grown metallic; aspen leaves were fluttering upside-down. Valerie watched ten yards out where the creek was broken by a volcanic cone, a silvery fish erupting from it, flipping, smashing back into the froth. The line zig-zagged and shot straight out with the automatic reel spinning. "I've got him!" she shrieked. "Holy cow is he strong!"

"Don't get excited," Nathan said. "Let'm run a bit — don't panic. For God's sake, don't panic — he's humongous!"

The fish flashed like lightning, head-high above the water.

Valerie shut her eyes. She felt the throbbing pull, the jerks, the beating of her heart. She felt drizzle on her face, moistness trickling between her breasts, and the baby; the baby was turning.

"I can't," Valerie said, sensitive to the fish's battle for life.

Nathan looked at her.

Valerie opened her eyes, shivered helplessly.

Nathan nodded.

He scrambled down around the bridge abutment, trailing the line through his fingertips, clearing past the signpost and branches. "It's okay," he said. "Reel it in just a bit."

Valerie reeled slowly, jerkingly.

On the bank, Nathan lost control. The wind looped the line everywhere, snagging it on branches and rocks. He snatched for the leader. His boots slithered across moss and went into the water while he tottered, regained balance, slipped again and fell.

Valerie yelped.

Nathan was up quickly, clinging to the fish line. The trout was desperate now, in shallow water. It spotted Nathan and gave a last-ditch flip and roll, darting for refuge among sunken rocks.

Nathan spiked his hand down, missed; grabbed again. He caught the fish behind its gills. It jerked in his hand like a small shotgun. He lifted, held it high. It jerked twice more and then fell limp...

Its full length, from the gills in Nathan's fingers to the tailfins, stretched past his elbow. "Whew," Nathan said, admiring it. It was iridescent in rainbow colors, brilliant even in the flat light of the closing fog. "Look at it," he said.

Valerie looked, eyes wide, throat tight.

Nathan crouched, his wet shirt sticking to the sinews of his shoulders, his boots black with creek water.

Valerie was petrified. She had seen him snap fish to kill them instantly.

Nathan held it gently in the backwash and jiggled the hook free, waited while the fish sucked water through its gills and gathered its strength and bearings. Nathan let go. The trout picked a direction and suddenly shot away.

Nathan was busy gathering line when Bancroft returned.

"The hell you doing?" Bancroft said.

"Got tangled up here," Nathan said, probing bushes.

"You folks, you're loonies," Bancroft said. "Better go get your fish in a supermarket."

Nathan signaled Valerie to finish reeling, then turned to Bancroft. "The lady in the raft. What was all that business?"

"No life preservers," Bancroft said flatly.

"No kidding? For that you wrote 'em a ticket? You said yourself, the water's shallow!"

"Kids drown in bathtubs," Bancroft said.

Nathan rolled his eyes. "What everyone says, it's true. You'd ticket your own mom."

"That broad in the raft," Bancroft said, "wasn't anything like my mom. You should've heard her language."

"Can't blame her. You're a prick, Bancroft."

"If I'm such a prick," Bancroft said, "I'd be writing citations for both of you."

"Citations for what?"

"Valerie, she left her line unattended while coming down to throw sand on your hat. You, for swimming in the creek."

"Who says I was swimming in the creek?"

"How'd you get all wet?"

"Never mind. I slipped. Go away, Russ."

"I intend to."

There was something about Bancroft. Nathan had known him all his life and could never tell when the man was serious. The game warden gathered the reins and mounted his big horse. It came awake, sidestepping as Bancroft settled onto the saddle and cupped his hands over the horn. The drizzle had stopped, and neither the horse nor Bancroft seemed dampened. Nathan felt soggy.

"One more thing," Bancroft said. "The coal business... "

"I know nothing about that, Russ."

"I know you don't," Bancroft said. "I'll take care of that one, okay? You just concentrate on the wilderness idea."

Nathan looked up at Bancroft. "What have you got in mind, Russ?"

Bancroft smiled. He jerked the reins. The horse snorted and lunged up the trail away from the bridge, hooves clomping loudly, haunches jarring through the saplings and out of sight into the fog.

***

They snuggled in a woolen blanket, down the road to Jackpine, Nathan driving. He said, "You haven't said a word about all the talk between Russ and me."

"If I said what I thought," Valerie said, "you'd get angry."

"No I wouldn't."

"Yes you would. Just be careful. That's all I'll say." Valerie paused, then added, "He's too... determined."

"Hey," Nathan said. "I've known him my whole life. The only way he does something... he makes *me* do it. You watch. He'll come around later about the coal business, too."

Valerie said, "I haven't known him my whole life, I admit. But I know Russ better than you, in certain ways. He's been changing. I warn you, he's serious about some things. Real serious in a quiet way, which is... bad."

"Valerie, for God's sake! You... "

"See? You're angry! I told you."

Nathan decided to shut up. They took several curves and drove out of the fog. Sunlight glazed the water drops on the hood.

"Nathan?"

"Yeah?"

"Why did you release the fish?"

Nathan steered, then said, "That was a whale of a trout, the biggest I'd ever seen come flying out of that creek."

Valerie snuggled against him, gazed up as he spoke, watched his eyes track the bends in the road.

Nathan said, "They get that big, you hate to spoil it. I think you must've caught that fish off guard—first mistake it ever made. So I gave it a second chance. What the hell."

Nathan stretched an arm around Valerie, drove with one hand. "I like to think that someday, when I'm old and grizzly, that fish will still be lurking around up there. He and I will meet again. Maybe then, I'll keep it." He grinned. "It was all a selfish act on my part, you see."

Valerie watched tree shadows flash past the windshield. The air streaming through the vents was fresh with rain and earth.

"You're a lousy liar," she said. "But that's okay. I think it was sexy."

Nathan felt the fizziness of her hair against his cheek. He said, "Sexy? You mean me? Or the fish?"

"Well..." Valerie smiled. "You fell all over yourself in the creek. Got soaking wet releasing that fish. Might have broken a leg or drowned. Not to save the fish for yourself. You did it for me. It was a trophy kind of fish and it didn't matter. You sensed my feelings and let it go."

"And to you, that's *sexy?*"

"You betcha."

Nathan smirked. "You want to prove it?"

Valerie drifted her fingers across his chest and breathed on his neck. "Prove it? Honeybear — I'll make a federal case out of it."

Nathan laughed. He liked Valerie's idea of a federal case better than Bancroft's idea.

Chapter 19: Dining for Dollars

THE LEARJET returned in late August. Chambers heard its turbojets echoing off the Jackpine storefronts, assumed Dexter and Bartz would come swaggering into the shop in twenty minutes. Instead, Dexter phoned in ten minutes.

"We have matters to discuss," Dexter said. "Are you free for dinner?"

"Just had dinner," Chambers said. It was one-thirty in the afternoon. He listened to Dexter's puzzled silence for a moment, then added, "Maybe you mean supper."

"Ah-hah," Dexter said. "Of course. My grandmother always called dinner supper, now that you mention it. She grew up on a farm."

Chambers said, "I usually eat supper, and dinner, with my wife."

"Nathan," Dexter said. "Spare the little woman her chores for one night. Bring her along. You choose the restaurant. Anyplace quiet. But please, no greasy spoons or spicy enchiladas. I have only two-thirds of a stomach left. Just pick us up whenever you're ready. Same motel where we met before. Parkway something-or-other."

"Parkway Motor Court."

"I'm sure that must be the one," Dexter said.

***

Valerie accepted the invitation with mild resistance and then decided to dress up. She selected a short shift that camouflaged her pregnancy and capitalized on her good legs. Balanced on higher heels than she had worn in months, she felt a little gangly. But the heels were slender, at least; not the thick clompers most women were wearing these days. She hated those.

Valerie had convinced Nathan to wear shined boots and a tweed sports jacket; she said the combination with his jeans and open-collared shirt was neither too dressy nor too casual for the occasion. Besides, it was sexy.

Steering his father's Chevrolet Impala toward the motel, Nathan felt like a teenager embarking on a double date. He clamped a hand on Valerie's stockinged knee and said, "You look kind of sexy yourself. Given your condition."

"I can accept that — I guess." She poked him.

***

The Pine Ridge Supper Club was situated to attract the summer crowd from Billings. Its log-raftered dining room provided a Continental menu and a spectacular view of Hellroaring Canyon.

"This is grand," Bartz proclaimed, gesturing out the large windows. "Have you told Nixon about this place? It's a better hideout than San Clemente."

"From what I hear," Chambers said, "Leon Jaworski will go after Nixon wherever he tries to hide."

"Ah," Bartz said, "you must've heard what our pitiful ex-President said today to a Tennessee Congressman — something about whether the people want to pick the bones of a carcass."

"That's what we do here at the Pine Ridge Supper Club," Chambers said. "So maybe you're right; Nixon would feel at home here."

They ordered drinks: a double vodka martini for Bartz, a German beer for Dexter, and Valerie found a Napa Valley Pinot Noir on the wine list. Chambers ordered a ditch.

"A 'ditch'?" Bartz asked. "The hell's that?"

"Plain old whiskey and water," Chambers said.

"I learn new things every day," Bartz said. He scooted his chair closer to Chambers and started listing some new things he had been learning recently about Jackpine...

Dexter faced Valerie. He said, "You're not a native here."

Valerie looked at him quizzically.

"You don't have freckles," he explained. "Western cowgirls have freckles."

"Not a freckle on my body," she admitted.

"I'll take your word for it."

Valerie lifted an eyebrow at Dexter.

Dexter smiled casually. Even with gold jewelry and pinstripe suit, he could make himself reasonably charming. He said, "I owe you an apology."

"Oh?"

"Talking to your husband earlier, I think I might have referred to you as the 'little woman.' For that, I apologize."

Valerie smiled at him. "I don't have buck teeth or pigtails, either."

"You certainly don't." Dexter flicked a gold lighter to his cigarette, exhaled. "So how come you look so worldly, like New York or San Francisco?"

"Perhaps because I lived near San Francisco before moving here."

"I see. Then I was right." Dexter squinted through his cigarette smoke. "So what brings you to the boondocks?"

"Escape," Valerie said — and decided to leave it at that.

Apparently Dexter understood. He nodded and said, "This would be the ideal place for escape — to or from." He paused. "There are so few people. Fewer complications, I suppose."

Valerie nodded slightly. "The distance across Montana is as far," she said, "as the distance from Milwaukee to Washington, D.C. I'm sure you have more people in Milwaukee than we have in this entire state. Your suburbs send more representatives to Congress than Montana does. We have just two."

"Really," Dexter said.

"I'm afraid so."

"Not much clout."

"I'm afraid not."

"Worse, I suppose, for a woman," Dexter said.

"How do you mean?"

Dexter shrugged. "I guess you know that yesterday, August twenty-sixth, was proclaimed Women's Equality Day by President Ford."

"Yes."

"Well? How do they feel in Montana about the Equal Rights Amendment?"

Valerie adjusted her posture slightly and said, "Mr. Dexter, don't be misled by all the pickups with gunracks and the macho struts of the cattlemen. In 1917, Montanans elected the first woman to the U.S. House of Representatives, an equal rights advocate named Jeanette Rankin. She was a woman's suffrage leader both here and in Washington."

Dexter lifted his brows. "You are well-informed."

"Does that surprise you?"

Dexter ducked his head. "Oops. I think I'm making a fool of myself."

*

Nathan was trying not to listen to Bartz prattle about the climate...

"It was hot in Milwaukee today — I mean hot. The clothes stick and you can't breathe for the humidity. Never gets hot like that here, of course... "

"Ninety-two, day before yesterday... " Nathan said.

"But that's dry heat. You don't feel it like we do... You ever been to the Midwest?"

Nathan thought about his sister Rebecca, living still in Chicago. It had been several years since he had seen her there. He had been en route to Pensacola to begin a naval flight school assignment. She had finished school and was working for some big architectural firm.

*

Valerie lowered her fork, not caring to eat any more. She asked, "Are you married, Mr. Dexter?" He wasn't wearing a ring.

"Call me Harold, or Hal."

"As you wish."

Dexter dappled some cream into his coffee and stirred. He said, "Divorced."

"I'm sorry."

"I'm not." His cuffs were brilliant white under the table lamp. "My wife has a townhouse and the kids. I have a furnished apartment and a mongrel cat. I consider it a fair exchange."

"Tell me about the children," Valerie said.

"Well, they're both girls. Attending Northwestern University. Debra and Janine."

"They're planning careers?"

"I somewhat doubt that. Probably just chasing young men on a fast track. They take after their mother." Dexter sipped his coffee. "Mrs. Chambers... "

"Valerie."

"As you wish." He said, "Valerie, would you mind if we walked a bit? I've been cramped in a small plane all afternoon. I need to stretch out and walk."

"Me too."

As they excused themselves, Nathan nodded blandly. He had concluded long ago that Bartz wouldn't get down to business until they were alone.

Now Bartz produced two fat cigars and offered one. Nathan declined.

"Your local newspaper," Bartz said, peeling the cigar wrapper, "and those terrible stories. What happened?"

Nathan sighed.

*

There was a stone path outside the restaurant leading to a rampart that overlooked the canyon. Dexter held Valerie's arm while she picked her high heels over the stones. They stopped on the overlook and gazed briefly into the darkening gorge where the winding road from Jackpine was a thin ribbon, barely visible. A few cars farther down needed head-lights to follow the curves.

Where they stood, though, orange sunlight was still glowing against the rocks and forming a halo in Valerie's hair. Dexter glanced at her hair, the way it danced in the breezes.

"You must be getting tired," he said.

She frowned slightly. "Do I look tired?"

"I don't mean tonight," Dexter said. He found a ciga-rette and fidgeted with his lighter. Before igniting, he said, "I mean — in general. Living here, where you don't belong." He struck the flame, sheltering it from the breeze.

Valerie lifted her gaze to the rock pinnacles across the canyon. "I'm an army brat," she said. "There's really no-where I belong. This is my fifteenth bivouac."

"Oh, I see."

"My father's retired now. I came out to help him get his ranch started. I didn't know anything about ranching — not then, I didn't. But I came, and I learned a few things. The hard way."

"And met your husband," Dexter surmised.

"Yes." Valerie smiled.

Dexter looked at her eyes. In the fading light, the hazel looked almost silver. She was a truly enchanting woman. He said, "Your husband. I think he played a trick on me. After I joked about *supper* being an old-fashioned word for *dinner*, he brings me to a fashionable restaurant called the Pine Ridge *Supper* Club. Do you think that was deliberate?"

Valerie shrugged. "I think he just took you to the one decent restaurant within sixty miles. But you never know."

"Is he also one of those macho men with a gun rack in his pickup?"

"Heavens, no." She laughed, her cheeks dimpling. "Well, at first he may appear that type. But he's not. He talks like a cowboy sometimes, depending on whom he's with or how he feels. It's unconscious, though. He has no intended pretenses. He has no interest at all in horses or six-guns. Yet... on the other hand, he does own a Jeep. And he sometimes listens to this foot-stomping, hog-calling, knee-jerk kind of country music. It drives me up the wall." She laughed again.

"You enjoy talking about him," Dexter observed.

"It's a little crazy, considering our differences," she said. "But I enjoy everything about him."

***

Joseph Bartz spread his arms on the table and settled back, working his thick lips around his cigar. The folds of his neck settled down over his collar, and he looked content.

Chambers drummed his knuckles on the tablecloth. He was getting tired of this.

"How much does it pay, being mayor?" Bartz suddenly inquired.

"A hundred and fifty," Chambers responded.

Bartz jerked his eyebrows and took the cigar from his mouth. "That's terrible," he said. "A hundred and fifty dollars a week, for such a demanding position?"

"Per month," Chambers said.

Bartz said, "You're kidding me."

"Nope." Chambers stopped knuckling the tablecloth. "The aldermen, they get just a hundred even. They're just as busy as me. The city attorney gets one-twenty, and he's got the most ability. I can't hardly complain, can I?"

Bartz lifted a shoulder. "So, what about the store? How do you make out there?"

Chambers gave Bartz a sideways glance. "That's none of your business."

Bartz flicked ash from his cigar. "Sorry. Didn't mean to get personal. I just thought, since you revealed your mayor's salary... "

"That's public record."

"I see."

Bartz shifted his bulk on the chair and gazed around the dining room. There were few people now. The gigantic stone fireplace was cold. The bartender was dumping ice.

"How've you been doing with our project?" Bartz asked. "Have you been moving ahead? Making progress with the town council? How about the public?"

Chambers had noted the subtle change in mannerism, the way the man's brain clunked into a different gear. Finally.

"Haven't made any progress," Chambers said. "Haven't even convinced myself."

"Oh my." Bartz twirled the cigar. "Nathan... before we go any farther, why don't you say what's bothering you. Maybe I could set your mind at ease."

"*Everything* bothers me. You could set my mind at ease by backing off a bit. Give me time to think and investigate."

"We don't *have* time, we explained that. Public hearings are scheduled and money has been committed. A great deal of money. Delays are costly, Nathan. The interest rates... "

"Those are your problems, sir, not mine."

Bartz squinted at Chambers. He leaned back and came forward again. "That's a narrow view, considering what this project means to the town. What it could mean for you."

Chambers thumbed his nose, then rested his hand. "Make your point."

"Hmm." While holding his cigar, Bartz used his free hand to begin rearranging items on the table. "Well," he said. "You're obviously the sincere type. You're worried about the future, as we all are. You're concerned about all the possible impacts of this project, good and bad. Let me tell you something... "

Chambers waited, watched the ketchup bottle trade places with the mustard jar.

"Nathan, don't try to predict the future. Don't try to guess what's right for the whole town. You'll only get confused. You know that? No matter what you do, half the people will say you're wrong."

Bartz traded the sugar cubes for the peppermill. "You have a child coming. There's plenty of future to worry about right there. Think about yourself, your wife, and your child. What is more important than a man's own family?"

Bartz looked up at Chambers for a reaction. None.

"The point is," Bartz continued, "our ski project presents an opportunity you may never see again." He rapped his thick fingers on the table. "Hear that? That's opportunity knocking."

Chambers gave Bartz a sharp stare.

"What I'm trying to tell you," Bartz said, "is that we can help you out. We can't expect you to carry the ball for nothing. The rest of us are highly paid. But we all depend on you.

You should be rewarded as we are. Let's decide on what's fair, considering your family, your position, and all the rest."

Chambers interrupted. "Is this a new disease going around? I'm seeing it all month on TV. First, there's a former Illinois governor goes to prison for a race track scandal. Next, a TV reporter lists fourteen Nixon aides who've pleaded guilty or been convicted of crimes. Then I see Hubert Humphrey's old campaign manager is accused of taking illegal contributions from milk producers..."

"Look, Nathan..."

"A lawyer in Texas pleads guilty on bribing John Connally with more milk money, and now Connally goes to trial."

"Nathan," Bartz said urgently, "can I finish?"

"Wait. There was another one. I think a California lieutenant governor had to resign and was sentenced for perjury. In just a matter of weeks, Mr. Bartz, we have governors, senators, presidential aides, and a former Treasury Secretary staring at iron bars." Chambers leaned across the table and in a mock whisper said, "Is that how you want to help me out, Mr. Bartz?"

Bartz had begun to perspire, but he managed a grin. "Please. Let me finish. The cases you cited are a perfect illustration of what might be called business as usual in America. The financial interplay between politicians and businessmen is both necessary and commonplace. It is so commonplace that a small fraction of the players slip up, do something stupid and get caught. But that's not what we're about here. I'm not trying to corrupt you — nothing like that. I'm only suggesting some decent compensation for your personal efforts."

"Bullshit."

Bartz looked horribly offended. "That's unfair, Nathan. I understand how you'd be concerned by the scandals in the news. But that's big-time politics involving huge organizations and special-interest groups. They will forever be at war with one another. But we're not part of that, you and I. We are simply two well-intentioned servants to our respective private and public constituencies. You see? Together, we are seeking to find a common ground for progress. It's all for the common good of my business associates and your fellow citizens. Nathan, without any danger to you whatsoever, I can show you how to make money from personal investments that are not related directly to the ski project. There wouldn't be any conflict of interest, then, you see?"

"Bartz, I wasn't born yesterday. There's no reason in the world you'd want to help me make money except to buy my loyalty to your project. That is conflict of interest. Period."

Bartz dropped his cigar into the ashtray. "Ah, me. Evidently, you're afraid the national press will swoop into little Jackpine to investigate your sudden great wealth. That's ridiculous, Nathan. The income available to you with my help is not enough to arouse curiosity even within your little local bank. However, Nathan, we are talking about enough to make a difference in your child's future. Aren't you curious about that?"

Chambers nodded his head. "Well, now I must say I am curious. I've never been able to quit a mystery book before the end."

Bartz smiled. "All right then. Let me figure it out here, based on a certain investment portfolio that comes highly recommended by my broker." He took a notebook and pen from his jacket pocket and bent over the table.

***

Dexter helped guide Valerie up the stone path. It was none too soon for her. With the sun down, the air became chill, and her short dress was inadequate. When he stopped her just outside the door, she was impatient.

"Let me give you this," he said.

She looked at his embossed silver card.

"Wait," he said. He took it back and wrote a phone number on the back side, using a Mont Blanc pen. "For any assistance," he said, and gave it to her.

She immediately felt much colder.

***

Chambers looked at the numbers. "Forty-two thousand a year — from a five thousand investment?"

"Well," Bartz said, twirling the cigar stub. "That's just gross. From that, you'd need to subtract the broker's commission, federal and state taxes, certain transaction fees. But hell, compared to a hundred and fifty a month... "

Chambers raised his brows. "Who would I have to kill?"

"Pardon?"

"You know what I mean."

"Yes. Well, the fact of the matter is," Bartz said, "you'd owe very little in return. We both know this project will happen sooner or later. We merely seek your assistance in making it sooner. What harm is that? You were inclined to support this at the beginning."

"Suppose I took your investment advice but then decided to oppose the project?"

"What?"

"Suppose I oppose it?"

"That poetry or something?"

"Are you going to answer me, or what?"

"You should know the answer without asking," Bartz said, waving his hand beneath the table lamp. "The investment portfolio is a special one, its growth dependent on the good will of officials at The Wisconsin Trust. Without performance, resources would be committed elsewhere, and the fund eventually would dry up." Bartz's rings glittered in the lamplight as he wagged his hand. "But we know you won't actually oppose us. Why would you? We've got the only game in town." He put out his hand. "Deal?"

Chambers hesitated, then gripped the hand.

***

Valerie and Hal Dexter, returning to the table, saw Nathan rising to his feet with an abruptness that had toppled his chair. Bartz was red in the face and holding his right hand with his left.

"What's this?" Dexter inquired, suspiciously.

Chambers nodded toward Bartz. "I banged his hand on the table. If he weren't such a feeble old fart, I might've kicked his butt across the room."

"Joseph?"

Bartz, wheezing on choked cigar smoke, wagged his head and made a thumbs-down gesture toward Nathan.

"We're leaving, Val," Chambers said. "Let's go." He took her arm and started pulling her away from the two men.

"Nathan," she said, resisting.

"What!"

"We brought them in your father's car."

"Damn, that's right."

"It's fourteen miles to town," Valerie told Dexter. "Maybe you need to patch things up here."

"What can I say?" Dexter shrugged.

Nathan said, "You could say nothing to me from now on. You could ride in the back seat with your mouth shut and listen to country music played loud. You could hitch another ride. Up to you."

Dexter silently counted to ten. He said, "We'll catch another ride."

"Suit yourself."

Nathan ushered Valerie to the door. She turned to Dexter just before going out and waved. As she waved, two little pieces of paper flitted from her hand to the floor. Dexter knew, of course, what they were — the remains of his business card.

"Joseph," he said. "You blew it. You blew shit out of it."

Bartz shook his head. "So did you."

"So did I," Dexter agreed.

The worst part is, he thought, *I knew it was going to happen. I warned Bob Taylor. He wouldn't listen.*

"Let's ask the bartender how much a ride will cost. And how late we'll have to wait."

"You ask," Bartz said. "I'm no good at bribes."

Chapter 20: August Moon

THE FIVE-YEAR-OLD IMPALA purred smoothly up the steep road and glided to a halt in front of the abandoned West Side mine. Nathan patted the steering wheel, pleased with the car's power.

Beside him, Valerie gazed at the lights of Jackpine, scattered like fallen stars in the dark valley. Overhead, small gray clouds paced a full moon.

"The August moon," she said. "I love it. It makes everything look peaceful, yet mysterious."

"Not bad for an old Chev with a lot of use," Nathan said. "Took that climb like a goat."

"It's different in winter," Valerie said. "Then, the moon's so bright on the snow, you can read a book. But now the shadows are long and dark. That old mine frame looks like it could move. Creep up on you in the dark... "

"Too bad it doesn't eat grass instead of gas," Nathan said.

Valerie looked at him. Her wondering eyes reflected the glow from the instrument panel. "Nathan, what are you talking about?"

"This car. It's got power, but it's a guzzler. I hate to think of Pops trading it in for one of those little Japanese cars." He shut off the engine and the lights, canceling the reflections in Valerie's eyes.

It was silent until Nathan said, "They wanted to bribe me — in case you wondered what happened back there."

Valerie nodded. "That seemed obvious."

Nathan said, "It came to over forty thousand dollars — you believe that?" He looked at Valerie. Her eyes picked up a glint of light from somewhere and flashed at him in the dark. He said, "Bartz made note of the fact that we'd have money for our kid. I was thinking about his college. Maybe he wouldn't have to join the military like I did, to get there."

"He could be a girl," Valerie said quietly.

Nathan looked out the window. The old mine frame was like a ghost from the past, its windblasted boards like the brittle bones of long-dead miners. The thing struck him as a vision of Jackpine's future without industry. "And I want Jackpine to have a ski hill. I want that no matter what Bancroft says. Don't you agree?"

"Yet, that was a violent thing you did, hurting that poor man's hand."

"...God, you're right. I don't know what came over me."

"I'm not saying he didn't deserve it," Valerie said. "I just thought you were more of a pacifist, after saving the fish."

"Jeez... a pacifist with a temper. Peace is really a fragile thing among humans. I'm no better, even after the war."

Silence.

Nathan turned to her. He tried to see her face in the dark, saw only her thick hair backlighted by moonbeams. "Valerie?"

Her chest rose and fell. "I don't know. I really don't."

This puzzled him.

She said, "Maybe I'm just bored. Maybe it's because I'm pregnant... " Valerie fumbled in her handbag. "If a woman doesn't belong to the P.E.O. or the Eagles Auxiliary and doesn't have a job in this town, there's not a hell of a lot to look forward to — if you know what I mean."

Headlights from another car abruptly swept across Valerie's face, revealing glittery moisture in her eyes. Chambers turned, saw the intruding vehicle was a Dodge Charger stripped down to a coat of gray primer, with chrome exhaust pipes belching smoke and rumbles. Inside, three high school boys and two girls shouted and tossed out beer cans until one youth said, "Hey, it's the mayor, for Christ's sake!" The car spun on the gravel and roared down the road back towards Jackpine.

Valerie said, "You see? I'm not the only one. Those kids have nothing to do except drink beer and park and cruise mainstreet. Now they'll tell their friends they saw the mayor and a woman parked at the old mine. And it will travel all over town." She shook her head.

Nathan ran his hands along the steering wheel. "It's another reason for a ski hill. Give both adults and kids some jobs... some recreation activities."

"It won't cure the heavy drinking," Valerie said. "It won't stop high school girls from getting pregnant. The town still won't have any culture."

"Culture? This is something new. Since when have you been looking for culture?"

"Since I discovered the town doesn't have any. And I don't mean little old ladies pretending to be discussing books while drinking tea and eating cake. All they do is spread gossip and get fat."

"How long have you felt this way?" Nathan asked, concerned. "What is it that you want?"

"I don't know. I just know what I *don't* want anymore. I don't want to hear any more gripes about the high cost of farming. I don't want to know about another store going out of business. I'm sick of talk about the last big snowstorm and whether or not it was bigger than the one back in 'twenty-nine."

Nathan stretched an arm around Valerie's shoulders. "That's not all there is, Valerie. I'm telling you."

Valerie resisted his embrace. "I'll tell *you*, Nathan — for a woman, that's all there is."

Nathan let go of her, flipped his hands in the air. "Hell. I should've taken the money!"

Valerie reached. "Get over here." She pulled his head to her cheek, stroked her fingers across his ears. "Forget my bitching," she said softly. "There's nothing I hate worse than a pregnant housewife feeling sorry for herself. Let's play."

Valerie squirmed sideways, her legs splaying wide. Her chest came under Nathan's jaw. He kissed her neck, intending to work downward. But the position was awkward, and his knee struck the steering column with a bony thunk.

"Oww — damn!" he said.

"Aw, hon."

"It's the funnybone," he complained, "which ain't *funny*." He rubbed the spot. "At least it's a big car. In a tiny Toyota, I might've crippled myself."

"Let's head for our bed," Valerie suggested. "Lots more room there."

"Now there's an offer I won't refuse."

When the car reached the highway, Nathan touched Valerie's knee. "Are *you* okay?"

"Getting better by the minute."

Nathan paused, then said, "Let's just take care of each other. And let the rest of the world go to hell."

"You've got my vote," Valerie said.

Chapter 21: Montana Midnight

A CLOUDBURST streaked the windows and splattered the sills of the small house on Juniper Street. Windblown branches tortured the shingles, and distant thunderbolts punctuated the quiet music inside.

In the glow of a bedside lamp, Valerie rested against the headboard, sheets pulled over her breasts, and watched Nathan dozing beside her. An hour ago at the old mine, she had come close to fulfilling her promise to Doc Fuller and had started to engage Nathan in a discussion of her discontent. But at the first sign of his discomfort, she had quit. She had taken him to bed. And even though she had enjoyed the sex, she found herself right back where she had started.

Nathan stirred. "What's that music you're playing?"

"Liebestraum," Valerie said. "By Liszt."

Nathan smiled. "I thought so. Mom used to play it a lot. Had an old seventy-eight RPM record and wore it out."

"Don't you like it?" Valerie thought the score was exceptionally romantic.

"I like it fine. Puts me right to sleep..."

And it did.

Lightning turned the windows stark white, casting rain-streaked shadows across the walls. The flash shimmered on

Nathan's face. Then a heavy thunderclap shook the house and the power went off. The room went black.

Valerie shuddered. She scrunched down against Nathan, grabbing him, holding tightly.

Awakened, Nathan said, "Did that big bang scare you?"

"Hold me," Valerie said. "This isn't funny."

"You're not usually so frightened by thunderstorms. What's wrong?"

"I don't know."

What it was, actually, was the ghostly shimmering on his face, followed by the sudden blackout and deathly quiet when the record player stopped. It gave Valerie an eerie feeling. She said, "Nathan... "

"Yes?"

"Don't ever go far away from me."

Another flash, briefer and not so bright, showed a gentle frown on Nathan's face. "I'd never go away. You know that."

"Don't fly in airplanes without me," Valerie murmured. "Don't go up in dangerous storms."

"What are you talking about?"

"Promise," Valerie said.

"I promise."

Valerie's tension eased.

Valerie listened to the thunder rolling over the mountains, the slick of car tires going past on wet pavement, the rain pelting the roof.

Nathan was hearing, deep in thunder, noises like the catapults over his bunk aboard the aircraft carrier in the South China Sea. Waiting his turn. There were target coordinates he would program into the onboard computer.

Glowing numerals that would direct the missiles, boring in to bombard the coordinates...

***

IT'S OCTOBER, 1970: Coming home to Montana.

Nathan expects changes; the Western Airlines jet has landed him in a city reeling with changes — new shopping centers and subdivisions, new offices and banks in what the Billings Chamber of Commerce calls "The Magic City" and "The Midland Empire."

The changes become fewer as a bus rumbles southward. Hay bales are spread on familiar green fields which fade to amber as the highway climbs the rising landscape toward the mountains. Twisted cottonwoods are shedding brassy leaves as the bus roars past. Then golden aspens and, finally, twelve miles out of Jackpine at 5,000 feet, the scrubby jackpine evergreens begin showing up, eventually dominating, laying upon the rising slopes like an olive-black carpet. Higher up, brilliant snow etches a jagged outline of peaks against an ice-blue sky.

The dinosaur bus makes rumbles in its metal belly as it slows near the outskirts: JACKPINE, MONTANA—ELEV. 5555—POP. 1555. A count not precise, but indicative of a certain local attitude.

The same old grain elevator stands flaked in the same old whitewash. The green Northern Pacific freight depot droops its eaves over rusty rail and weedgrown ballast — trackage abandoned after the railroad's merger with the Burlington and Great Northern; and the Standard Oil storage tanks are surrounded by the same rusty chainlink fence.

Mainstreet — so hopefully named Broadway all these years — is flanked by littered gutters, frost-cracked sidewalks, hodgepodge storefronts. Chambers notices the double doors still sag on the Safeway supermarket, and broken venetian blinds remain hanging haphazardly behind the windows of the old stone courthouse.

The bus, brakes squeaking, drops Nathan directly in front of the Chambers hardware store. As the bus rumbles on, Nathan waits, duffel bag over his shoulder, to breathe once more the ever-crisp mountain air. He pushes open the stubborn door of the hardware store and immediately feels back home among the smells of saddle leathers and copper-coated nails.

An excited father rushes Nathan home without bothering to lock the store. Along shaded streets resembling a faded home movie, most of the Victorian-style houses have been aging gracefully, but there is a crusty look to the asphalt pavement, laid without curbing to weedgrown parkways. Junked cars are planted in a few sideyards, and one vacant lot is crowded with dented washtubs, tractor tires, bedsprings, and splintered lumber. Dead limbs hang from untrimmed trees, and children's broken toys and bicycles litter many lawns.

"You're awful quiet, son," Woodrow Chambers says from behind the steering wheel.

"Just taking it all in, Pops. The town looks older than I remembered."

"You had to be away to notice that," Woodrow replies, flicking turn signals as they approach Custer Avenue. "Jackpine was always old."

In front of the gray-shingled house, Nathan sits still, studying the steep-roofed dwelling where he had grown up among flowered wallpapers, coffee and bacon smells, model airplanes, and dozens of nooks and mothballed closets.

Getting out, Nathan slings a firm arm around his father's beefy shoulders, and together they mount the creaking wooden steps and thump across the broad front porch. Woodrow opens the screen door and nudges his son into the cool vestibule. "Jessie!" he calls to Nathan's mother, his voice ringing in the hollow spaces. "Come see who I dragged home!"

Jessica Chambers comes into the hallway from the kitchen, wiping her strong hands with a dish towel. "Woody! What in the world? I... Oh, my God! Nathan baby!"

"Hi, Mom," Nathan says. "You haven't changed a bit."

***

They talk about many things during supper, but little about the war. Discussion of Rebecca, Nathan's sister, deals with her job in Chicago and her ongoing affair with a married man.

"She's going through a tough phase," Nathan insists. "She's level-headed, though. Stop fretting about her."

"And what about you?" Woodrow asks. "You still want to be a bush pilot in Alaska?"

"I haven't wanted that since I was fourteen. Remember?"

Woodrow nods. "Then it's engineering, I suppose. In California?"

Nathan sits back. He has spent years studying aeronautical engineering on an R.O.T.C. scholarship, has repaid the scholarship with service in the navy, with time in Vietnam.

"Nope," Nathan says. He can't explain it, but the idea of wearing a white shirt and tie, doing numbers on computers, no longer has any appeal. He imagines a landscaped office surrounded by a parking lot full of little sports cars in the sun of Silicon Valley; a two-hundred-thousand-dollar tract house with a hot tub and a wet bar and a balloon-payment mortgage; a health club membership, a fancy jogging suit, a wife who invites friends for quiche and California wine.

Paying for all this would be work on air-to-ground missile guidance systems that may errantly choose to select some primitive village and blow the limbs off skinny kids.

"Look, Pops. It was hard for you, getting me to college. I hate like hell to waste it. But I'll be damned if I'm going to California or anywhere else right now. Vets aren't exactly heroes in those places, anyway."

"What will you do then?" Woodrow asks quietly.

"Stay here, I guess, near old friends, real people. Get my feet on solid ground... " He stops. "Dad, I can't help build any kind of war machines. Not anymore."

"Well... " Woodrow looks at his feet, shakes his head.

Nathan sits back, crosses his legs. "It's not that I oppose national defense. I just need a break, and I'd like to try helping out this town, somehow. Help it grow a bit. Maybe work in your store, if that's okay with you."

Tears are in Jessica's eyes. Woodrow's voice is scratchy as he lifts his glass. "Let's toast to that," he says.

***

Then comes Valerie Ensign.

Valerie's father, a retired army colonel, comes across as a glad-hander, boastful, loud, affecting a southern military drawl. Valerie's mother, Geneva Ensign, is a no-nonsense woman with narrow hips and broad shoulders who likes to display her collections of pottery and glassware from around the world.

Valerie is their only child, and she has grown up to seem as aloof as those mountain sheep that click up impossible slopes, then gaze from the top at the tiny world below. She has hair that flows like the mane of a running mustang, eyes that sometimes flare like propane flame. She avoids other women, helps her father in the field more than her mother in the kitchen.

Nathan learns Russell Bancroft has been visiting the Ensign ranch, and that disturbs him. Years ago, there was a pretty blonde in high school named Lana French. Bancroft went after her as soon as Nathan went off to college; then dropped her without warning and headed for school himself. The girl picked up Roy Yancey on the rebound, entered a doomed marriage, fled town. She hadn't been back since.

It isn't long before Bancroft finds himself in disfavor at the Ensign ranch. Coyotes have been prowling the perimeter of the colonel's winter range, which is public land on lease, and the game warden refuses to kill the animals. Bancroft also enforces the federal ban on the use of a predator control known as "ten-eighty." The colonel is incensed. Valerie, caught in the middle, turns her attentions elsewhere.

Nathan sees Valerie strutting in town, narrow hips in rhythmic motion, tapered legs encased in tight Levis. She attracts stares from the men, envious glances from the women. Initially, she's direct with Nathan, as with everyone, but treats him as someone not really worth investigating.

Until one day her eyes soften suddenly; they begin surveying the details of his face...

***

A LIGHT has struck Nathan's face; music has attacked his ears. "The hell's that!"

Valerie touched his cheek. "It's okay, hon. The power just came back on. I forgot to turn everything off."

Nathan gazed around him. Valerie was up, hurrying to shut off the record player. She came back and snuggled under the covers with him. "You were so sound asleep. I'm sorry. Were you dreaming?"

"Uh, yeah." With incredible detail, he realized.

"Want me to rub your back?" she asked.

"What time is it?"

"Midnight. On the dot."

"What day?"

"None. It isn't any day."

Nathan blinked. "Hey, am I still dreaming?"

"I mean, it's midnight. Yesterday is gone," Valerie said. "And tomorrow isn't here yet. We're at *midnight*."

"Fine. That sounds like a good place to be these days."

Valerie's hand drifted across Nathan's shoulder. He exhaled and enjoyed the feeling. He said, "Val?"

"Yes, hon?"

"Why don't we just stay here?"

PART TWO
THE FIRE

Chapter 22: Mines and Memories

THE J.C. PENNEY catalog store had closed in 1964, leaving a vacant building between the Montana Power Company utility office and the Horseshoe Bar. In September ten years later, the building acquired new occupants. Three men installed desks and file cabinets and hung venetian blinds. They did not hang a sign.

Curious townspeople speculated the men were connected with the ski project. Wall charts and maps were visible through the blinds.

Benjamin Bayliss wouldn't settle for speculation. He boldly went inside and spent fifteen minutes there. He hurried to the courthouse, came back, and questioned the men for another ten minutes.

Chambers caught up to Bayliss on the sidewalk. "Geologists," Bayliss announced without breaking stride. "For the coal company. They won't say if it's feasible to reopen the mines. Just testing." He smirked. "Know what that means?"

"No, "Chambers said. "What's *your* best guess?"

Bayliss stopped. "Of *course* it's feasible! It's just a matter of finding the cheapest places to poke their holes." Bayliss resumed his hasty walk.

"A hundred miles east," Chambers said, "they're stripping coal off the surface. Why would anyone want the expense of mining underground?"

Bayliss arrived at the door to his office. "Expense? Have you forgotten the tough strip-mining legislation passed this summer in Congress? The bill that caused two thousand miners to walk out in protest? Where've you been?"

"I know, Ben, but..."

"By comparison," Bayliss said, "there are no reclamation laws when they go underground. Royalties are cheap. And the last federal underground mining law was written back in the Eighteen-nineties."

"Ben, there are plenty of mining laws. The oldtimers still gripe about some of the shutdowns caused by all the laws... "

"Those laws," Bayliss said, "concern mine safety. Not the pollution or social impacts." He put a hand on Nathan's shoulder. "The late 'Forties... heck, you were only five or six years old then. I was still back in Missouri. But I learned a lot from the newspaper morgue. You should look through those old clippings yourself."

"Hard times," Chambers said. "I know that."

"*Hellish* times. After the explosion here, they closed the mines. Six hundred men without jobs. Half stayed, tried to live on pensions. The rest moved out, leaving two hundred vacant houses on the market. Stores closed and more people moved away. Real estate prices fell through the floor. Taxes skyrocketed because high school bonds had to be paid. But enrollment dropped. Teachers were fired, courses were cancelled. Athletic competition was ended."

"Everyone still talks about it," Chambers acknowledged.

"Worst of all, the mining companies didn't even try to clean up their mess. The slack piles are still there. The sludge has ruined several creeks and the old shafts are full of water and snakes."

"Yeah, that too," Chambers said. "Couple of kids got killed in one of those shafts a few years ago. I helped some men board up the hole. But the boards get knocked down again. Sometimes the ground caves in above the tunnels. A rancher loses a steer." He pushed up his hat, gazed toward the West Bench slack heap.

"If it happens again," Bayliss said, "it'll be worse. Now the railroad's gone. They'll have to move the coal by truck. Imagine those huge dusty trucks roaring down mainstreet every night. Then in a few years, they'll shut down again."

Bayliss banged open the door to his office and went in.

Chambers leaned against the building, thumbs hooked in his pockets.

Then Bayliss was back. He said, "Did you see that NBC report last month about Rock Springs, Wyoming?"

Nathan scratched an eyebrow. "I don't think so. What about it?"

"Because of the energy crisis, Rock Springs is a boom-town. New coal mines, oil exploration, soda ash production, construction of a major powerplant. Now their schools are crowded, the streets are jammed, the sewer system is over-loaded, and people are living in tents and trailers. Think about it."

Bayliss went inside and slammed the door.

Nathan watched a crippled old miner enter the super-market with his food stamps. He knew the man would come out later with a loaf of bread and some canned dog food.

The man didn't own a dog. He'd trade the rest of his food stamps for cash to buy wine at the state liquor store.

It was a common way of life in Jackpine. Everyone knew it. No one talked about it.

Chapter 23:   Ed Cahill, Asst. Warden

LAUGHTER ECHOED off the corrugated aluminum walls inside the airport hangar. Two dozen men on rickety folding chairs had just seen Jonas Barclay immobilized by the assistant warden from the Montana Department of Corrections — using two fingers. "It's all in the pressure points," the assistant warden said.

The trainees laughed again as Jonas wobbled to his chair like a crippled duck. The group included the police, firemen, county sheriff and deputies, several merchants and ranch hands, Bancroft and Chambers, and now *six* aldermen. Guilio Bastoni, a baker, had been appointed as Nathan's successor.

Assistant Warden Edmund Cahill was a deceptive man of middle age — small, smiling, with kindly eyes and graying hair. But his stomach was flat and his muscles firm under a knit golf shirt. "Now I'll show you the most damned fearsome weapon for crowd control ever devised by man."

All eyes followed as Cahill moved with panther-like strides and picked up a wooden pole. "Remember your Robin Hood stories?" He twirled the pole. "Little John taught Robin some respect with a staff like this."

The men, amused, hunkered forward.

"Suppose a couple three of you come at me."

The hangar was still.

"All right, six of you then!"

Chuckling, the men prodded one another until Sheriff Merlin Gabe stood, hitched his belt, and flexed his heavy arms. "I'm game," he announced. "Come on, you pipsqueaks — you ain't *all* afraid of a little old man with a long cane."

Smiling sheepishly, Cahill said, "I promise I won't cripple anyone — not permanently."

Roy Yancey lifted his egg-shaped body and tugged at his belt. "Okay, I'm game!" He nudged Vincent Fox. "Come on, Vince!"

Fox shrugged and stood up. He chucked his gum at a corner.

"Very good," Edmund Cahill said. "Let's try this in kind of slow-motion. You three come at me together, not too fast, and I'll just demonstrate a few techniques here." He hefted the pole. "Whenever you're ready."

The trio shuffled uncertainly. Then Yancey charged, head down, screaming, *"Bonzaaii!"*

Cahill moved casually, a sweep of his staff catching Yancey at the knees and toppling him into the front row of firemen. A vicious chop at Fox's collarbone, then a menacing thrust at the sheriff's neck, and all movement froze.

Cahill had assessed each man. He knew Yancey would be foolhardy, Fox squeamish despite his arrogance, and Gabe the dangerous one. He concentrated his eyes on Gabe's and pressed the pole against the sheriff's throat. The sheriff glugged... and shrugged.

"Okay. Thanks, men." Cahill lowered the staff. He waited as the three fellows, taking slaps and hoots from the others, maneuvered back to their chairs.

"Now hear this," Cahill warned, spinning the staff in his hands. "That was a dangerous demonstration. Not dangerous for *me*, mind you" — smiling kindly — "but it took all my skill to avoid hurting those fellows. *You* there... " he indicated Yancey, chagrined and rubbing his knee. "You might've gotten your ass in a sling after that ridiculous Bonzai charge. This staff is meant to break bones. When you men use it, you *will* break bones. You won't be good enough not to." He looked at Gabe. "And Sheriff, if anything's worse than an ass in a sling, it's a neck in traction. You had me worried there. For a minute, I thought you meant business. That would've been unfortunate, because you'd be choking on your Adam's apple."

Gabe said, "I ain't totally stupid. I reckoned you meant business, too."

Alderman Kermit Czarnowsky thumbed his nose. "You ask me, this stuff seems kinda rough. Why can't we just do the job with tear gas or firehoses? Some of us are gettin' too old for hand-to-hand combat."

"Yes," Cahill agreed. "Some of you are better off behind a firehose. But firehoses are clumsy. And you can't control the drift of tear gas. Sometimes you need a selective weapon, and a harsh one. This is it, fellas. This is it."

"Well... " Czarnowsky said. "Like when, for instance?"

Cahill stared him straight in the eye. "Like when they come at you with ax handles and tire chains, or knives and broken bottles. Or worse."

Czarnowsky shriveled down.

"Remember, men," Cahill said. "You fellas are there to preserve the town. The mob is there to destroy it. It's no time to be squeamish. You get a dozen men marching in a phalanx with these poles. You march right into 'em and show you mean business. You crunch some bones if you have to. Then if you're tough enough and lucky enough, the mob will scatter."

Patrolman Buck Chism raised a hand tentatively. "What you're sayin', I understand, is that we oughta make a show of force. Not pussyfoot around. Right?"

Cahill nodded. "You need to know mob psychology. Usually, they're like buffalo. Keep 'em timid and nobody will get hurt. But let 'em realize for a minute they pack all the muscle, and they'll stampede you into the ground."

Cahill hoisted the staff again. "The beauty of this item is that you can be selective with it. You can take out the troublemakers right away, without hurting any so-called innocent bystanders. Of course, there's no such thing as innocent bystanders in a mob. None I've ever seen, anyway."

He paced. "You'll hear some comments about police brutality. Let me tell you about that. Mob brutality is a lot damn worse. A mob is the most brutal life form on this planet. It can kill, burn, destroy, and loot with mindless fury. You men must be ready to stop it cold. Stop it before it passes the point of no return — that point where destruction doesn't end until the mob burns itself out."

After a moment of silence, Vincent Fox said, "Maybe the poles aren't enough, Ed. Maybe we should get us some machine guns."

Cahill forced a smile. "The idea is to stop short of guns. If you're forced to use guns, your situation is lost. People will get slaughtered. You included."

Chambers spoke up for the first time. "Ed, the crowds we get in Jackpine — they're not convicts. Mostly just cowboys and some tourists, a few rowdy youngsters. We start punchin' those sticks at 'em, they won't likely ever come back. I don't think we had that objective in mind."

Cahill shrugged. "You have to judge the crowd you're dealing with. Sometimes, most times, you can talk to them. You can pull a Wyatt Earp — just walk right into them and arrest one loudmouth, and everybody else breaks up. However, from what I understand happened here last Fourth of July, you men had no inkling what to do. You ran around like Keystone Kops."

That brought Chief Driscoll to his feet. His resentment showed in the color of his face. "I might point out," he said, "that we been handlin' mobs of drunks and bums for something like twenty-three years now. This was the first time we had any real trouble. And I think the reason was like you said. We pussyfooted around with a couple of streakers when we shoulda throwed the bunch of 'em in the slammer. Could've nipped the whole damn business in the bud." He sat down heavily, deliberately not looking at Chambers.

Cahill detected this resentment among the local officials. He diverted the issue. "Well, I'm not here to second-guess your actions last July. I came to help prepare you for the next time. Some of it may seem too brutal for ordinary crowds, and you'll have to judge each situation for yourselves. But it's always best to be prepared for the worst.

That way, you won't get all shook up over the lesser difficulties."

He looked them over and smiled. "Look at it this way. You men wouldn't have any trouble chasing off a flock of chickens. That's because you're bigger, faster, and smarter than they are. You know damn well you don't have to shoot those chickens or club 'em to death in order to get them scooting. Right?"

The men laughed.

"Well, it's the same principle. I intend to make you bigger, tougher, and smarter than any mob you'll ever face. You'll have confidence, and it'll show. You'll master this science of crowd control until you can meet each situation with MEF — Minimum Effective Force. Like chasing chickens."

"Sounds good to me," Yancey said. He nudged Fox. "Man-o-man, Vince, can't you just see them hippie faces? Here we come, you turds! Poles up the ass! *Long* poles!" Yancey's belly was bouncing with laughter, his eyes watering. "They'll have so much shit in their pants, Vince, we won't even need to grease the ends of them poles. *Yahoo!*"

Fox didn't think this was all that funny, but he grinned back at Yancey and said, "Yeah. Sure."

Chapter 24: Arnold and Geneva Ensign

WOODROW CHAMBERS put an extra leaf in the dining table and laid a roaring fire on the hearth. It was the last week in September, with a cold rain sweeping down the slopes west of Jackpine.

"That fire looks good," said Colonel Arnold Ensign, clapping his palms as he entered the parlor. "We might get frost tonight on our summer range, Woody, you know that?"

Woodrow handed Arnold his favorite drink, Kentucky bourbon sloshing in a fat glass. "You still got cows up there?"

"About thirty head." The colonel sank into a soft chair. "Forest Service tells me I can't renew my lease on that pasture, once it expires. They claim it's over-grazed. Hell, how can you over-graze with just thirty head?"

"Where's the missus?" Woodrow asked.

"Hell if I know. She came in right behind me... Geneva? Where'n hell are you!"

Geneva Ensign's high voice came down the hallway from the kitchen. "I'm helping Jessica with the gravy. You noisy bulls just sit tight. We'll be along."

"Women *always* gotta gab in the kitchen, over their little secrets," Arnold said. "Glad my daughter ain't like that. Where *is* she, by the way? They get here yet?"

Woodrow got up and went to the window, peered out. "No sign yet. The rain's moving in fast... " He returned to his chair. "So. What's this about over-grazing? The Forest Service won't let you keep your lease?"

Arnold sucked bourbon through his teeth. "Damn fools. Woody, I went right to the district ranger. He says they need to save forage for the deer. You figure it out. I can't graze thirty head on a summer range big enough for twice that many. But they turn around and allow a big ski resort smack in the middle of an elk range."

"I didn't know that had been decided," Woodrow said.

Arnold gripped his knees. "Well, they need to go through some official motions. But it's in the bag, I tell you. Down at that ranger station, you can smell it in the air."

At the hallway entrance, Nathan said, "Smell what?" He entered behind Valerie and helped remove her jacket, displaying husbandly concern for her 'condition.' But she stepped with a lively gait to a stiff chair and sat demurely. "Stop gaping at the pregnant woman," she told the men. "Somebody bring a Schweppes for the baby."

"I'll get it," Woodrow said, hurrying to the cocktail cart. "Nathan, Arnold thinks the ski resort is a lock. Says the public hearing will be just for show."

Arnold raised his glass. "I also think you'd be smart to get a piece of the action, Nate."

"In what way, Arnie?"

"You know. Get some stock or something. Everybody else is."

"No can do," Nathan said.

"Why the hell not?"

"Dad," Valerie said, "that's a sore subject."

"Your wife's expecting a baby," Arnold said. "You ought to think about that child's future. If you need some investment cash, I'd be glad to fix you a loan... "

"Dad," Valerie warned, "Nathan would have a conflict of interest. We've been through it, and the answer is no."

"Conflict of interest? That's about big-city politicians. It don't apply here."

"Dad, please."

"Only conflict of interest I see here is over concern for your child's future... "

"Darn it, Dad, shut up!"

Ensign became slowly aware of his daughter's temper, aware that Nathan had clammed up.

"Hey, no offense," Arnold said, putting up a hand. "Hell, I don't mean to meddle. You kids got to do what's best for yourselves. I know that."

Geneva Ensign entered. A short, pugnacious woman, she had none of her daughter's tall dark beauty, but she shared Valerie's alert eyes and firm manner. "Arnold, I heard you shootin' off your mouth again. When're you going to learn to leave the kids alone?"

"Now Geneva..."

"Still thinks he's in the army," Geneva said. "Tries to run his affairs like boot camp. Drives our cowhands nuts."

Jessica Chambers appeared at the door. "Food's on the table, everyone. Come and get it."

The noisy chatter stopped as Woodrow sat at the head of the table and bowed his head. "Lord, thank you for this food and all your wonderful blessings." He cleared his throat. "We especially thank you for the little miracle being carried by Valerie. We pray it will be a healthy and happy child who will grow up in a peaceful and prosperous community. Amen."

Valerie raised her softened eyes to Woody's gentle smile. "Thank you, Grandpa. That was nice."

The meal progressed through rounds of small talk until dessert, when Arnold suddenly raised his voice at Nathan. "Say, Nate! That newspaper has been coming down real hard on the coal business. Can't you put a stop to that?"

Nathan looked up from his dish. "How do you mean?"

"Persuade that publisher to lay off. He's got everybody upset, and he's liable to spoil everything."

Nathan smiled. "It's freedom of the press, Arnie. I couldn't hush Bayliss even if I wanted to."

"And you don't?"

"Nope."

"Why not? It's industry, Nate. What are the youngsters going to do — join the army like I did? When I left Three Forks? Or like your sister, when she ran off to Chicago?"

Arnold had touched another sore point. Geneva opened her mouth, but Nathan spoke first. "The mines would create about two dozen jobs. Machinery does most of the work now. And those jobs are dirty. Wouldn't want it for my kid."

"That leaves just the ski mountain. And it don't seem like it would pay as much."

"The mines would last ten, maybe fifteen years," Nathan said. "Even before then, there'd be troubles and layoffs... "

"I think they'd also cut down some of the welfare around here," Arnold grumbled.

"Arnie," Nathan said evenly, "the mines *caused* the welfare around here."

Woodrow, listening in attentive silence, suddenly turned to Arnold. "Arnie, I have to agree with Nathan on this. If you had been here when the mines started closing in the 'Forties, I don't think you'd want to see anything like it again. It's not worth the risk, and I'm speaking as a local merchant."

"Don't forget the pollution," Valerie interjected. "This is beautiful country. Why would you spoil it?"

"Now there," Arnold blurted, "...that's *exactly* the kind of asinine nonsense that gets in the way of decent progress. It's *beautiful*, she says, don't *spoil* it. Bull! This land stopped bein' beautiful when the army came and slaughtered the buffalo, when the damn farmers plowed up the grassland and fenced the range. Or how about Anaconda and that big stinking smelter? Or the open-pit copper mine at Butte? If that ain't the world's ugliest, biggest damn hole in the ground, I'll eat my hat."

Arnold waved an arm toward the windows. "You want pretty scenery? Fine. There's thousands of square miles up in those mountains. Go crawl back in there with the back-packers. But down here, people got bills to pay. We can't *afford* the luxury of bein' beautiful. If we don't make a decent living off the land, we can't afford to live here at all. Might as well give it back to the Crow and Blackfeet."

"Arnold," Geneva said, "you aren't lecturing your troops!"

Ensign laughed. "All right, Genny honey, I'm just havin' some fun... "

She said, "Nobody's enjoyin' it except you."

"Oh, hell," he said. "It's just... I get sick and tired of these environmental wackos, like that game warden friend of Nate... "

"Arnie, you stop!" Geneva demanded.

"Say, I liked that fella at first. Seemed like a hard-workin' game warden who knew his job very well. I didn't even mind him sniffin' around Valerie that first year. Well... "

"Time to leave," Geneva said, pushing back her chair.

"But I damned well knew something was wrong when he refused to run the coyotes off my leased land. Claimed my own dogs were killing the sheep. Then he warns me about the Ten-Eighty poison. Threatened to haul me into court if I set those traps. I tell you, Nate... *Watch* him. That fella has spent too much time in the backcountry. He got to where he likes animals better than people."

"That's enough," Geneva commanded. "Jessica, Woody, it was awful nice of you folks to invite us, but we really have to run along. The rain may be turning to snow at our place. Come on, Arnie." She tugged his shoulder.

"Oh, all right," Arnold said. "Well, it's been a real swell evening. I sure did enjoy it."

"Bye, Dad," Valerie said without standing up.

Chapter 25: Lana French

NATHAN CHAMBERS shut off the ignition and studied Bancroft's cabin. It featured hand-hewn logs and a steep-pitched roof with solar panels. A windmill was rigged to a generator hut. A small watermill spanned the creek in back. Gurgling water and chirping birds were the only sounds.

There were two vehicles parked there; Bancroft's Ford Bronco and an unfamiliar yellow Mustang. Woodsmoke curled from the stone chimney.

Nathan went to the door and knocked several times. Eventually the door was pulled open and Bancroft looked out. "Hello, Nate. What's up?"

"I went back to the district ranger," Nathan said.

"About time. Come in."

Nathan entered and glanced around. "Got any coffee?"

"In a minute." Bancroft went to a homemade stove converted from an oil drum and felt it. Evidently it wasn't hot enough, because he opened the hatch and threw another log inside. This contraption was piped into a large fireplace, also built by Bancroft from shards of Wyoming lichen stone.

Nathan sat on a chair of lodgepole pine, cushioned with sheepskins. Across the room was the bedroom door. He saw a shadow move across the space between door and floor. Someone, the driver of the Mustang, was in that room.

The door opened abruptly and Lana French emerged, tucking her blouse into her slacks. "Hiya, Nate," she said.

Nathan took just a moment to recognize her. Her hair was platinum now, her eyes green with makeup, lips pink. She had taken off about twenty pounds since divorcing Yancey. Nathan said, with genuine surprise: "Lana! I didn't know you were back."

"How couldja miss me? I been here since July. I seen you a number of times."

"You've changed some."

"How's your wife?" Lana asked. "I hear she's pregnant."

"She's fine," Nathan said.

Bancroft gave Lana a smart swat on her buttocks. "We need some coffee," he said.

"Ouch, you brute!" Lana jabbed him back. "What'm I, your maid?" To Nathan, she said, "You'll be lucky to get coffee before dark. He expects me to heat it on that stove. It takes forever."

"Do it," Bancroft said.

"Yes *sir!*"

Bancroft sat. "She's mad because I won't buy an electric coffee pot. Why waste electricity? I can heat coffee on the same fire that heats the room."

"Heat, he calls it," Lana said. "I like froze to death here last night. Yancey was a dope, but he kept me warm at least."

This all seemed very strange to Nathan.

Years ago, Lana French had been a high school cheerleader whom Nathan had dated numerous times. On other occasions, she had dated Bancroft and almost every other boy in town. She had married Roy Yancey while Nathan and Bancroft were attending their colleges. It had lasted a year, and she had gone to Seattle. Now she was back, different and yet the same, and living with Russell Bancroft. It had to be the best-kept secret in town.

"Lana thinks I was born a century too late," Bancroft said.

"At least!" she said.

"Only because I'm mostly self-sufficient. I get along fine and don't need to depend on an industrial civilization."

"Oh yeah? Let's see you get along without your little truck."

"Might need to, Lana. The world's running out of oil."

"And how about your magazines and books?" Lana said.

"Fortunately," Bancroft said, "paper is a renewable resource, and they're working on inks that won't use petroleum." He touched a copy of Scientific American. "I admit this is one modern product I would miss."

"You're such a drag sometimes," Lana said.

Bancroft said to Nathan, "You're probably wondering why we're together."

Nathan shrugged.

"She's helping me with paperwork," Bancroft said.

"Hell, I knew that," Nathan said.

"No, really. She's pretty good at it."

"Among other things besides," Lana said.

"In Seattle, she did paperwork for a food broker. Nine account executives, she says. Those are traveling salesmen who go around to grocery stores, stocking candy bars. She kept them all pretty happy, she says. I believe it."

"Russ," Nathan said, "I need to get going pretty soon."

"How's the coffee doing?" Bancroft asked.

"Don't ask me," Lana said. "If I watch it, it'll never boil."

"You said you got back to the district ranger," Bancroft said to Nathan. "Finally."

"I had a lot of doubts," Nathan said. "I spent a lot of time coming up with the right questions."

Bancroft frowned. "Did you ask the ranger about the Wilderness Act?"

"I did. He said they've been doing a wilderness study for several months — in the primitive area. That's well back from Wapiti Mountain."

"They picked the smallest area they could. Damn them!"

"I asked about Wapiti and the Beartooth Face. He said they can't start a wilderness study there until the Bureau of Mines does a mineral study first. Maybe next summer," Nathan told him.

Bancroft stalked back to the stove. He stared at the pot of water. It was simmering; so was he. "The ski permit will be decided long before then."

"Maybe not," Nathan said. "The public hearing was postponed. Until December."

"Postponed?" Bancroft brightened. "Great! How come?"

"Request of the developers," Nathan said. "The ranger says it's because the promoters need more time to complete their environmental studies. I think it's because they need more time to build public support."

Bancroft nodded. "I agree. At least you accomplished that much."

"Accomplished what?"

"You slowed 'em down."

"I didn't do a damn thing."

"That's what slowed 'em down."

Nathan stood, ready to leave. "Anyhow, that's everything I learned. Not much chance to get the wilderness enlarged beyond the primitive area. But we gained a little time."

Bancroft glanced at Lana. She was by the window, looking out, drumming her fingers on the sill. He turned back to Nathan. "Well, it's a start," Bancroft said. "Now we'll need to create even more delays for the ski project."

"How?"

Bancroft studied Nathan. Then he said, "I'm going to enlist some reinforcements. The Montana Wilderness Association, the Sierra Club... "

"To do what?"

"To help the cause. They can bring national attention to this problem. They're well organized. They have clout. They can obstruct this development on a lot of different levels — the courts, the press, the legislature... "

"Now wait a damn minute." Nathan jabbed a forefinger. "Russ, I am opposed to that sort of meddling. It would tear the town apart. Bringing in outsiders, extremists — you know how the folks around here would boil over that. Forget that crap."

"Crap?" Bancroft gonged the stove with a fist. "I'll give you a definition of crap. Crap is what those robber barons are feeding us so they can steal a fat profit. Those guys are the extremists, buddy. They're extreme in their greed... and extremely ruthless."

"Russ... "

"Listen, Nate. Those developers have the money and the clout to tromp all over us. We need to get some clout on our side, create some kind of stand-off."

Nathan nodded. "We've got five weeks until those hearings start. Before turning this into a full-scale war, give me a chance to see what I can do."

"What can you do in five weeks? You had all summer and did nothing."

"I'll tell you when I get back from Chicago."

"Chicago?" This caught Bancroft by surprise. "Why are you going there?"

"To ask more questions," Nathan said.

Bancroft stood board-stiff at the door and watched Nathan drive down the gravel road.

"The coffee's hot," Lana said.

"Too late," Bancroft said. "I don't want any."

Bancroft went to the bedroom and stared at the stacks of paper on the floor and the mimeograph machine on the dresser. Lana followed, rolling up her sleeves. She pulled her blouse out of her slacks and sat on the floor amidst the papers, started folding and stuffing the sheets into envelopes. "Get cranking, will ya," she said. "Let's get this over with."

Bancroft started cranking the mimeograph.

"Who licks the stamps?" Lana asked.

"I was hoping you would," Bancroft said.

"At these wages?"

"You've got the tongue for it," he said.

"I wouldn't mind if these were wedding invitations," she said.

"Shut up and lick," he said.

Chapter 26: Rebecca Chambers

REBECCA CHAMBERS stood at the observation windows in the Northwest Airlines lounge at O'Hare International Airport. She watched as her brother's DC-10 treaded among a maze of fat silver jets squatting under murky clouds.

Her fear of not recognizing him dissolved when he came through the boarding tunnel. Nathan looked different in a tan business suit with cordovan shoes and maroon striped tie. But he was the one who stood erect, when others scurried at a forward slant; his eyes were alert, while the others were vacant; his skin was weathered, and the others pale.

Rebecca waved, but Nathan didn't see her. He was eyeing a dude in white cowboy hat and glossy black boots standing near the cocktail bar.

"Nathan, hon," Rebecca said, reaching up to tap the high shoulder.

Nathan whirled and grinned. "Becky! By thunder!" He dropped his overnight bag and swept her off the floor. "How's my favorite sister? You look... great!"

Rebecca caught the hesitation as she hugged him. "Jeez, put me *down* — people will stare."

"Nuts," Nathan said, lowering her gently. "Nobody looks at anyone around here." He took a good look at her. "Wow."

A multi-colored headband surrounded Rebecca's long taffy hair, center-parted and straight. Cheekbones stood out on her gaunt face. A lime-green shift ended six inches above her knees, showing thin legs anchored in thick-heeled shoes. A sash hung loosely around her hips, and her breasts jiggled with every step along the concourse.

"You can't afford a brassiere?" he whispered.

"Christ," she said, stopping. "A brother isn't supposed to notice things like that."

"Can't help it. Neither can anybody else."

"Grow up, would you? You're in the big city now." Rebecca steered him down the escalator and past the luggage turntables, outside the terminal and into the parking maze where, eventually, she found her battered Oldsmobile Cutlass. She fumbled for her keys, inexplicably nervous the whole time.

The traffic was thick and fast along the Kennedy Expressway as the Cutlass bored toward the Loop. But most headlights were flowing through the murk in the opposite direction. "Rush hour," Rebecca said, flicking on the radio. "I'd better check the traffic 'copter reports."

A horn blasted in Rebecca's ear as a big Mercury angled in from an entrance ramp. "Up your ass!" She honked back and floored the accelerator, shifted lanes, cut ahead of the Mercury. The driver flipped a finger as the Cutlass sped past.

"Take it easy," Nathan said.

Rebecca switched off the radio. She hadn't been able to hear her brother in the wind whistle, engine roar, and broadcast cackle. "The helicopter's way north, on the Edens," she said. "Two lanes are blocked up there, probably an hour-long backup."

"How can you stand it?" Nathan asked, watching her shift lanes again to pass a slow-moving Datsun.

"There oughta be a crackdown," she said. "Driving below fifty during the rush hour. It's insane. They cause more accidents that way... What'd you say?"

"Forget it. Just drive."

By the time the Cutlass pulled in front of a row of brownstones on the Near North Side, Chambers was ready for a drink and said so.

Rebecca laughed. "Come on, country boy. Let's go calm you down. My pad is less than a block from here."

It was refreshingly quiet on the third floor where Rebecca kept a three-room apartment. They had to climb the stairs, though; the elevator was out of order.

"Take a load off," Rebecca said, throwing a series of deadbolts and chain-hooks on the door. She kicked off her shoes and went barefoot to the kitchen.

A picture of himself caught Nathan's eye. It was framed and placed prominently above a small writing desk. He went for a closer look and studied it.

Rebecca came to his side. "You looked so young then," she said.

"That's when I entered the navy," Nathan remembered, accepting a glass half full of scotch. He watched her sit down on a long sofa cluttered with bright satin pillows. She drew her legs under her and sipped her drink.

"What is that?" Nathan asked, pointing to a large vinyl lump on the floor.

"A beanbag."

"A what?"

"Sit in it, dum-dum."

Nathan sat, immediately sank. He spilled some of his drink. "If this isn't the damnedest thing. Is it supposed to be furniture?"

"They must have beanbags in Montana," Rebecca said. "Surely by now."

"If so, they oughta shoot 'em. How do you get out?"

"Don't. Just relax." Rebecca smiled. "Tell me about Mom and Dad. And all about Valerie and the baby."

"Well, not much to tell," he replied, settling back. He then spent half an hour telling her. Rebecca listened eagerly, spread out on her sofa. A change came over her face. There was a softening, something less like the Chicago working girl and more like the Montana kid Nathan remembered from long ago.

"You should come home," Nathan said.

"What?"

"You heard me. Home." Nathan waved his hand in a sweep that took in the apartment and the city. "This can't be much fun."

"Christ, how would you know?" Rebecca swung her feet to the floor. "I'm having a ball!"

"Okay," Nathan said.

"I mean it. How can I make you and the folks understand? I hate sleepy old Jackpine. What can I do there?

Marry some poor cowboy slob and raise ten screaming little brats?"

"I don't know. What do you do here?"

"Lots. This is an exciting and beautiful city — pretty as the mountains in some ways. Fantastic architecture, and culture, and the people are totally friendly — in a different sort of way than Jackpine. Here, they're nice to you, but they know when to leave you alone."

"Sure. Like when you're being mugged?"

"Be a smartass."

Nathan shrugged. "So. You look at architecture? Absorb culture?"

"Damn right. And lots of other things besides." Her eyes challenged him.

Nathan hesitated. He had heard a similar phrase, not long ago. "What other things?"

"Listen, not what you're thinking," Rebecca said. She put down her glass. "I may not be a virgin, but I don't screw around indiscriminately."

"Well, that's good to hear," Nathan said.

"Look. I'm doing terrific. I make over three hundred a week. I own a sporty car and pay my rent. I have a closet full of clothes and a talented — *and* quite successful — man. A man who's passionate for me. What else is there to want?"

"This passionate man. The architect? The same guy from a few years ago?"

"What is this, the third degree?"

"He's married, right?"

"Well, sort of," Rebecca said, taking a swig of scotch.

"Sort of? How can a guy be sort of married?"

"He's in the process of getting a divorce, dammit."

"That's what you said before. Aren't you kind of ashamed to bust up a guy's marriage? Hurt the wife and the little kids?"

"Christ." Rebecca collapsed backwards on the sofa. "There's no kids! And Nancy's a bitch! She's clinging to Evan only because of his money!"

"Sounds like a dead end," Nathan said. "He leads you along for years now. Still goes home to the wife every night."

"Not every night. Oh hell." Rebecca sat up. "I don't want to talk about this. Here, take my glass and fill it up."

Nathan accepted the glass and went into the kitchen, where the neatness of the apartment ended. The porcelain sink was full of soiled plastic dishes, and a carton of milk was souring on the linoleum countertop. Skim milk, he noted, pouring it down the drain. He looked for a garbage can, found it under the sink, overflowing with yogurt containers. He jammed in the milk carton, hunted up the scotch bottle among a cluster of condiments.

Pouring, he wondered how much Rebecca drank. He wondered if his own child would be living like this someday.

He carried the drink to Rebecca, thanked her for her hospitality, and asked if he could borrow the couch for a night's sleep.

Chapter 27: Sheldon Kaplan

BEFORE LEAVING Jackpine, Nathan had spent days seeking an appointment with Bartz or Dexter, but they were always "in conference" or "away on business" and had never returned his calls. He finally had succeeded in making an appointment at the Chicago engineering firm assigned to the ski project. He had told them he possessed vital information concerning the development.

The morning after his arrival, Nathan phoned Clarkson Dross Associates to confirm his appointment. Rebecca had left early for work, accommodating her house guest to the extent of hot water for instant coffee and a packet of Carnation Instant Breakfast. Chambers stirred his coffee while a secretary kept him on hold. Eventually, a nasal, rapid-speaking male voice came on the line.

"Mayor Chambers? Sorry to keep you waiting. Sheldon Kaplan here. Listen, sorry about the appointment. We've been tossing you around the office like a football, and it looks like I'm the fella who caught you last. Trouble is, I'm on roller skates. Any chance we can postpone this until next Wednesday?"

Chambers refused to be put off. "I had an appointment for today. Came fifteen hundred miles, and I've got a business and a town waiting for me. What's your problem?"

"Okay, okay," the nasal voice said. "Lemme think. How about this evening? Say seven-thirty. I gotta work late, I can skip dinner. That suit you?"

Chambers agreed and took directions on getting into the building and then dialed Rebecca at her office.

"Fine," Rebecca told him. "Evan and I were planning to take you out to dinner. We can make the side trip first, no problem."

***

A low overcast had darkened the evening as Nathan rode south on Lake Shore Drive in the sealed cocoon of Evan Black's cream-colored Eldorado. He watched the silent drift of white headlights on the left, the darting red taillights in front, listened to a stereophonic boom from twin rear-seat speakers. Up front, Rebecca sat half-turned in her bucket seat and pointed out passing landmarks — the brightly lighted Water Tower beyond blinking rows of Michigan Avenue traffic signals; the Chicago River aglow with reflections from the Wrigley Building.

Nathan was deeply aware of the close-in towers surrounding him, fractionally lighted against the invisible sky. But only after they swerved into a Randolph Street parking garage, did he really begin to feel the high-pressure congestion of the Loop. He winced at the screech of the Eldorado racing up the concrete ramps in the hands of a young parking attendant; wrinkled his nose at the sweet caramel scent of a Wabash Avenue donut shop; ducked from the clattering roar of an overhead commuter train on the elevated tracks, showering down pungent odors of iron and ozone.

At windy intersections, Nathan joined the jostle of pedestrians scurrying across like the skittering litter scraps at their feet. Horns blared, turn signals blinked, brakes chirped everywhere. It was a world of hard steel and monumental concrete — a world that diminished human life to something fragile, passing, and cheap.

"Exciting, isn't it?" Rebecca asked hopefully. "Can you see why I just can't go back to Jackpine after this?"

"Well, I don't much care for it," Nathan said.

Alongside them as they walked, Evan Black seemed quietly detached from the surrounding bustle. He was thick-haired with mutton-chop sideburns; had an overly handsome face well-doused with cologne; wore a shiny double-breasted suit. He held Rebecca's hand like a walking stick, flipping it about casually. "I believe we've arrived," he said, his round head inclining toward an entrance.

Nathan looked up at the tower.

"We'll go in with you," Evan said. "Wouldn't want you getting lost, eh?"

They entered another cocoon, a dead-silent lobby with a sleepy guard at a gigantic desk rimmed with polished brass. Nathan spoke to him and was directed to a bank of elevators marked for floors 18-34. The high-speed rise brought them to a bright corridor strewn with cleaning carts and vacuum cleaners. They explored the silent halls until finding a triple-doored suite bearing the silver-lettered name of Clarkson Dross Associates. The reception room was furnished with teakwood and green ferns. The conditioned air was cool and sweet.

"Now what?" Nathan wondered. The inner door was locked and no one seemed to be around. Then he remembered the instructions and picked up the phone on the reception desk, punched in the numbers of Kaplan's extension.

"That you, Chambers? Hang loose, fella. Be right there."

Shortly, the inner door opened and Sheldon Kaplan appeared: short, fox-like, mid-thirties, frenetic. Gold jewelry contrasted with his rumpled shirt, unkempt tie, bent cigarette dangling in his fingers. Chambers made introductions, but Kaplan paid little heed. "This-a-way," he said, turning to the inner door.

Kaplan led them past a series of glass-walled offices filled with opulent furniture, each like a Michigan Avenue window display. They came to an ornate teakwood door which Kaplan opened to a dark cave. "Damn," he said. "The cleaning crew shut everything off. Stand still. I gotta find a light switch."

Chambers peered inside and glimpsed Kaplan's shape feeling around in the gloom. "Ouch-shit!" A piece of furniture clattered.

"You okay?" Chambers called.

Then lights started coming on — high fluorescent banks blinking in succession like the score on a pinball machine, systematically lighting up a space the size of a gymnasium. The area was sectioned with rows of modular steel partitions, each cubicle identical with suspended desktop, hinged drawing board, shelves of reference manuals, orange bulletin board. There was no sign of human activity — no ashtrays, pencils, or coffee cups. Clearly there was a place for everything, and everything was in its place.

"Reminds me of a feedlot," Chambers said, and Kaplan laughed.

They came to Kaplan's cubicle, and Chambers smiled. This one was different. Kaplan had to shove aside bundles of paperwork to make room for his elbow as he sat. There was a rubber figurine of Daffy Duck, an "Uncle Sam Wants You" poster replacing the usual progress charts, and rows of cactus plants instead of manuals.

"So," Kaplan said, motioning to stools for his visitors. "As you see, you get to bypass all the bigshot assholes and meet with the action man. That's me. What can I do for you?"

Evan Black, using the edge of his hand to sweep an already spotless stool, sat down and carefully tested the swivel. Satisfied, he shook a hundred-millimeter cigarette from a silver case and tapped it on his watch crystal. "All right if I smoke?"

"Sure." Kaplan looked around, shrugged. "Here. Use this for an ashtray."

"Your rubber duck?"

"Turn it over. It's hollow."

"Aren't there some ashtrays in here?"

"Gone with the clean-up crew. Aw, go ahead — the duck doesn't bite."

Evan shrugged and inverted the duck. He appeared extraordinarily foolish tapping ashes into the duck's ass and knew it.

"Chambers —" Kaplan spoke with impatience. "I realize this is a fascinating place. But can we get on with it?"

Nathan stopped looking around and fixed his eyes on Kaplan. "You first. Tell me the current status of the Jackpine ski project."

"You don't know?"

"Since August, I haven't heard anything. The public hearing was postponed — that's all I know."

"Why ask me? You should question the developers," Kaplan said, becoming cautious.

"I tried. All I hear is silence. I'm being stonewalled, Mr. Kaplan."

"It's Shel." Kaplan swiveled back and forth on his stool. "It doesn't surprise me. Spears is like that."

"Who?"

"Spears. Hey — that's who we're talking about, right?"

"I don't know the name. The guys I met are Dexter and Bartz... Wisconsin Trust."

"Shit. Pardon my French." Kaplan flipped a hand, rapped his desk with a knuckle. "You know from nothing about Spears Industries?"

"I'm here to learn."

Kaplan shook his head. "No-no. You're here to tell *me* stuff — stuff vital to the master plan. That's what you said when you called."

Chambers nodded. "All right — here it is. You guys have got to scale down the plan. Way down. Otherwise, there's going to be large-scale local opposition."

Kaplan crossed his arms. "So?"

This indifference angered Chambers. He thumped a fist on Kaplan's desk. "If it comes to a battle, maybe there won't be *any* ski resort. Is that what you guys want?"

"Hey," Kaplan said, eyebrows lifting. "I couldn't care less. Look here, Chambers, the politics ain't our business. Spears pays us to draw pictures. Your beef, it's strictly with him, not with us... Anyway, you ask me, that resort doesn't belong in your town in the first place. The conditions are too marginal."

"Marginal? How do you mean?"

"I mean you don't get enough early-season snowfall. And you get Chinook winds that erode whatever snow base you do get. That's no good. You gotta have a solid packed base to open for the holiday season, or you're dead. That means you have to groom the slopes like a golf course. It means seeding against erosion, bedding the slopes in straw, and blasting away every last stump and boulder. You got boulders up there the size of cars. You know how much dynamite we're talking? Your town's gonna shake, rattle, and roll like World War Three — for nearly a year." Kaplan let this sink in, then added, "And that's just to open Phase One. Against the cost of all that grooming, that resort won't break even until it reaches full capacity — after Phase Three. And that's why it can't be scaled down. No matter how much you object."

"It's all or nothing?"

"That's right, cowboy."

"Where can I find this Spears guy?"

Kaplan chuckled. "Forget it. He hides out in a big house on Sheridan Road in Winnetka. It's one of those little estates surrounded by a stone wall and a pack of vicious Dobermans. You wanna try, be my guest. The FBI can't get in there."

Nathan sagged from the weight of his frustration.

After ten seconds of silence, Kaplan picked up a drawing pencil and threw it viciously against the partition, leaving a mark. "Aw, shit."

Chambers and Rebecca stared at him. Evan Black, startled, dropped the rubber duck.

"I'd best explain something," Kaplan said. "There's a client relationship involved here — like doctor and patient, you know? So maybe tomorrow I'll be pounding the streets for another job, in the middle of a recession yet. But what the hell, I'm sick of this rat warren. Feedlot, you called it."

Chambers said, "Shel — I don't understand."

"Me neither. Maybe I feel sorry for your little apple-pie town. Maybe it's your pretty sister here. I dunno. All I know is that Mr. Ernest Lucius Spears was a bastard slumlord when I grew up on the West Side, and I've got no stomach for protecting his selfish interests."

Kaplan jerked a roll of blueprints from a bin and laid them out on his desk, placing drafting tools to hold down the corners. He said, "Your ski project is only half your problem. Take a look at this."

Chambers, rising, stared at a complicated layout for something resembling a factory. It was like nothing he had ever seen. "These printed specs — they look like they're written in German," he said.

"Bright boy. It's a schematic for a German liquefaction plant. The Krauts built a few of these, and I'm supposed to adapt it to the topography east of your town. If it ever gets funded, it would be the first in the nation — what they call a pilot project."

Chambers, a hand suspended over the drawing, said, "A... *liquefaction* plant?"

Kaplan nodded. "It turns coal into oil — heats it under four or five thousand pounds pressure and injects it with liquid hydrogen. This particular plant would accommodate twenty-five thousand tons of coal per day and — well, depending on the quantity of petroleum packed into the coal — it could produce thirty-nine thousand barrels of crude. Theoretically."

"A day?"

"A day."

Chambers whistled.

Rebecca's eyes widened. "How *big* is that plant?"

Kaplan worked a finger into his ear and wiggled it. A thin smile creased a corner of his mouth. "Honey, you'd see the stacks for fifteen miles. Maybe more."

Chambers sat down. "I've got some trouble catching up with this. We were talking about a ski mountain. Now you show me some kind of magic oil factory. Are we still talking about the same people — about Spears and whoever?"

"We are." Kaplan snapped his fingers at Evan Black. "Say, old sport. How's about one of your cigarettes? I'm all out." He reached, pegged the cigarette between his lips, lit it with a match, waved out the match, dropped it on the freshly vacuumed floor. "It's like this, cowboy. Spears is like Genghis Khan — hell-bent to conquer. If he doesn't seem consistent in his goals, at times, it's only because he wants everything."

"You've lost me," Chambers admitted.

"Okay, imagine this," Kaplan said. "Some chiefs at The Wisconsin Trust want to back a ski development. Our Ernie Spears — a major stockholder and senior board member — he likes the idea. But he doesn't trust the Trust executives to handle it. He takes a western tour and picks the location himself, then forces the board to accept his choice. He's good at that."

Kaplan paused to draw on his cigarette. He continued: "Of course, he doesn't care if the town is the best possible location for a resort, because he discovered something else on his tour. This town has these old coal mines, and there's a worldwide energy crisis. His eyes light up with dollar signs.

"For the next two years, while The Wisconsin Trust is paying the expenses for extensive surveys and environmental studies, Spears is consolidating a few coal companies and investigating the latest technologies. He learns about liquefaction, and that's where we are today."

Chambers nodded. "I suppose he's also heading the consortium that bought the coal rights."

"Right on. Using the bankrupt coal companies he had bought and consolidated."

Rebecca uncrossed her legs and gripped the sides of her stool. She said, "I'm confused. Dirty coal mines and ugly factories don't seem compatible with ski resorts. How can this man expect to accomplish both projects in the same town?"

Kaplan looked at her. "Good question." He turned back to Nathan. "Can you guess the answer?"

Nathan nodded sadly. "He doesn't plan to stick around for the conflict?"

Kaplan looked impressed. "You're sharp. That's how Spears got rich on the West Side. He bought cheap property and started up some rehab plans, using other people's money. When the projects went down the tubes, Spears was long gone. The other investors were left holding the bag."

"He's a crook," Rebecca said.

Kaplan rolled his eyes. "Don't be so kind! He's old Beelzebub himself, and he's picked your town to loot and burn. The Wisconsin Trust boys don't know that, and I can't prove it. My only advice to you is — find yourself an exorcist."

"Jesus Christ," Chambers muttered.

"He'd be good," Kaplan said. "If you know where to reach Him. I don't."

Kaplan escorted them through the corridors. The elevator doors parted, and Rebecca and Evan Black stepped aboard. Kaplan held Chambers back. "Cowboy, don't ever call me back, you hear? If you want any more information, ask that lawyer back home who works for Spears."

"In Jackpine?" Chambers frowned. He felt a disturbance in his stomach. "There isn't any Jackpine lawyer who works for Spears."

"You're not awake," Kaplan said. "He probably doesn't advertise it, but he's there — a lawyer named Foster."

Chambers relaxed. "You've got wrong information. There's no lawyer in town named Foster. There's only Tom Applegate and Webster Forsythe."

"Oh yeah, that's him. Forsythe. Webster. How could I forget a name like that for a lawyer?"

"You're still wrong. It can't be Web Forsythe," Chambers insisted.

"Why not?"

"He's city attorney. Representing Spears in this situation would be a conflict of interest — a *blatant* conflict. Maybe worse."

"Uh-oh," Kaplan said. "I shot off my mouth once too often. Just ignore it."

Chambers leaned a fist against the corridor wall and looked hard at Kaplan.

"Look, it's only a name I heard," Kaplan said apologetically. "I'm trying to help. I don't know your local politics. Not my job."

Chambers inched closer. "Who else, Shel? What other names have you heard in connection with Spears?"

"I dunno," Kaplan said, hanging his head.

"Dammit... Shel, you know what I have to deal with. You said yourself, Spears is *evil!* Help me find all his little devils!"

"All right." Kaplan sucked air and said, "There's just one other name I heard. I think he's a rancher, owns a chunk of land earmarked for the base lodge. They've been working on an exchange — the land in trade for stock."

"Okay. His name?"

"Hang on... The name, it's some military guy, a colonel — the name for a... "

Chambers waited, not wanting to hear it.

"A flag," Kaplan said. "That's it, an ensign. Actually, a Colonel Ensign."

Kaplan looked at Chambers. "What? Are you okay?"

Chambers, his expression hard and bleak as a tombstone, shook hands and boarded the elevator. The slamming doors, the sinking feeling, were appropriate.

As they dropped, Rebecca questioned him. "He mentioned Valerie's father, but so what? Why are you looking so devastated?"

"Because I'm going to have to force Web Forsythe's resignation when I get back — then hand in my own."

Rebecca's mouth fell open. *"Why?"*

"Because my father-in-law is involved financially in the ski project. That means I'm tangled up in a conflict of interest the same as Web. There's no way I can fire him without taking the same exit."

The elevator hit bottom.

Nathan followed his sister and Evan Black along mysterious streets to the The Pump Room. He sat down in the midst of grandeur without seeing it... and ate elegant cuisine without tasting it.

Chapter 28:

Meanwhile, Back at the Fort...

FROM 29,000 feet, the Great Plains resembled a wrinkled brown skin on the old earth, a skin sequined with scattered lakes, criss-crossed with thin scars of highways. The thick haze of the East had ended at the Missouri River, and now Chambers could examine each detail of the dry earth as if studying an ancient tapestry under a magnifying glass.

On the uncrowded DC-10, Nathan had a row of seats to himself and nothing to do except think. He tried to visualize how wagon trains had crept across the expanse, struggling under constant attack by weather, by raiders, by diseases — choking in dust one day, floundering in wild rivers the next. Now he sat in pressurized and air-conditioned comfort, stereo headsets if he wanted them, while the Douglas jetliner raced the sun westward and the land unraveled beneath the wing like a piano roll.

A lot of progress in just a hundred years.

A flight attendant presented him with a covered plastic tray containing something made of compressed chicken and rice, a covered bowl of soup, a tiny fruit cup, a hard roll and a butter pat. He automatically declined a premixed cocktail and then had second thoughts and ordered a double Bloody Mary.

Nathan had pondered how he would confront Webster Forsythe and fire the old man for betraying the city's trust; how he would explain to Valerie that her father had ended Nathan's brief stint of public service; how he might handle Russell Bancroft...

Chambers and Bancroft had been friends since second grade in Woodrow Wilson Elementary School — that red-brick blockhouse of a building that still stands with its creaky wooden stairs. How many times had Nathan raced Russell down those stairs to the play yard?

The mines had been closed several years by then — but one year too late for the Bancroft family. Russell's father, Oliver Bancroft, had been among the 43 victims of the great explosion. It had forced Russell's mother to work the rest of her life at dirty, menial jobs.

Woodrow Chambers had tried during the late 1950s to make life a bit easier for Nathan's friend. After buying a horse for Nathan one summer, Woodrow had acquired another for Bancroft's use, so the boys could ride together.

Often, Nathan and Russell had joined up with Lana French to ride among the jackpines and junipers, up steep and rocky trails enclosed by timber. The horses wheezed, and balked at deadfall, but the three youngsters had urged them on, their second-hand saddles creaking noisily among the silent pines, until they either reached one of the high lakes or were forced to turn back by ice-hard snowdrifts blocking the trail.

The ride down was always wild and dangerous, the horses eager for the corral and heedless of the whooping young riders. Rounding a switchback at full gallop, Nathan had toppled from the saddle and — clinging to the reins — had pulled the half-ton mare with him. The entire mountainside had seemed to lose stability as boy and horse tumbled down the slope, rock chunks cavorting alongside, pine needles stabbing his face, bark scraping his hands, branches cracking like rifle shots.

After the dust and turmoil had settled, Nathan had been surprised to find Lana scurrying anxiously down the slope to help him while Russ, still astride his gelding, wrists crossed on the saddlehorn and a faint smile showing under the brim of his big hat, merely nodded and rode away.

***

The flight attendant removed Nathan's tray and said, "Seatbelt, please."

Nathan came to attention, knowing the plane had entered its landing pattern. Ahead of the wing, he saw the low purple ripple that marked the Beartooth Range. Directly below, two tall smokestacks jutted from immense block-like buildings at the fringe of a tiny town. That was Colstrip — the controversial strip mines and twin generating plants of the Montana Power Company.

As the plane descended, the Colstrip complex became clearly visible, down to the strange blue-green color of the powerplants. Newspaper photos of the massive draglines, the soaring stacks, the huge coal-fired generators, and the deep strip mines themselves had portrayed Colstrip as a monster spread all across eastern Montana, devouring whole acres of rangeland in single bites.

But from the air, Colstrip looked strangely insignificant against the far-flung plains of the nation's fourth-largest state — as puny as the early pioneers must have seemed against the vast buffalo herds...

In the DC-10's final curve toward Billings, the Colstrip complex slipped under the fuselage and out of sight. The Yellowstone River sparkled, looking close enough to touch. The Rimrocks flanking Billings loomed into view and slipped behind as grass and then the runway came up swiftly. The big tires chirped and smoked, and Nathan Chambers was back in Montana.

***

Parked directly in front of the Billings Logan Airport terminal, Valerie scurried from the Jeep and welcomed Nathan into her arms. He hugged her, kissed her lips, helped her climb aboard, tossed his bag in the rear. He strutted to the driver's side, started up, and wheeled the Jeep around the parking lot, past the old Northern Pacific locomotive display, out to the edge of the Rimrocks. From this lofty point, they overlooked the sprawl of Billings and the misty Beartooth Range some sixty miles southwest. "Nice day," Nathan said.

"Yes," Valerie agreed. "Much nicer, now that you're home. Especially after breaking your promise."

"Promise?"

"Flying without me," Valerie said.

Nathan glanced at her in surprise. "I thought we settled that before I left!"

"Don't worry about it," she said. "You're back and I'm fine." She smiled at him. "Just don't do it again."

Nathan shrugged and turned down 27th Street to descend the Rimrocks.

Valerie said, "But other problems are waiting for you. We have a real-live demonstration in Jackpine today. You know — pickets, people with signs. They've been marching on the sidewalks all morning."

Nathan sighed. "For some reason, I'm not surprised. Tell me more."

"Well, they're all strangers here. I saw a bus with California plates, cars from Colorado, Washington, Oregon... from all over, I guess."

"And what's their beef? What do they want?"

"Well, I saw a van with a mural on it, a sign painted 'Friends of the Earth,' and symbols I didn't recognize and slogans I didn't take time to read. I guess they're environmentalists opposed to the ski project or whatever."

The Jeep rolled beneath the King Avenue overpass and climbed the Interstate 90 entrance ramp. In minutes they were cruising in open country, well above the new national 55 mph speed limit. Prior to the energy crisis, there had been no daytime speed limit on Montana highways other than "safe and proper."

"How are the local citizens reacting to this?" Nathan asked.

"Mostly, everybody's just curious. Except Burleigh Driscoll. He's buzzing like a hornet. He wanted the city council to call an emergency meeting."

"Did they?"

"No. Webster Forsythe called me, and when I said you'd be home this afternoon, he convinced the others to wait."

"Good ol' Web," Chambers said.

If there was a note of sarcasm in his voice, Valerie didn't hear it. She said, "Nathan, you're over the speed limit... "

Nathan shrugged. "Hell. Nobody can hold fifty-five on these open roads."

"Be sure to explain it to that officer," Valerie said, nodding to the rear.

"Whoa!" Nathan let up instantly on the accelerator, let the Jeep coast while the Highway Patrol cruiser loomed in his mirror. He heard again the knocking in the engine, began to suspect a piston rod. The patrol car paced them all the way to the Laurel interchange, then turned off.

"Boy, are you lucky," Valerie said.

"Yeah. Well, maybe. It depends on what I find in Jackpine."

***

The Jeep swerved to a stop at the north end of mainstreet alongside a trio of young people wearing armbands and distributing leaflets. Chambers rolled down the window and accepted a leaflet from a girl in denim and leather, with straight blonde hair and huge sunglasses. He noted the headline, "Save the Wilderness," dropped it on the seat and drove on.

In the next block, the Jackpine police car sat double-parked with its lightbar flashing and Chief Driscoll fidgeting beside it. On the sidewalk, about thirty demonstrators paraded back and forth with placards. A television camera truck, from KULR-TV in Billings, was against the curb, its crew members nowhere in sight. Merchants leaned against their storefronts and watched. Across the street, shoppers paused to stare, then hurried along into stores.

Chief Driscoll showed no expression as Chambers walked over. "I see you're back," he said. "Nice trip?"

"What's up?"

Driscoll nodded at the demonstrators. "Just what you see. Nothin' too serious, so far. We're expectin' worse, though."

"How worse?"

The chief touched Nathan's arm. "Stand back. Let this traffic go past... " He waved a few cars to proceed. "Well, from what I hear, this is just the first arrivals. There's more comin' in tonight."

"More? From where? Who are they?"

"Buncha outa-state radical hippies, that's who." The chief sneered at them. "The Highway Patrol ticker says a few dozen carloads was seen crossin' state lines since yesterday morning. Officers are checkin' some, followin' others. No arrests. I figure we'll have maybe two hundred of these idiots spendin' the night here."

Chambers looked toward them mildly. "They could have trouble finding places to sleep, then. There's maybe a hundred motel beds open. All the rest are closed for winter."

Driscoll eyed the marchers less mildly. "I got six jail cots. Twelve more in the county jail."

"Where's the TV crew?" Chambers asked.

"Havin' lunch at Monti's place. You want to see 'em? They were asking for you. Maybe you could watch yourself on TV tonight."

"No way, Chief. I was wondering how to avoid them." Chambers added, "I heard you wanted a city council meeting. Can it wait until morning? I'm beat."

"Whatever you say," Driscoll said.

"Let's meet at eight o'clock." Chambers turned to leave.

Driscoll called after him. "When you get a minute, stop at the firehall, wouldja?"

"What's at the firehall?"

"Riot headquarters," the chief said. "There's a helmet for you. And one of them big long poles."

Chapter 29: Watching, Waiting...

TWO FIGURES approached the geology office in the former J.C. Penney catalog store.

One approached from the alley — a staggering figure, pausing repeatedly in the fading light to lean against a wall or a garbage rack. This figure carried a bottle and swigged from it during each pause.

The other figure was on the street side, parked in a four-wheel-drive vehicle, waiting while the demonstrators lowered their placards and began moving away in various directions.

Eventually, the street became quiet. And still the man sat in the vehicle and waited. He, too, had a bottle. But his was not for drinking. It lay on the seat beside him along with some rags, and it was covered by his hat — the broad-brimmed gray hat of a Montana game warden.

Russell Bancroft sat until the twilight became dusk and the dusk became night, and the people on the street became fewer and fewer.

Chapter 30: Crowd Control

NATHAN HEARD the phone ringing in his sleep and rolled over on the couch, his head filled with Chicago traffic and jetliner motion. But Valerie pushed his shoulder and said something about the chief of police.

Nathan cracked open an eye and peered at her. "What!"

Valerie had knelt beside the couch, her brows knitted with concern. She said again, "Burleigh Driscoll phoned. He said those people are coming to our house. They're on their way now."

Nathan sat up and gazed around the den, faintly illuminated by the desk lamp. "Hmm. What people?"

"The demonstrators," Valerie said. "They're marching up the street from town. They want to confront the mayor, and they're carrying torches. Burleigh said he's rounding up the police auxiliary."

The phone rang and Valerie responded. "Hello? Who is this? Hello?" Then she hung up. She stood dead still for a moment, staring at the phone.

"Who was it?" Nathan asked.

"Whoever it was, he wouldn't say anything." Valerie sat down and folded her hands. "Not one damn word, just breathing... Nathan, I hate that!"

The phone rang again. Valerie jerked.

"Stay," Nathan said. "I'll get it." He hoisted himself and went to the desk, waited while the phone rang twice more, then lifted it. "This is Chambers," he said. "If you… "

He heard a click and the dial tone.

He slammed the phone down.

Valerie wrapped her arms around him.

"It's just kids," Nathan said unconvincingly. He slipped out of her embrace, plucked the receiver off the cradle and jammed it behind a chair cushion.

From the street, they heard a brief hoot from the police siren. A beacon swept across the curtains. "They're here," Valerie said, moving to the window.

Outside in the dusk, the patrol car's lights flashed at a group of people trudging up the street with placards and torches held high. From the other direction came three pickups loaded with helmeted men. The trucks jerked to a halt directly in front. The men dropped the tailgates and jumped out, gathering long poles from the cargo beds.

"Back shortly," Nathan said.

Valerie snatched his sleeve. "Where the hell do you think *you're* going?"

He nodded toward the street. "They came to see the mayor. They won't go away quietly until they do. So… I'll go and oblige them."

"Nathan, don't be crazy!"

"Hey… don't take this so seriously. These are people who work hard to protect birds and bunnies. How dangerous can they be?"

"That's not funny!" And then, because he looked so confident and amused, she cracked a tiny, helpless grin.

"That's better," he said, tweaking her nose. And he went straight out the door.

Crossing the lawn, Nathan felt Valerie's eyes on his back and resisted the inclination to turn around and look at her. He walked straight ahead and stepped onto the asphalt before realizing he was in his socks.

"Nate! Hey! Wait up!" That was Roy Yancey's voice. The paunchy alderman, ridiculous in a riot helmet, was scurrying up alongside. Vincent Fox was behind him, adjusting his own chin strap. "We'll stay with you," Fox said.

Chambers stopped. "No thanks. You stay here and watch the house. And Valerie. Okay?"

Fox looked skeptical, his eyes squinting just under the helmet rim. "What if you need help?"

"I won't." Chambers walked off.

"It's your ass!" Fox called.

Chambers had to pass the patrol car and saw Chief Driscoll inside, strapping on his helmet. With his big square head, he looked ready to butt skulls with a buffalo.

"Evenin', Chief."

Driscoll turned, surprised. "The hell you doin' out here?" The chief threw open the car door and squirmed out. He stared at the mayor from head to foot. "You nuts? You ain't wearin' a helmet. You got no pole. By damn, you ain't even wearin' shoes!"

"I'll need a few minutes with these folks," Chambers said. "Don't make any waves yet."

"Those thugs are liable to bust your ass, Nate. You go back in your house and let me handle this! You hear?"

Chambers ignored the chief. He went onto the street and strutted toward the marchers with their torches and signs, now about twenty paces away.

Driscoll searched the scene, saw Fire Chief Berlinsky among the men behind the trucks. "Spud! Get the hell over here!"

Chambers stopped and waited. His eye caught the glow of a cigarette beneath an elm to his right. The man nodded at him, and Chambers looked harder. It was Bayliss, standing with a camera around his neck. "Big story, Ben?"

"Front page," Ben answered. "Smile at the birdie." The camera flashed.

Chambers, eyes half blinded, turned to face the street.

The crowd swarmed upon him.

***

Thirty yards away, Valerie slipped out the front door with her husband's boots. She could see him in the torchlight, the crowd closing in. She saw the volunteers in their big helmets, nervously shifting into a wedge formation, their poles colliding. Driscoll and Berlinsky were at the patrol car, shouting and motioning. When she looked again toward the crowd, she couldn't see Nathan...

***

There were two, Chambers discovered, who spoke for the rest. The blond man had frizzy hair and beard, emblems sewn onto his leather vest, wide eyes about level with Nathan's. The woman was black-haired, pointy-looking, wearing plain denim and no makeup.

Beyond them, most of the demonstrators wore headbands, tie-dye, broad belts, metal studs and copper pendants. Their chants and crowd noise drowned the blond man's words until he turned to the group and fiercely waved his arms and shouted. "Hold it down! I got the *man* here! Knock off the noise!"

It helped. Chambers could hear himself now. "Did you say you have some kind of petition?"

A strobe light flashed — Bayliss shooting pictures. Mixed with the torchlight and the police beacon, the flash produced an uncanny visual effect.

"This spells it out," the woman said, proffering some stapled pages. "Your council will reject the ski proposal for obvious environmental reasons. We also demand passage of a local resolution supporting a Beartooth wilderness."

"Demand?" Chambers frowned. "Lady, you're not in any position to make demands here. You could try asking politely, though."

"Now you listen... "

"No," Chambers said. "You listen first. Even if we agreed with this petition, we'd have no impact. The Custer National Forest including the Beartooth Range is under Forest Service jurisdiction, not ours. Go take your petition to the feds."

"Bullshit!" the blond man said. "Don't cop out on us, man!"

Chambers responded patiently. "The National Forests belong to the people of the United States. This is a national matter, not a local issue. Get wise."

The woman said, "A local council resolution would have a lot of influence with the feds. They always apply a weighting factor for local opinion."

"But you're not talking about local opinion, lady. You're talking about your own opinion."

The crowd grew noisy again and Chambers couldn't hear her response. He thought he knew it anyway.

***

Patrolman Chism stopped Valerie on the lawn. "Mrs. Chambers! You shouldn't be out here, ma'am. Please go back in your house."

"But I.. " She lifted Nathan's boots.

"Please, ma'am, this could get serious. Things could blow apart at any second. People could get hurt! You gotta get back inside — right now, ma'am!"

Valerie stood firm. "This is my property, Buck. I'll stay right here."

"But Mrs. Chambers... "

"I insist you go help my husband. It looks like they have him surrounded."

Chism wavered, glancing at the crowd. Then he saluted. "Yes ma'am."

***

The blond man spoke earnestly now.

"It's the damned *builders*, man. They don't think about this stuff — how you can't build nothing without destroying something first. Know what I mean? Like, say you want to build a house. Say you build a house and there's this tree in the way. Don't you think you should at least look at this tree — see what's in it — before you chop it down?"

Chambers nodded patiently. He realized he was dealing with a splinter faction — eager, but not bright, not organized.

"Yeah, man," said the demonstrator. "You could find a nest of squirrels and birds, all kinds of insects and critters. It's like a whole *ecology* — a whole *world!* And you could destroy it all for the sake of a few square feet of a bathroom. Know what I mean, man?"

"Sure," Chambers said.

"Same like with factories and stuff, man. Somebody has got to stop and look, you know? Society don't take the time, and we get whole forests destroyed so builders can put up some piece of gingerbread shit. Rivers and lakes get polluted so we can make plastic bottles. And the air, man. Even the *air* gets ruined because of shit like hair spray and stuff like that. Know what I mean?"

***

Chief Driscoll clenched Spud Berlinsky's shoulder. "Look what they're doin'," he said. "They got him almost surrounded. You get the men ready — you hear the signal, they move! You got that?"

Berlinsky nodded, hustled back to the auxiliary, his arms signaling for attention.

The chief drew out his revolver, spun the heavy cylinder with its load of .38 soft-point slugs. He jammed it back into its holster. He saw Chism watching him, imitating him. They nodded at each other.

And Chism started easing toward the crowd.

***

Chambers said, "No way, folks. I understand your emotions and all, but the Jackpine council won't adopt your petition or pass any resolution without a clear indication of support from our constituents. And we're a long way from that."

The woman said, "Mayor, if you won't act, we will. We have resources you can't imagine. You and your family and this whole town will feel pain like you wouldn't believe! You still want to argue?"

Chambers sighed. He felt the crowd pressing on all sides. He said, "You got a joint, lady?"

The woman looked mildly surprised. "What if I do?"

"Stick it in your ear," Chambers said.

***

Buck Chism tried to decide. The mayor was among all those people — alone, trapped, defenseless. The auxiliary couldn't move unless the mayor was out of there. He recalled the crowd control lessons, couldn't think of examples covering this situation. But he had to think of something. Mrs. Chambers, so pretty and pregnant, was depending on him. And the chief was pacing, stalking, eager to take control as soon as someone hauled Nathan Chambers away from danger. And then, from the training sessions, he remembered... Wyatt Earp.

His mind made up, Chism strapped his revolver to his wrist and raised it high, then started shoving his way through the outer fringes of the crowd.

***

Chambers explained, "Our folks are divided on these issues — but nobody can tell 'em what to think. Not me. For sure, not you. You got TV coverage, your pictures in the papers. You delivered your petition. I say, quit while you're ahead. Push too hard, it's liable to backfire in your faces. Trust me, I know these folks."

"Now look, man... " the blond man began.

"I said my name was Nathan. Chambers."

The fiery look in the man's eyes dissipated. He wagged his beard, allowed a sliver of a smile. "Okay... Chambers. I'm Neely. Rod Neely. You got guts, man."

Chambers extended a hand. They shook.

"Mr. Neely," Chambers said, "you want to support a wilderness, I got no quarrel with that. You want to attend the hearings, be our guests. You could submit any information that would help, and all of it would become part of the record. Sometime in the next several months, our city council might even adopt your resolution. No guarantees, but we just might. Meanwhile, though, you got to stay peaceful as a possum. I mean it."

Neely shrugged. "Well, hell yes, man."

Chambers turned to the woman. "You still want to argue?"

Something happened at that moment.

While the two men and the woman faced one another, groping for a patch of common ground, there was a distinct shift in the crowd. Its motion stopped pressing from the outer edges toward the center. Instead, it expanded outward. The noise level intensified, became a roaring chant. The crowd began shouting — *"Oink-oink-oink! Oink-oink!"*

Neely frowned at the mayor. "What's happening, man?"

Chism's helmet appeared among the hair and headbands, and Chambers saw the revolver gleaming in the torchlight, barrel pointed straight up.

The pistol cracked!

It cracked twice again!

***

Valerie scrambled to her feet, a heart-stopping thud in her chest. Pressing a hand to a tree for support, she saw Nathan's head drop, saw the helmeted phalanx of the auxiliary march into the torchlight, long staffs jabbing violently into the crowd. The roar was terrific. Placards were swung, torches thrown. Some people fell.

Valerie's legs had lost feeling, and she stumbled back to the porch and sank onto the steps.

***

Chism yanked at Chambers, pulling him from the melee. Chambers, angry and limping, shook free. "Let the hell go, you asshole!"

The patrolman was stunned. His hands fell, the revolver dangling. "Yessir. I'm damn sorry, sir."

"Hell," Chambers muttered. "Go report to the chief."

***

Driscoll yelled into his bullhorn, trying to direct his forces. The remnants of the crowd disappeared like startled fish. Broken placards and fizzling torches littered the street. Bayliss flashed his camera as auxiliary volunteers hoisted their staffs and cheered. The last demonstrator hopped a fence and fled into darkness.

There were no stragglers, no arrests.

Chambers saw his neighbor joining the cheer.

"That you, Abe?"

His neighbor came over. "Hell of a show, Nate. You all right?"

"Pissed off," Chambers said, limping on a trampled foot.

"By golly," Abe said. "That sure was a mangy-lookin' bunch! Your volunteer police took real good care of 'em, though. That was a damn smart idea, organizing that auxiliary. I'm real *proud* of you, Nate!"

"Good night, Abe." Chambers hobbled across the lawn.

Valerie waited on the porch steps, still holding Nathan's boots in her trembling hands.

Nathan eased down beside her and rubbed his foot. He saw the boots. He said, "Too late for those."

Valerie didn't respond.

"Damn!" Nathan said. "If Chism would've just waited a couple minutes..."

Valerie dropped the boots and lifted herself, scurried inside and slammed the door.

Nathan exhaled, limped across the porch and crept through the door.

He found her in the dark parlor, sobbing. He went to her and knelt alongside. "Sweetheart... "

She shouted, "That was the *ugliest thing I ever saw!*"

Nathan reached out, gently overpowering her resistance and gathering her into his embrace. "I doubt anybody was hurt, except for bruises."

Valerie peered into his eyes. "Oh? What about you? You're limping!"

"Hell. Some damn clod stomped on my toes."

When she neglected to show any sympathy, he gave her a slightly pained expression. Still no reaction.

He tried, "They do *hurt* some, honey."

Valerie's eyes flashed at him. "Well? It serves you right! You asked for it, you blithering idiot! And don't call me *honey!* I am not excrement from a *bee!*"

That did it. Nathan broke into hearty laughter.

Gradually, Valerie succumbed. She hugged Nathan and gently laughed with relief.

Their joy was brief.

A high-pitched wail assaulted their ears, rising to nerve-rattling volume. It took a second for Nathan to recognize the sound.

"It's the civil defense siren!"

"Good grief!" Valerie moaned. "What *now!*"

The siren raked all across the town, driving shivers up Nathan's back. He twisted away from his wife and bolted to the front window.

In the direction of mainstreet, an orange glow flared above the treetops. A huge billow of smoke puffed up, reflecting the hideous light. A shower of red sparks reeled upward into the night.

Valerie stared through the curtains. The spectacle grew in brilliance, lighting up a whole section of sky. "My God, it's a huge fire," she said. "It's gigantic!"

She heard no response from Nathan.

She turned sharply, suddenly aware that she had spoken to an empty house.

Nathan had left her again.

Chapter 31: The Fire

BROADWAY was strewn with tangled firehoses and black-ened debris. Ponds and streams of dirty water, backwash from the hoses, reflected a kaleidoscopic dance between fire bursts and the swirling beacons of the two pumper trucks.

The front of the building was a sheet of white and or-ange, except where thin black structural members remained standing at odd angles. It was the geology office, the former J.C. Penney catalog store, going down forever.

Chambers treaded among the firehoses, wearing neo-prene boots and fire helmet, struggling into his turnout coat. He saw Fire Chief Spud Berlinsky directing his men through a bullhorn. From atop city hall, the civil defense siren continued to wail for volunteers.

"Hey Spud!..." Chambers shouted for attention.

Berlinsky lowered the bullhorn and yelled into Nathan's ear: *"Nate!... Hey, I think this was arson!... You can smell gasoline clear to the curb!"*

"Damn!"

"Judging by the way the building blew up... I'll bet it was a Molotov cocktail!"

"God Almighty!... How can I help?"

The fire chief surveyed the deployment of his men and equipment. He had two hoses blasting into the front of the store, a third trained on the roof of the adjacent Horseshoe Bar. The Montana Power office on the other side did not appear in immediate danger. *"Tell you what,"* Berlinsky shouted, *"get those two guys by the hydrant... and go around to the alley!... Check the back!... Take a couple of extinguishers and air-packs with you!... They're in the rear transverse compartment — number one pumper!"*

"You got it!" Chambers moved, snapping the storm flaps on his coat.

The men at the hydrant were Alderman Nels Christofer-son and Chuck Vreeland, a local Pepsi Cola distributor. At Chambers' directions, they dislodged the extinguishers from the pumper, but they couldn't find any airpacks.

"Dammit," Vreeland yelled as they rounded the corner to the alley, *"when we catch the sons-of-bitches that started this... there's gonna be a lynch mob!"*

Christoferson: *"Any clues, Nate?"*

Chambers: *"I just got here, Nels!... Watch out for broken power lines!"*

Vreeland: *"Clues, hell!...We know it was that mob you busted up on your street tonight — getting their revenge!"*

They reached the back of the building, smelled the sickly odor of burning paint and old wood. Spray from the roof of the Horseshoe Bar fell like misty rain and muddied the alley.

Christoferson: *"The fire's spread back here already!.. Look!... You see that?"*

Darkness shrouded the rear of the building except for periodic glows from fiery smoke clouds overhead. Then Chambers saw what Christoferson had seen — bright flashes between the slats of a boarded-up rear window.

A deep passageway in the back of the building led to a wooden stairway and a rear door. Chambers shouted, *"Let's check it out!"*

They felt severe heat in the passageway. Smoke stung their eyes and nostrils, and the civil defense siren rang in their ears.

Vreeland: *"I wish someone would shut off that goddamn siren!"*
Christoferson: *"I wish we had those airpacks!"*

Chambers tested the doorknob with a fingertip. It was *hot*. He shoved his hand back into the monkey-grip glove and turned the knob slowly. He eased the door open a crack — and flame billowed out. *"It's an inferno in there!"*

Flames erupted through the wall over their heads. Christoferson yelled, his words drowned in the roar of fire and the wail of the siren.

The men hoisted their extinguishers and shot against the flames. They continued spraying desperately as they stumbled back through the passage.

Abruptly, the civil defense siren howled down, lost pitch, went silent. It left a ringing in Nathan's ears.

In the alley, Vreeland said something, his voice hollow and crisp in the sudden silence.

Chambers said, "Hold on. I hear something."

They listened to the crackling and roaring of the fire, the gurgling of water.

"What did you hear?" Vreeland asked.

"Like a scream... " Chambers said.

Chambers stared into the passageway, now arched over by wavering sheets of flame. Burning wood chunks began dropping, some landing on the wooden steps.

Then Chambers saw a sight that stunned him — a hand, a wrinkled human hand, feebly poking from under the stairs. "Aw, *God,*" he groaned. "There's somebody in there."

Vreeland: "I don't see... "

Christoferson: *"Hey!* Where you *going!"*

Chambers charged the passageway. His companions jumped after him, catching an elbow and a shoulder. Nathan fiercely attempted to yank loose. "Let go, damnit! There's somebody under the stairs!"

Christoferson threw an arm around Nathan's neck. "The walls are caving! Get outa here, Nate!"

With a roar the passageway disappeared, consumed by blinding light.

No more could Chambers see the stairs. Or the hand.

He saw only brilliant white fire, felt only intense dry heat, heard only his own breathing — his choking, gasping breathing.

Chapter 32: Webster 'Web' Forsythe

THE FIRE VICTIM was identified just prior to 7 A.M., when Chambers put down the phone and went back to the bedroom for a shirt. Valerie sat on the bed, watching him fumble with his cuffs. He had burn ointment on his face, mingled with stubble from a difficult shaving job and lines of exhaustion near his eyes.

"Who phoned?" Valerie asked, her voice tremulous.

"Web Forsythe," Nathan answered. "I asked him to come over, soon as he can." He stopped buttoning his shirt and slumped down next to her. "What a mess. The cops sealed off the highway at both ends of town. They're questioning any demonstrators who try to leave."

"All of them? That could take hours — days!"

"Got to do it," Nathan said. "There's an arsonist loose. And Web said the crime involves murder, too."

"Dear God," Valerie leaned against Nathan.

"They identified the body, the fire victim," he said. "It was Erwin Wooster."

"Wooster — the drunk?"

"That's him. Too bad. Went under the stairs to sleep off a binge, I suppose." Nathan fastened another shirt button.

"Too bad?" Valerie looked at Nathan with moist eyes. "It was horrible! That poor man... "

"You're crying for him," Nathan observed. "You hardly know the man... *knew* the man."

She sniffled. "Someone should. He had no family. His life was so *sad...* "

Nathan nodded. "And there's more bad news." He took her hand and explained what he had learned in Chicago about Webster Forsythe. "When he gets here... I'm going to fire him."

Valerie said nothing for a moment, sat with lips parted, eyes unfocused. "I don't understand that," she said. Cocking her head towards him: "You mean Web has broken some law? No way. It must be a mistake."

"No mistake," Nathan told her. "Conflict of interest, clear-cut and simple."

"But Nathan... " Valerie withdrew a few inches from her husband. "He's been practicing law here since before you were born. He's lived in Jackpine all his life. He — his *father* practiced law here... "

Quietly, Nathan said, "I learned about *your* father, too."

An ironic twist formed on Valerie's mouth. "*My* father? What has *he* to do with any of this?"

"He's made a deal with the developers, trading some of his land for shares of stock. Did you know that?"

Valerie frowned. "No. He never mentioned it, not to me. Why? Is it important?"

Nathan shook his head. "Valerie, his dealings in the ski resort reflect on me. We're in the same family. If he had sold his land for cash, it might've been all right. But trading for stock — it's conflict of interest again. Same thing I'm firing Web for. But now it applies to me."

Valerie's lower lip quivered. "How can it be a conflict for *you?* You didn't know anything about it."

"Try explaining that to everybody. Remember those editorials in Ben's newspaper? Wait 'til he learns about *this!*"

Valerie took a long breath and shook her head.

"I need to resign," Nathan said. "But now I can't. Not in the middle of this crisis... They'd appoint Yancey. It's the worst thing that could happen. Damn, and if I *don't* quit, and this leaks out, they could throw me in jail."

"Over my dead body! And damn my father! This is just like him! Always interfering! *Br...brother!* Wait 'til I see him!" She slammed her fists against the mattress.

The doorbell chimed.

Nathan stood. "That must be Web. You okay?"

"Hell no," Valerie said. She flipped a hand. "But go invite him in."

***

Chambers took Forsythe into the den, where they had coffee and agreed on a one o'clock time for the emergency council meeting. Then the attorney said: "Well, Nate. Looks like we're going to have a busy few weeks. I'm going to be spending a lot of time in court — if we catch the bugger."

Chambers nodded silently.

"Under the state's new Criminal Code, effective since last January," Forsythe continued, "it looks bad for whoever set the fire. Wooster's death means I'd have to prosecute the case as a felony murder. That's a capital offense in this state. There's no plea bargaining, you see. I'd have to go for a conviction on deliberate homicide, and that's going to require a lot of preparation. We've only had two other murder cases in this county's whole history."

Chambers formed a cage with his fingers. "You think we might catch him?"

Forsythe made a soundless chuckle, a jiggling of his hunched shoulders. "Probably not. But say, your police chief was on the ball last night. The fire wasn't going ten minutes before he had the state police setting up roadblocks. Whoever did it might still be in town."

"Web," Chambers asked, "how long can we keep those folks bottled up with a roadblock?"

The attorney held a donut and stared into space. "That's a good question. You get involved with civil rights there. You have a legal right to pursue the investigation, of course, and question all possible witnesses and suspects. But you can't search their cars without a warrant, and I'd certainly suggest running them through the process as speedily as possible."

"Has anyone tried to leave this morning?"

"Dozens. But the rush is expected later. The majority have been staying in the campgrounds south of town — haven't folded up their tents yet. Burr says they're having a good time, hiking, watching birds... "

"Hell. And here we sit. A man dead, a building burned to the ground."

"And folks talking about a lynching." Forsythe nibbled his donut.

Chambers wondered about that. "Web, what is the mood in town this morning?"

"Well... " Again he stared spaceward. "They're not selling souvenirs and postcards to the visitors today. It reminds me of those hot, dry summers, when the forest is tinder-dry and ready to explode. Everyone's just sitting around, waiting for a spark... "

Chambers watched Forsythe dig out his pipe, poke it into his tobacco pouch. "Web... I have a complaint against you. A serious one. Official."

Forsythe's hands trembled a little. "Go ahead," he said.

"You've been doing work for the ski project."

The attorney shrugged. "I won't deny it."

"What kind of work, Web?"

Forsythe struck a match to his pipe bowl. He drew on it, twice. The match almost singed his quaking fingers. He blew it out, set it carefully on his saucer. "Research, mostly. City and county ordinances. Environmental laws. Anything local that could affect their plans."

"Why?"

"Why?" The attorney peered at Chambers over the rim of his eyeglasses. "Nate, do you realize that the City of Jackpine pays me one hundred and fifty dollars a month? And city business takes eighty percent of my time. A man can't live on that — especially a man well past retirement age."

"But you have a private practice, Web. A successful one."

"I did, at one time, yes. Then the folks who could afford a lawyer left town. My present-day clients are old widows trying to collect miner's pensions. A few ranchers need me to arbitrate an occasional dispute over water rights. Some businesses ask me to collect their delinquent accounts... "

Forsythe paused to relight his pipe while Chambers waited.

"Maybe it sounds like I'm making excuses," the attorney continued. "But it's been a long time since I administered an estate that netted me more than a couple thousand dollars. Between the city and all my old friends who expect legal advice for free, I'm just not making out."

"You could've charged more. You could've quit the city job to give yourself more time... "

"I thought of both — and couldn't do either. Look, Nate, I have some loyalty to Jackpine and all those people I grew up with. I couldn't quit and I can't try to milk them."

Chambers nodded. "But you can betray them?"

Forsythe leaned back with an expression of defeat. "That's how you interpret it. I don't."

"Hell. It's the way the *law* interprets it. You oughta be the first to realize that."

"Yes, yes." Forsythe nodded. "I realize what the *law* says. Believe me, it's not all that cut-and-dried. There's lots of gray area. I could take you to my office and show you hundreds of foolish and contradictory laws... You know, the longer I practice, the more I think modern law is idiotic. Sometimes, I think we'd be better off with just the simple Ten Commandments."

"Then we wouldn't need any lawyers."

"Oh, we'd need them. But to plead mercy, not seek loopholes and technicalities." He gave up trying to keep his pipe smoldering and put it down on the table.

Chambers said, "How can I show mercy to you, Web?"

Forsythe let his shoulders sag. "Just think of this, Nate. No matter what work I've done for the ski people, I never let it really conflict with the interests of the city. I kept my duties to Jackpine foremost. I'm from the old school, you know. From a time before we needed laws to tell us whether we had integrity or not. I might've stretched the ethics of my profession, but not the dictates of my conscience."

"Web, I know damn well you're an honest man. That's not the point."

"And I'm saying the conflict of interest statutes are intended to protect the public from corruption, which is not the issue in this case. Certainly not after thirty-odd years of public service at lower wage than our garbage collectors."

"I know how you feel, Web."

"No you don't. Nate, I admit we're all in the same boat. We work hard for our community, make many personal sacrifices, and we know — at least we *should* know — that nobody gives a damn. We're not going to win any medals, Nate. There'll be no testimonial dinners for us. But that's because we'd have to give testimonials to three-fourths of the town. Sacrifice isn't rewarded in Jackpine. It's *expected.*"

"And... you're saying we should collect our own rewards?"

"I'm saying we try to save ourselves in whatever way we can. That's all. That's my crime. Trying to survive. And staying off welfare."

Chambers spread his arms. "Damnit, Web. What'm I going to do with you?"

Forsythe chuckled. "Now *there's* a conflict of interest! You ask me to advise you on how to deal with me. Well... " He sighed. "I admit that I allowed a situation to develop that gives the *appearance* of conflict of interest. Whether it actually existed is beside the point, as far as your duties are concerned. Therefore, it must be dealt with. So. How about if you accept my resignation and we let it go at that?"

Chambers eyed the attorney in silence. Then he said, "You understand, I have no choice, Web."

"Of course. Anything else would make you guilty of collusion."

"Your resignation... I'd need it right now."

"Immediately?" Forsythe's eyes filled with wonder. "Who will settle this mess with the fire?"

Chambers had asked himself the same question — about himself and Web both. "I'll put you on as a special counsel. From the emergency reserve budget. Just for the fire situation. Your other responsibilities to the city will end. How about it, Web?"

Forsythe straightened and stared at Chambers over his eyeglasses. Then he nodded, said, "Yes. We'll work it out."

Chambers held out a hand. "Thanks, Web."

Forsythe shook it. "It's all right. I'm going to need the work."

Chapter 33: Anxieties

ON THAT OCTOBER morning, Jackpine's preoccupied officials missed the weather report.

A major winter storm was building over Oregon and Washington and heading inland toward the Rockies.

A mass of Pacific moisture had started moving in a chain of low-pressure cells from the west. A Canadian cold front began pushing down from the north. These weather systems would converge over the Continental Divide, a geographical line that included the mountain range twenty miles west of Jackpine.

That meant, according to the U.S. Weather Service, that higher elevations in the Rockies would be hit with heavy snow followed by subzero cold. It would happen, said the meteorologists, within the next forty-eight hours.

What that meant to most Montanans was a typical autumn preview of the winter ahead, an interruption of Indian Summer.

What it meant in Jackpine was much worse. Hundreds of visitors, anxious to flee the mountains ahead of the storm, would be impeded by roadblocks.

Nathan Chambers had spent an hour that morning trying to get a feel of what was happening on mainstreet. The smoldering ruins of the geology office had attracted a cluster of people, held back by four members of the police auxiliary. Other members, in riot helmets, patrolled in pairs along both sides of the crowded street.

In the hardware store, Nathan found his father peering out the display windows. The rifles and handguns had been removed.

"Expecting trouble, Pops?"

"Hmm? Oh, you mean the guns." Woodrow hunched his heavy shoulders. "I locked 'em up. No sense leaving temptation in plain sight."

"Dad, how many guns would you guess we had in this town?"

"Hell — probably two, at least, for every man, woman, and child." Then Woodrow said, "You consider getting some help? The National Guard maybe?"

"No." Nathan spoke firmly. "It's bad enough we've got men in riot helmets all over the street."

"Touch-and-go situation. Maybe you could get *some* kind of help standing by. How about the Highway Patrol?"

Nathan considered it. "Well, maybe. I'll look into it."

Strutting towards city hall, Chambers encountered Dallas Carpenter. She stopped him on the sidewalk to complain about the closing of her bar.

"Who closed it?" Chambers asked.

"Burleigh Driscoll, who else?" Her face expressed anger beneath her jumble of red hair. "There's a thousand thirsty people out here, and he tells me I can't serve no one. I coulda throwed him on his fat can!"

"He figures these folks are mean enough without getting drunk, Dallas."

"They'll get one helluva lot meaner if we don't do nothin' about their thirst, Nate."

"They can get soda pop at Safeway," Chambers said.

"Nate, if them folks look to you like soda pop drinkers, you're dumber than Driscoll!" She turned and marched off.

Other complaints, other sounds followed Chambers as he worked his way to city hall. Honking horns, shouts, arguments, a periodic burst of the police siren as Driscoll cruised the street and issued stern warnings to assorted knots of troublemakers.

The mayor's office was quiet when Chambers sat and phoned the attorney general in Helena to request standby units of the Highway Patrol. "I can have eighteen officers there in two hours," the AG told him. "However, that might not be enough if the situation degenerates. I'll be seeing the governor shortly. If you like, I can pass along a request for the National Guard."

Chambers declined. "Things aren't that bad. I'll let you know if we get into worse trouble."

"Don't wait too long," the attorney general warned.

Downstairs in the firehall, Chambers observed a dozen pairs of eyes staring at him from under riot helmets. Extra deputies, firemen, and several aldermen had scattered about the garage, some playing cards, some reading magazines. They all looked up when Chambers trotted down the stairs.

"How 'bout it, Nate?" The question came from Roy Yancey. "Are we gonna get the National Guard?"

"Eighteen Highway Patrol cars are standing by," Chambers said. He shifted his gaze beyond the open door to the city's two fire trucks parked outside, gleaming in the morning sun. The crews had dried and remounted the firehoses after the night's workout.

"But no National Guard?" Yancey asked.

"Roy," Chambers said, "I got a lot to do before the council meeting. How about lending a hand?"

Buck Chism said, "I think we might need the Guard, sir."

"I can use your help, too, Buck."

Chism blinked, stood, came forward. The others turned back to their magazines and games.

"Buck," Chambers said, "you go find the chief. Tell him I want radio reports back here every fifteen minutes."

"Yes sir, you bet. Uh, reports on what?"

"Everything. I need to know what's happening with the roadblocks, the crowds in town, any kind of disturbance. Got it? Now move." He turned to Yancey. "Roy, you run down to the newspaper and get Bayliss to print me some public notices. The special meeting at one o'clock — we can't hold it in here. Not enough room. Let's clear the kids out of high school and set up the gymnasium."

"The gymnasium?" Yancey seemed bewildered.

"This meeting will be open to the public."

"Holy Christ, Nate! We'll get mobbed!"

"That's why we need the gymnasium. Tell Bayliss I need those handbills in one hour. Let him decide the wording."

Yancey's face was puckered in dismay. "I dunno about this, Nate... "

"Roy, you listen up. Explain this to Bayliss. I want to get everybody off the streets. I want the people inside where we can talk to them. Maybe it'll keep 'em from smashing windows."

Yancey pulled at his nose.

"Next," Chambers said, "get over to the school and make arrangements for the gym. Call me if there's any hitches."

"I sure hope you know what you're doin'... "

"You got any better ideas?"

"Well, the National Guard... "

Chambers almost booted Yancey through the door. "You're wasting time. Get the hell *moving*, Roy."

Yancey flapped his arms, waddled out the door.

Chapter 34: The Culprit

FIRE CHIEF Spud Berlinsky paused inside the gymnasium, his potato head cocked in wonder. The crowd surging through double doors at each end of the basketball court had become huge. Auxiliary police served as ushers; sheriff's deputies patrolled at strategic points; and there was the school band, perched on a section of bleachers and pounding out brassy music.

Berlinsky climbed the steps of a portable stage and joined a huddle of city officers. "Whose idea was the band?" he asked.

Chambers turned. "They were here for practice and hadn't heard about the dismissal. They offered to stay."

"You gonna let 'em?"

"Why not?"

Berlinsky nodded. "Let music soothe the savages, huh? You think it will help?"

"Spud," Chambers said, "at this point I'm looking for *any* kind of diversion. How about you doing your magic tricks?"

"No thanks, Nate. I'll leave the magic to you." He went to find a chair.

Chambers, wishing he *had* a few tricks up his sleeve, checked his watch. One o'clock. He waited awhile for the crowd to settle down, then signaled the band director. The musicians launched into the national anthem, bringing the assembly to its feet. Chambers took the microphone in his hand and waited.

The anthem was followed by massive silence. Chambers heard his own breathing amplified by the public address system. He coughed and said, "This special meeting of the Jackpine City Council is called to order."

Tension filled the air, and Chambers observed that townspeople and visitors had seated themselves on opposite sides of the gym. The space between them seemed to crackle with hostility.

"This is an emergency," he said, "so I won't bother with any formalities. We all know what this is about. The state fire marshall is here, and he found ample evidence to confirm last night's fire was arson. Erwin Wooster was killed, and the coroner has ruled his death was caused by the fire. Under state law, that makes his death a felony murder."

The crowd began murmuring. There were angry hoots from the local side of the gym, directed at the visitor side.

Chambers raised his voice. "Before you jump to any conclusions, I think you'd better hear a few more facts."

The noises ebbed.

Chambers said, "I'm going to point out four people. Two are local residents, the other two are visitors. First, Dallas Carpenter, would you stand up? There she is."

The local side of the gymnasium produced a round of applause embarrassing to Dallas. Chambers gave them a moment, then said:

"Dallas was ticked off at me this morning, and I don't blame her. We closed her bar — after she had spent half the night contributing free beer to firefighters with parched throats. She hauled the beer cases to the fire herself."

She received loud cheers. Chambers turned and exchanged a few words with Kermit Czarnowsky.

"I just learned Mrs. Czarnowsky isn't here for her introduction. She's at home, exhausted. This lady is about sixty years old, and last night she kept bringing sandwiches to every man and woman on that fire."

After waiting for the second round of applause to end, Chambers continued.

"Now I'd like you to meet a young lady from Tacoma, Washington, Debbie Thornton. Miss Thornton, please stand."

All heads swiveled to seek out Debbie Thornton, who revealed herself as a small blonde in the bleachers left of the stage.

"This little lady came here as part of the demonstration, but last night she worked as a volunteer firefighter. Early in the battle, when we were short of manpower, she pitched in and helped roll out the hoses. That right, Spud?"

Berlinsky stood. "That's right. And she was one hell of a worker!"

Applause, although not overwhelming, came from both sides of the gym.

"Next," Chambers said, "a guy named Chuck Steward." He pointed to the young man, rising a few rows behind Thornton. "Chuck and five or six of his friends, they ran jugs of hot coffee from Monti's over to the firemen. They came here from Montana State University at Bozeman. This fire wasn't theirs, and they'd never been here before. But they pitched in regardless. I had to drag Chuck off the street to get him here. The rest of his buddies are still recovering from their workout, sound asleep in Greenwood campground."

After a pause, Chambers said, "I'll bet we could find a lot more folks like that, if we asked around. On both sides of this gym. Now let's remember one more thing. The fire probably was started by one person. Just one."

The silence, the reflection, lasted for a moment. Then:

"Mr. Mayor!"

Chambers turned toward the shout and saw Ivan Bezdicek standing halfway up the center section of bleachers. Bezdicek was waving his arms violently.

Reluctantly, Chambers said, "You got something constructive to say, Ivan?"

The bar owner's words were indistinct, and several persons called out for him to speak louder.

"I said," Ivan yelled, "that was a good speech and you made your point. But it don't help us catch the arsonist. We know damn well the fire wasn't started by somebody local — and if there'd been a wind blowin' last night, we coulda lost the whole town!"

Chambers responded with an edge in his voice. "I'll ask again, Ivan. You got anything *constructive* to say?"

"I sure do." Bezdicek waved toward the opposite bleachers. "How do we know those people who helped with the fire didn't set it? Maybe they were just coverin' up, or makin' an excuse for hangin' around to watch. None of them had any business bein' here in the first place. If they hadn't come, none of this woulda happened. I say we oughta run 'em out of town right now. Quicker they're gone, the less likely they'll get their shit kicked out!"

Instantly, pent-up angers erupted from both sides of the gymnasium, and people began surging towards the floor. Deputies and auxiliary police pushed back with nightsticks while Chambers tried to restore order with gavel whacks and commands over the P.A. system. Nothing had any effect — until something simple and extraordinary happened.

From the school band, a small freshman boy with large eyeglasses strutted onto the stage with his trumpet and blew a deafening, endless squeal into the microphone. Enhanced by electronic feedback, the wail reverberated from the cinder block walls and stunned the crowd to near immobility. Another band member picked up the cue and struck an explosive barrage on his kettle drum. It was more than enough distraction to give the deputies an edge, and they quickly drove the agitators back to their bleachers.

"I'll be damned," Berlinsky muttered to a shaken Driscoll. "The *kids* had the magic. Cool!"

Chambers, palms sweaty on the microphone stand, spoke out with all the self-control he could muster. "Ivan, I'm paying you a visit later with the sheriff, and you'd better figure on spending your weekends away from home. Anyone else who wants to start a riot can expect the same accommodations!"

He inclined his head toward the school band. "I'm thankful these youngsters know how to behave like adults, even if their parents don't. Thanks, guys."

The students responded with a drum roll and clash of cymbals.

"Back to business. I'll remind you that we have an investigation underway. The visitors are plenty anxious to get home on their own, without assistance from any local idiots. But they're bottled up by roadblocks. It's taking about ten minutes to clear each car. At that rate, the last of these folks won't be gone until noon tomorrow — and only if most of them are willing to spend the night in a traffic backup."

"Mr. Mayor?"

This time the voice was quieter, coming from a middle-aged man in a bush jacket, standing four rows behind the platform.

"It better be constructive, mister."

"Mr. Mayor, I don't know how constructive. I hope it will be informative."

"Go ahead," Chambers said.

"Sir, I came here with a small group of people from California. We're members of the Sierra Club and... "

"I'm sorry," Chambers said. "I didn't hear all that. Did you say Sierra Club?"

"I did," the man said. "And we didn't just barge in. We were invited. So... "

"Invited? By whom?"

"By your own local group — your 'Save the Wilderness' people."

Chambers frowned. "Never heard of 'em. Not in Jackpine."

"Well," the man said, "I have the invitation right here. It has a local address and local postmark." He held up a paper.

"Could I see that?"

The audience passed the paper from hand to hand. Along the way, two others scanned it and nodded recognition.

Chambers looked at it, frowned, stuffed it into his shirt pocket. "I'll keep this, if it's okay with you."

"Fine with me," the man said. "I just want you to see that we came with the expectation of doing some simple fact-finding. We had no idea that it would become a major disturbance. The Sierra Club membership does not endorse any manner of illegal disruption or violence. And now we simply wish to leave before the storm arrives. That's all."

The man sat down.

Chambers turned to the microphone... suddenly veered back to the man. "Mister... What's that about a storm?"

"It was on the radio this morning. A big winter storm. Heavy snow above four thousand feet. It seems likely we could be stranded here unless we get out beforehand."

A murmur rolled through the gymnasium. Chambers abandoned the microphone to confer with Driscoll and Berlinsky. "You guys know about this?"

"Thought you knew," Driscoll said. "They're expectin' high winds, heavy snow, the works. Should hit us tomorrow morning. Cover half the state."

Chambers wondered how far the motorists would need to travel to get clear. "Below four thousand feet — any problems there?"

"Black ice, probably," Berlinsky said. "I don't think many of these visitors have chains or snow tires. I almost feel sorry for those California folks."

"Damn." From the corner of his eye, Chambers became aware of an anxious stirring among the visitors and locals alike; but he didn't see the man approaching the platform from behind him.

"We've got to let those folks out and lift the road-blocks," Chambers said.

Driscoll scratched his jaw. "I dunno, Nate. We let that firebug slip through, we're liable to have another riot on our hands."

"Just minutes ago, our folks wanted to *throw* 'em out."

"That was different," Driscoll said. "Kickin' them out is one thing, lettin' them escape is another. Hell, I don't know what to do."

The sound of boots clumping up the platform steps startled them; they turned.

"Let me handle this," the man said.

***

Russell Bancroft had mounted the steps with quick, purposeful strides. He wore faded Levis and a hunting jacket. In place of the usual game warden's hat, he wore a battered Stetson. He approached the microphone.

Chambers said. "Russ, the hell you doing?"

"Relax, friend. This will all be over in a minute."

Bancroft put his mouth to the mike. "Now that everyone's had a chance to bicker," he said, "it's time for the truth. That fire wasn't started by anybody from out of town. It was started by me."

Amid the general astonishment, a strobe flashed. Bayliss had shot a picture of Bancroft and, behind him, Nathan Chambers looking awestruck.

"I don't plan to state my reasons here. They were personal," Bancroft said. "But I do want to make it clear I had not expected to hurt anyone. I'm sorry about old Wooster. Damn sorry. It's something I'll never be able to live with."

Bancroft gazed at the high steel beams and heard his voice echoing from the vaulted ceiling. "Anyway, there's no need to keep anybody stuck here. These visitors had nothing to do with this, and they should go home. And you neighbors... go back to your own affairs. And... " He turned and stared at the stricken police chief. "Burleigh, you can have me whenever you catch me."

With that, Bancroft spun on his heels and trotted off the stage.

His boots made hollow clicks on the gymnasium floor as he charged toward the south end. He pushed the metal lockbar with a screeching sound and went through. The door hissed slowly and closed with a heavy slam that echoed from the wall at the opposite end.

"Well... " Driscoll's voice sounded dry and choked. "What're we waitin' for? Let's go get him."

Chambers fished the mimeographed letter from his pocket and glanced at the "Save the Wilderness" lettering across the top — and at Bancroft's signature at the bottom.

He crumpled it and walked off the stage after Driscoll.

No one needed to adjourn the meeting. In minutes, hundreds of departing shoes had smudged Bancroft's letter into pulp.

Chapter 35: The Yellowstone Parkway

TWO HIGHWAY PATROL cars blocked the Yellowstone Parkway a quarter-mile south of Jackpine.

Officers Ron Travis and Neal Pomeroy questioned a middle-aged couple in a Dodge camper who claimed they were heading for Yellowstone National Park and the Grand Tetons. They insisted they were passing through and had not been in town during the fire. They also objected to being stopped twice — coming into town and on the way out.

Officer Travis agreed to let them proceed without further delay; but he took a minute to warn them of the approaching storm. He said the storm would close the pass, and it would remain closed until next spring. It would be the same, he added, for most high passes within Yellowstone.

As the camper pulled away, Officer Pomeroy waved the next car forward. Off-road movement caught his eye, and he nudged Officer Travis. "Look out there, Ron. Isn't that Russ Bancroft's rig?"

Travis looked, saw a four-wheel-drive Bronco slewing recklessly through the sagebrush. "Yeah, I'm sure that's him. What's he doing out there?"

Pomeroy wagged his head. "If it were someone else, I'd guess he was trying to bypass our roadblock."

Both officers grinned as they turned to check the next car in the line.

At that moment, the radio sounded in Pomeroy's car. Travis said, "You wanna get that, Neal?"

Pomeroy trotted to the radio, checked in, acknowledged. He quickly returned to Travis. "You're not gonna believe this," he said.

The officers conferred, then dashed for Travis's patrol car. It squealed away with lights flashing, leaving the line of motorists wondering what was going on.

***

Police Chief Burleigh Driscoll clipped his radio mike back in place on the instrument panel and said, "Okay, they spotted him. They're in pursuit."

Chambers nodded. "Let's go, Chief."

"Might be a rough ride," Driscoll warned.

"Rougher for Bancroft, if we don't get the hell moving."

"You called it. Hang on." Driscoll switched on his lightbar and powered the police car through a tight U-turn in front of the gymnasium. The horde of people pouring out and milling on the sidewalk watched as the car sped away.

***

Climbing the switchbacks of the Yellowstone Parkway, Bancroft estimated he had a five minute headstart. It wasn't much margin for the Bronco, built more for trails than highways. But if he could reach the perpetual snowfields on the high plateau, he could cut cross-country on a long descent into backcountry. There, he'd be able to elude discovery for a long time.

Turning a tight curve, he had to downshift to gain enough power on the upgrade to pass a groaning pickup with Wyoming license plates. He swerved back just in time to avoid a massive Allied Van Lines tractor and trailer rig hauling downgrade in low gear with airhorn blasting.

Bancroft eased up on the accelerator as he approached the S-curve. Then he floored it, sending the speedometer to 40, then 45, in a sluggish attempt to overtake a dirt-crusted station wagon. He wanted to pass before reaching the next hairpin. The needle crept to 48. The starving carburetor gurgled for air.

***

Patrolman Ron Travis flicked on his siren, sending out shrill whistles to bounce off canyon walls. "If there's anybody coming down that next turn, I sure hope he hears us," he said. "Hang on... "

Patrolman Neal Pomeroy put his hands out to the padded dashboard as the cruiser swung into a wide sloppy skid around aptly-named Breakneck Curve. Travis was spinning the wheel back and forth, trying to control the fishtailing. He was rapidly overtaking the Dodge camper destined for the parks. "Goddamn it. Don't stop on the road! Pull over, you idiots!"

The camper slowed almost to a halt, leaving Travis no choice but to steer around it. "Goddamn, he's afraid of the cliff!" The cruiser went into a broad skid, its rear bumper sparking against the rocks on the uphill side.

"Jee-zus!" Pomeroy yelled.

Travis straightened out with skillful use of accelerator and steering. "You coulda taken your own car," he snarled.

"Hey, I'm not complaining," Pomeroy said.

"Why'd you insist on riding with me anyway?"

Pomeroy looked embarrassed. "I'm low on fuel."

***

The line of cars extending from Jackpine shifted like a serpent toward the shoulder as the police car blared down the center of the highway.

"Reminds me of when I was a kid," Driscoll said. "Trying to pass a ninety-car freight before it got to the crossing. I took chances like that when I was a kid, you know? No more. I learned the turtle was smarter than the hare."

"What do you know about those Highway Patrol guys?" Chambers asked. "Are they trigger-happy?"

"Naw. Not unless they're shot at. Then look out."

"I'd feel better if you'd get back on your radio, ask them to take it easy. No sense anyone getting hurt."

Driscoll fished a stick of gum from his shirt pocket, handed it to Chambers. "Unwrap this for me, wouldja?"

Chambers took the stick, tore the wrapper off.

"Thanks," Driscoll said. "There's more in the glove box if you want some."

"Would you get on the goddamn radio?"

The chief steered in silence, chewing. "Look," he said. "City cops got no business tellin' the Highway Patrol how to run their show. It ain't professional. But... if it'll make you feel any better... "

Driscoll reached for the radio.

***

Bancroft passed the 10,000-foot altitude marker and settled back behind the steering wheel. Keeping the accelerator floored, he could barely maintain a 33 mph climb in the thin air. He knew the supercharged police cruisers could do a lot better. The question was whether he had enough of a headstart.

Bancroft crossed to the downhill lane to see over the guardrails to the switchbacks below. He heard a siren and — yes, there was the Highway Patrol car, lights blinking, coming through the S-curve two flights down. Below it, entering the first hairpin, was another police vehicle — Burleigh Driscoll, probably.

The blare of a car horn bearing down on him jolted Bancroft back to his own side of the road.

***

Despite his driving intensity, Officer Travis managed occasional glances down the canyon walls as the cruiser hugged the guardrails. "Remind me," he said. "We gotta come up here some time when we're not in such a hurry."

"When do we *ever* have time?" Pomeroy asked.

"Well, we oughta make time. I know a New York cop, never went to the Statue of Liberty. Crazy, you know? But here I am, patrolling close to one of the world's most scenic highways, and I don't get to see it. Except like now."

Pomeroy fixed his gaze on a wall of rock rushing at them with alarming speed. "I ain't complaining, mind you," he said. "But I'd be grateful if you'd pick some other time to look at scenery!"

***

Barreling through the first hairpin, Driscoll made it clear that Chambers faced no less danger than Bancroft. Driscoll had an unnerving way of plowing into the turns, hitting the brakes and skidding out. "Damn!" Chambers complained.

"I warned you it'd get rough," Driscoll said, chewing gum. "This damn car, it don't have suspension for this high-speed stuff. I kept asking the city council. Each time we put out for bids, I asked to get a car with heavy-duty suspension. Well, you know how that goes."

"I hear about it every day," Chambers grumbled.

"Hell," Driscoll said. "I'm lucky I got all-weather tires. Once, I went after a thief in the alley behind the appliance store. He was on foot and I had the car. There was maybe an inch of snow, and I sat there spinning on cheap tires. The thief scoots off like a deer. Goddamn punk outran the police car on foot!"

The car sailed halfway into Breakneck Curve, and again the chief slammed the brakes and skidded out.

"That ain't the only thing," Driscoll continued, chewing vigorously. "The lightbar on the roof. You know about that?"

Chambers wagged his head.

Driscoll said, "It don't belong to the city. It's mine, bought and paid for outa my own pocket."

"Jeez! Are you telling me the city can't afford a lightbar?"

"Well, it couldn't back in 'Sixty-four. I don't think you was here then. That's when I bought this set. The old one was shot, we didn't have the crime control funds from the state back then. So what could I do? I paid for the goddamn lights from my own pocket. Two hundred and sixty bucks. Never been reimbursed, neither."

Driscoll chewed and stomped into the next hairpin.

The Bronco, its paint chipped from a scrape with a guardrail, gained speed on a short downstretch. The needle barely touched 48 mph.

Bancroft passed the 11,021-foot summit. Ahead was a shallow drop, another switchback to a lesser height; finally the snow-covered Beartooth Plateau.

The Highway Patrol cruiser entered his rearview mirror, several hundred yards behind and gaining.

Bancroft pressed hard on the accelerator and watched the needle quiver at 54 mph.

***

The temperature had dropped inside the patrol car. Pomeroy turned up the heater switch and said, "This chase is getting old, Ron. How about, if we get close enough, I could take shots at his tires?"

"Forget it," Travis said. "You heard Driscoll's request. And that's a fellow peace officer we're chasing."

"Yeah, well... I was just thinking out loud." Pomeroy gazed at the flashing guardrail, the canyon below — deep enough to swallow Manhattan's skyscrapers with barely a trace — and the snow-covered peaks beyond. Overhead, a small patch of blue showed in a deck of gray clouds. Some heavier and blacker clouds were snagging onto the distant peaks of the Absaroka Range.

"Say, maybe we should alert the Park Service. Have the rangers block the road at the other end?"

"Nah," Travis said. "He won't make it that far. We almost got him now."

***

The gap between vehicles diminished to less than 200 yards as the Bronco ascended the last switchback. The speedometer dropped to 40, 38, 37...

Bancroft glanced at his outside mirror. He could make out the two officers inside the cruiser. Then he remembered — to engage four-wheel-drive traction for the snowfields, he'd have to stop and lock the front wheel hubs.

He slammed the brakes hard as he hit the plateau, yanked the parking brake and leaped from the vehicle. It took only seconds to twirl the hubs into the locked position, but in those seconds the Highway Patrol car had closed all but fifty yards of the gap.

Bancroft jerked his Weatherby rifle from the Bronco's gunrack.

Through the sights, he saw Pomeroy yell at Travis.

Bancroft squeezed the trigger. The shot was good enough. The slug skimmed off the front bumper and ripped through the left front tire just below the rim. The Highway Patrol vehicle veered toward the cliff.

***

Travis had steered left around the last curve, and the tire's rupture sent the cruiser skidding. The rear end engaged the guardrail and wrenched it loose from its 8X8 posts. The rail had barely enough stretch to contain the vehicle as its rear end broke into open air above the 4,000-foot canyon. The rear tires spun in gravel, sending rock chunks out into space.

Pomeroy held his breath as Travis jerked the wheel hard right and gunned the engine. The tires grabbed pavement and chirped, and Travis steered back to center and stabilized the vehicle.

He resumed the chase on three good tires.

"Holy shit," Pomeroy said, his armpits soaked.

***

From the instant Bancroft had grabbed his rifle until Travis regained pursuit, less than thirty seconds had passed. It was barely enough for Bancroft to jump into the Bronco, shift gears, pop the brake, and hurtle down the highway.

Now the cruiser filled his rearview mirror, its siren screaming and lights flashing, its front end bucking.

"Now?" Pomeroy asked Travis, his sweaty fingers clutching the butt of his revolver. The inside of the car was a rattling steel cage, pitching violently. Pomeroy said, "A bullet in his tire would even the score."

"Tell me," Travis growled. "Are you as good with a handgun as he is with a rifle — while aiming from a seat that's bouncing like a goddamn air hammer?"

"I could find out."

"Forget it. It's bad procedure. I'll force him off the road on that flat spot just ahead... "

***

Bancroft watched the cruiser pulling out. He needed more time to reach the turnout. At the moment, there was no opposing traffic.

The patrol car came alongside, swerving, slamming the Bronco with a solid metal crunch. Bancroft looked over. The two officers stared back.

Another slam. A piece of door moulding snapped off the cruiser and clattered onto the highway.

Bancroft turned hard right. The Bronco leaped across the shoulder onto snow-covered tundra. It bucked crazily... and kept moving.

Skidding at a forty-degree angle, the cruiser smeared gravel on the shoulder and rocked to a halt, its blown tire shredded and smoking.

Travis and Pomeroy barged from the car, revolvers out. Pomeroy lifted his weapon and sighted, his fingers damp on the grip. The Bronco bounced and rocked like a wounded buffalo...

Pomeroy lowered the revolver. "Screw it."

Both officers holstered their weapons.

"On four good tires, I might chase him," Travis muttered.

"You wouldn't get fifty feet," Pomeroy said. "It's a long walk to civilization."

Travis kicked at the smoking remnants of the tire and the blackened rim. The hubcap was gone. "Damn. Let's get the jack out."

***

Pomeroy turned the tire wrench on a wheelnut as Driscoll's car pulled onto the shoulder. Chambers marched toward Travis, who held the spare.

"Where is he?" Chambers asked.

"Westward," Travis said. "About a mile off."

Chambers searched the snowfields, caught the Bronco's movement as it crested a rise, then disappeared over the far side.

"Hey Neal," Travis said. "Watch that tire when you go to pull it off. It's hot as hell."

"I know, I know," Pomeroy said.

Chambers turned to them. "Need help?"

"No, we're okay." Travis rolled the spare into Pomeroy's dirt-smeared hands.

Chief Driscoll, panting in the thin air, ambled toward them. "What happened to you guys?"

"Bullet in the tire," Travis said, clapping dirt off his hands.

Driscoll, surprised, inclined his head in the direction where the Bronco had last appeared.

"Yeah," Travis said. He turned to Chambers. "Shot by your good buddy."

Chambers bit a lip. "He was your friend, too, Ron."

"Yeah, well... " The officer squinted across the gray expanse. "That's history. Right now, he's an armed and dangerous fugitive."

PART THREE
THE STORM

Chapter 36: Ernest Lucius Spears

THE LEARJET hit the runway hard enough to jar Dexter's teeth. Bartz grabbed the armrests and held tightly while sweat oozed from his neck. Neither man said a word. They didn't dare. The pilot was Ernest Lucius Spears. Himself.

"Goddamn wind shear," Spears griped. "Crappy location for an airport."

Spears, lean as a fence post with a face like a coconut, had brown hair cropped tight to his skull, military fashion. His eyes had an indistinct color, like the washed-out jeans he wore. He also wore scuffed sneakers and a blue workshirt split open to his sternum. A mass of steely chest hair spilled from the gap.

While Spears shut down the Learjet, a green Ford station wagon idled near one of the hangars. Against it leaned the sagging figure of Webster Forsythe. He waited, chewing his pipe stem, as Joseph Bartz scurried from the plane followed by Hal Dexter. Spears came out last.

"Well, Forsythe," Spears said, not shaking hands. "I hear things are pretty goddamned fucked up around here."

The attorney pinched the pipe from his mouth. "You could say that, I suppose."

"I *could* say that? I *did* say that! The hell's going on here? The hell am I paying you for?"

"Your mining office is a total loss," Forsythe said calmly. "The records are destroyed... "

"Yeah, months of investment shot to hell. Let's get going. Tell me the rest on the way. Joe, you sit in front. Hal, get in the back seat with me."

By the time the car reached Jackpine's city limits, Forsythe had explained all that Spears wanted to know. Dexter and Bartz had remained silent throughout.

"One other thing," Forsythe said. "I'm no longer the city attorney."

Spears slammed a fist on the armrest. "Why the hell not?"

"Nathan Chambers found out I was working for you. I don't know how. In any case, the conflict of interest is obvious. He forced me to resign."

Spears tapped Bartz on the shoulder. "Joe, what's your assessment of this Chambers guy? What is he, a Boy Scout?"

Bartz squirmed sideways, looked back at Spears and Dexter. "I'm afraid he's gotten difficult, Mr. Spears. In the beginning, he seemed fine. But now... "

"Never mind," Spears said. He glanced out briefly at passing storefronts, then tapped Forsythe's shoulder. "Forsythe, I need to know exactly what we're dealing with. You understand I don't need you as a legal counsel. I've got more lawyers than I know what to do with. Your only value was your position as city attorney. With that ended, you're just dead weight."

Forsythe made no comment, but his fingers twisted on the steering wheel.

"On the other hand," Spears added, "I could use an expert on local morals and customs. How well do you know this Chambers?"

Forsythe stretched his wrinkled neck enough to catch a glimpse of Spears in the rearview mirror. The eyes stared back, coldly.

"It depends on what you want to know," Forsythe said.

"Don't feed me that crap," Spears said. "I want to know *everything*. His background, ideas, ambitions, and his weaknesses. Especially his weaknesses. Like who he sleeps with."

"There isn't much to tell," Forsythe said. "Nate Chambers, by your standards, is a pretty ordinary fellow."

"Which makes him a schmuck. Easy pickings." Spears snorted.

Forsythe drove into the Parkway Motor Court and stopped. He shifted into park but didn't shut off the engine. He dug out the room keys and handed them to Bartz.

Spears climbed out of the car, said to Forsythe: "Well? You coming in with us? Or what?"

Forsythe hesitated a moment — then switched off the engine.

Chapter 37: Three Musketeers

ON THE MORNING of Thursday, October 31, under an overcast sky, Jackpine children hurried to school wearing Halloween costumes under their winter coats. The streets otherwise were quiet and normal — except for smoke still rising from the ruins of the fire.

At the top of a flight of stairs, Nathan Chambers hesitated before knocking on the door of an apartment. He became conscious of the silence in the empty Teton moviehouse below. The last time he had been to this apartment, years ago, there had been a racket of motion picture gunfire beneath his feet.

Nathan knocked.

In a moment the door opened to reveal Lana French in a housecoat. "Well, if it ain't the famous Nate Chambers, at long last." She winked at him under a stiff lock of platinum hair.

Nathan nodded. "You said you have something for me — from Russ."

"Aren't you gonna come in, honey?"

"Better not," he said.

Lana frowned. "I won't bite."

Nathan went in. The old apartment was much the same, one large room with a kitchen alcove and bathroom at the back. But there was less furniture, less clutter. Lana wasn't sharing the place with anyone now.

"How you doin'?" she asked him.

"Fine. I'm in a hurry, Lana."

"It figures." Lana buttoned her housecoat and walked in slippers across the throw rugs to a small table next to her unmade bed. She picked up a large manilla envelope and fingered its edges. "The three of us — you, me, Russ — we used to be like Musketeers. I wish it coulda been like that forever."

"You were the first of us to get married," Nathan said.

"And you were the first to take off. You were gone a long time, Nate."

"There was a war on."

"I wasn't married when you got back," Lana said.

Nathan held out a hand. "Could I have that?"

Lana fidgeted with the envelope. "Why don'tcha come and get it?" She cocked a hip at him.

"For Christ's sake, Lana."

"Oh here!" She threw it at him.

Nathan failed to catch it. He stooped to retrieve the envelope, saw his name on it. He said, "What are you so upset about?"

Lana came closer, her hands clasped behind her, green eyes peering up through wisps of hair. Her mouth trembled slightly when she spoke. "It's all your fault, you ask me. If you'd been a little faithful, it wouldn't have happened. You big jerk."

Nathan looked at her in wonder.

"Oh, don't look so dumb!" she snapped. "Russell wanted you to help him in this stupid fight over the environment. He wanted your help so bad, and he didn't get it. So he went on his own and did somethin' foolish. Now he's wanted for murder, for Christ's sake, and you coulda stopped him, Nate. You could've!"

"Lana..."

"Oh hell!" She gripped his arms. "I'm just all mixed up. Forget it. It's all past history now. It's been my rotten luck to go for guys I can't have." She looked into his troubled eyes. "Go on home to your nice wife. I hear she's a good lady, even if she ain't from around here. S'long, Nate. It was nice knowin' you, once."

"You're going somewhere?" he asked.

Lana nodded. "As far away from here as I can get. There's nothin' here anymore except old memories."

Nathan saw in her, at that moment, something of his sister Rebecca. He put a gentle hand on Lana's shoulder. She responded quickly, hugging him. She kissed his cheek, leaving a small red smear. She pressed her fingertips against his shoulders and then turned away.

Nathan went out the door, clumped down the steps and out to the sidewalk. Next stop was the police station.

Chapter 38: Two Tough Statements

IN A TINY OFFICE cluttered with radio and Teletype
equipment and thick green record books, four men sifted
through the pages of Bancroft's confession.

Nathan Chambers read each page first, then circulated it
among Police Chief Burleigh Driscoll, Fire Chief Spud Berlinsky, and Ben Bayliss. The newsman made notes.

Bancroft had written in longhand on lined notebook paper. The report began with details of his activities on the
night of the fire. He had filled his Bronco with supplies and
survival gear, including two five-gallon cans of gasoline and
his Weatherby rifle. He had parked outside the geology office and waited.

While the demonstrators were picketing, Bancroft approached one and suggested the march to the mayor's
house. He then returned to his vehicle and waited for them
to discuss the idea. It wasn't long before the pickets
marched off.

When the street was nearly deserted, Bancroft went into
the Horseshoe Bar and phoned Chambers to make sure he
was home. When Valerie answered, he hung up, waited a
minute, then dialed again. This time Chambers answered,
and Bancroft was satisfied.

At 10:30 P.M., seeing no pedestrians, Bancroft hurled a brick through the plate glass window of the geology office. He reached inside and tore down the venetian blinds. Then he struck a kitchen match and ignited the gasoline-soaked rag emerging from a 32-ounce glass Pepsi bottle and tossed it inside.

"That cinches it," Chief Driscoll said, reading this. "The fire marshall found pieces of the Pepsi bottle and the brick. It all fits."

In further detail, Bancroft described his motives. As a state law officer, he had probed the ownership and operations of the mining companies which had employed the geologists. They had operated under a corporate charter issued to Consolidated Energy, a consortium linked to Spears Industries. The head of that was E. L. Spears, who controlled several other companies including the Davison Clay Pipe Manufacturing Company of Sioux Falls, South Dakota; Ski West Tours of Denver; the Hunter Automated Machines Company of Reno, Nevada, makers of coin-operated vending machines, pinball machines, and slot machines; and 28 percent of The Wisconsin Trust in Milwaukee.

Bancroft explained his personal grudge. Among the independent mining companies absorbed by Consolidated Energy was the Wyo-Mont Coal Company. Prior to its bankruptcy, Wyo-Mont had operated two Jackpine coal mines, including the West Side mine which had exploded in 1947 and killed 42 other miners and Oliver Bancroft. Although criminal negligence had not been proved, Wyo-Mont had shut down its operations rather than conform to stiffened federal safety regulations. And the former Wyo-

Mont president, the man responsible for the disasters, now served on the Consolidated board of directors.

Bancroft's confession ended with an apology of sorts. He said he had calculated his action to destroy the front office, nothing more. He blamed the unexpected spread of the fire throughout the building on its new occupants, who had illegally removed a fire-rated partition. "However," Bancroft wrote, "I do not deny that I am solely responsible for Erwin Wooster's death and am prepared for the consequences, if and when I am taken into custody."

Bancroft had scrawled his signature at the bottom.

Burleigh Driscoll got up and went to the adjoining city clerk's office. In a moment he returned with an aluminum coffee pot and a stack of foam plastic cups. "Anyone wants sugar or powdered cream, it's in the other room."

Ben Bayliss finished Bancroft's last page and slapped it onto the chief's desk blotter. "If it weren't for Wooster's death," he said, "I'd give this guy a medal."

Fire Chief Berlinsky reached for the coffee. "That fire was a danger to more than Wooster, Ben. He could've destroyed this town."

"Damn right," Chief Driscoll added. "If I'd seen him ready to throw that fire bomb, I would've shot him down. Made no difference who he was or why he acted that way."

Bayliss sighed. "I sympathize with his feelings, not his actions... So what's the plan, Burleigh? You going after him?"

Driscoll sat down, planted his feet wide. "I can't risk sendin' men out — not with that storm comin' up."

Chambers said, "There's another risk to consider. The danger to Russ. That's reported to be one hell of a storm."

"Hey," Driscoll said. "Bancroft's an old hand in the woods. I don't think he's in any big trouble."

"That plateau... it's a long ways from the shelter of any woods," Chambers said.

Bayliss had listened dourly. Now he leaned forward. "There's yet another problem of some possible interest to you guys. You know the Learjet came back last night — our friends from Milwaukee."

"So?" Chambers asked.

"What you don't know, probably, is that the big guy came with it — Spears himself."

Chambers said, "Spears? Here?"

"You betcha. And he's already fired a double-barreled blast at you guys."

Chief Driscoll glanced up from sipping his coffee. "What the hell does that mean?"

"You've all been naughty," Bayliss said, producing several sheets of paper. "Here's a statement he released to the press this morning. I'll read it to you."

*

"For immediate release; October 31, 1974; Jackpine, MT:

"Officials of Consolidated Energy today accused the city officers of this southcentral Montana community of condoning Vigilante-style actions against the mining firm's exploratory activities in the area, actions which destroyed a building and killed a local resident..."

*

Driscoll interrupted. "Vigilante? What the hell kind of horseshit is that?"

"Let me finish, Chief. It's all here." Bayliss returned to the document:

*

"E.L. Spears, Consolidated's chairman of the board, said a com-pany office was fire-bombed by a local man who boasted of his achievement at a public meeting attended by many Jackpine citizens and officials, including the mayor and chief of police. After making his bold statement, the man was allowed to walk out of the meeting. No attempt was made to arrest or detain him.

"Later, according to various sources, a lackadaisical pursuit was made, but the confessed arsonist was permitted to escape into the region of Yellowstone National Park. The state police who partici-pated in the chase claimed they were stopped by a flat tire. Park Service rangers in the vicinity were not alerted, and Jackpine's po-lice chief promptly called off the search, claiming poor weather."

*

Driscoll thumped his desk. "That's the worst buncha crap I ever heard! Poor weather, hell! That storm's a man-eater — it'll kill anybody who gets stuck in it."

"Including *Russ*," Chambers said. "Like I've been trying to *tell* you!"

"You guys wanna stow it? There's more to this," Bayliss said.

"Sorry," Chambers said. "Go ahead."

*

"Citizens here said the fire victim was an elderly alcoholic ~without friends or relatives, implying that his death is not widely mourned, or even of particular concern.

"However, some Jackpine citizens expressed shock and dismay at both the vigilante-type action and the non-action of local officials to

control or punish it. Webster Forsythe, the city attorney for Jackpine, was fired the morning after the fire-bombing by Mayor Nathan Chambers, apparently because the attorney had supported Consolidated's efforts in the community and would have been in charge of prosecuting the arsonist."

*

Noting that Berlinsky and Driscoll were dumbfounded, Bayliss stopped reading. "Any comment, Mr. Mayor?"

Chambers shrugged. "Sorry, gents. There wasn't any time to discuss that with you."

Driscoll stared at Chambers in disbelief. "It's *true?* You fired *Web?* The hell's gotten into you, Nate!"

"Easy, Burr. It's not like it sounds." Chambers tossed his hands. "Web was working for Spears and getting paid for it. That's a conflict of interest. Web knows that, and he agreed to resign."

"I don't get it," Driscoll said. "Web ain't no crook, never was. Why didja have to fire him?"

"The same reason *I'll* be quitting after this mess is over."

They looked at him.

Driscoll said, "Is *everybody* going nuts? Or is it just me?"

Chambers sighed. He leaned back in his chair and explained his father-in-law's involvement in the ski project. Bayliss set aside the Spears document to take notes, listening with deep interest.

"That's about it," Chambers concluded.

Bayliss nodded, picked up the document again. "You didn't have to tell us that, Nate. But I'm glad you did, especially considering the charges in the rest of this statement."

"There's more?" Driscoll wiped his nose. "I don't think I could take any more of that horseshit."

"But this is the best part," Bayliss said. He read:

*

"According to Forsythe, local sentiment favors reestablishment of mining operations in this depressed community, which has been stagnant since World War Two. However, a small group of opponents staged a demonstration the night of the fire-bombing. They met in a torchlight parade which was greeted by Mayor Chambers near his home.

"The mayor has been a life-long friend of the confessed arsonist, and local sources speculate that the mayor may have participated willingly in the torchlight demonstration, using it as a diversion from the planned arson attack. The parade had drawn all of the town's security away from the downtown area. Moreover, neighbors say the mayor seemed at ease among the demonstrators, talking and mingling with them.

"When the demonstration later got out of hand and was dispersed by the police, the mayor became angry with a patrolman and rebuked him for taking action. Still later, it was learned the demonstrators, many from out of state, had been invited to Jackpine by the mayor's friend, the confessed arsonist. That man is a game warden for the Montana Department of Fish and Game, bringing yet another law enforcement agency into question.

"As a result of these suspicions, Consolidated Energy officials today are in contact with the Montana Attorney General. A spokesman from that office is expected to announce shortly whether an investigation will look into official misconduct and other criminal charges against Mayor Chambers and various other officials."

*

"And that," Bayliss said, folding the statement, "makes a pretty strong accusation that our mayor is an accomplice before the fact — to arson and murder. In other words, in deep shit."

Chambers stared at Bayliss.

"I'll be glad to print your response, Nate," Bayliss said.

"It is bullshit, deep enough to drown a horse standing on a ladder," Chambers said. "Print that."

"Aw hell." Driscoll threw up his hands. "We *all* know it's crap! Nate, I ain't always gotten along with you, but I know the truth when I see it. Bancroft's confession clears you in my mind. Also, you sure's hell wasn't at ease among those radicals. You mighta looked it, but I could tell you was scared shitless."

"Thanks, Burr."

Berlinsky laughed.

"What *I'd* like to know," Bayliss said, "is whether you'll still support the ski project. Under these circumstances."

"What's that got to do with anything?"

"Answer, Nate. It's important. Believe me."

Chambers hesitated. He said, "I'm not sure if I'm opposed to a ski area. But I am strongly opposed to this one. I decided that when I visited Chicago. But I think I was, well... inwardly against it long before then."

"You're against a dream of yours?" Bayliss asked.

"Against a nightmare," Chambers said.

"Then your problem is half solved."

"I'm damn glad to hear that. Which half?"

Bayliss grinned. "I'm amazed you don't see it."

Chambers stared.

"The conflict of interest!" Bayliss explained: "There's no conflict if you oppose the project. You would stand to benefit from your father-in-law's involvement only if the project is approved. If you mean what you say, that you'd fight to sink it, then you're obviously not taking sides with either the developers or your father-in-law."

"Well, of course not."

"So why resign?"

"... Damn," Chambers said. "Where the hell have I been?"

Berlinsky smiled. "By glory, Nate. You ain't gonna wriggle out of this mess that easy, are ya?"

Chambers rubbed his eyes and shrugged.

Bayliss said, "Nothing, Spud, is ever that easy."

Chapter 39: One Desperate Hope

THE CONFERENCE continued.

"Ben," Chambers asked, "what does Spears plan to do with that statement?"

"He's already done it — released it to regional media and the wire services."

Chambers hooked his boot onto a chair rung. "Would the press accept it at face value?"

"Sure. Maybe not at face value, but it's a slick story. Lots of shocking ingredients for good reading. Of course, reporters will be looking for you, supposedly giving you a chance to refute it. Are you ready for that?"

"Shoot. Anything I say will make it sound worse." Chambers got up, went to the window and looked out.

Spud Berlinsky had been prowling the small office. He stopped and asked, "Why not sue the bastards?"

Bayliss flipped the document. "I've looked this over top to bottom. For the most part, they're quoting witnesses. Everything they say is based on fact. It actually happened. The order in which the facts are presented is misleading, as is the choice of words and the omissions. But you'd have no chance of proving libel. Even if you could prove them wrong on every count, it wouldn't be enough. You're public officials. You'd have to prove malice — deliberate libel. You'd have to prove they knowingly made false accusations." Bayliss swiveled on Driscoll's chair. "Care to try? When Spears can hire the best lawyers in the country?"

"I once thought *you* were bad news," Chambers remarked. "Compared to these guys, you're a pussycat."

"Golly, I'm touched!" Bayliss said, putting a hand to his heart. After a moment, he added, "'Vigilantes Ride Again' — it's like a movie title."

"The hell you talkin' about?" Chief Driscoll asked.

"The headlines." Bayliss sat up straight. "Spears was smart to mention vigilantes. It connects this situation to one of the most notorious chapters in Montana history. Editors will love it. You know, there's a lingering suspicion that vigilantes still ride the ranges. Some bastard finds his barn has gone up in smoke, the neighbors joke about it. They call it, 'The Montana Solution'."

The police chief snorted. "I don't care for that kind of talk, Ben."

Bayliss let his eyes drift spaceward. "Still, that could be the answer," he said. "Fight fire with fire, so to speak."

The fire chief looked up. "And I don't care for *that* kind of talk."

Bayliss smiled, enjoying this.

Chambers turned away from the window and said, "You got some kind of bright idea, Ben?"

"Finally some interest!" Bayliss stared at the ceiling where the blades of a fan whirled at low speed. "Yeah, I can picture pulling it off — with a helicopter." Bayliss stretched his arms, yawned, looked at Chambers. "Nate. Before your

phone starts ringing all day and night — wire service reporters asking if you beat your wife or burn up little old drunks
— maybe you should do something. Huh?"

Chambers sat down. "You mean, like jump from a cliff?"

"Don't get ahead of me. There's a form of action we
news guys sometimes call a theatrical stunt. It's all smoke
and no fire — excuse me, Spud — but often it works. Anyway, stunts make headlines. And that's what you want. Take
the initiative from Spears. Grab his football and kick it over
his goal post. You know?"

Driscoll slapped his thigh. "The man's gone off his nut!"

"Ben," Chambers said patiently, "get to the point someday. Okay?"

"Right. Here's what you do." Bayliss abruptly stood,
stepped in front of Chambers and pointed a bony finger at
him. "You get a helicopter and you go out there and pick up
Bancroft by yourself. You bring him back here for prosecu-
tion. You do that — blooey! The Spears statement is riddled
with holes."

The chiefs stared at Bayliss. Driscoll groaned. "Spud, get
one of your fire nets and throw it over this guy."

Chambers leaned forward, hands on his thighs. "Ben's
right."

"You're *both* nuts!" Driscoll yelled.

"No, Chief." Chambers stood again. "I'm thinking along
the same lines. Like Ben says, I can't sit on my ass waiting
for reporters to skin me alive. I can't leave Russ out there,
alone in a blizzard. I sure's hell can't ask others to get him
for me... But *I* can *do* it! With a helicopter, I can bring him
back."

"You ain't a cop!" Driscoll said, his face darkening.

"Exactly! That means Russ knows I won't shoot him, and he won't shoot me. Someone else goes up there, anything can happen." Chambers placed a hand on the chief's shoulder. "Look, Burr... I'm the safest choice here. Bar none."

Driscoll sighed. "But you'd never make it," he said. "The rescue choppers won't go that high. Even if they could make the altitude, they can't handle the wind. It's been tried before. Most of the time, it's no good."

"A Huey could do it," Chambers insisted, eyes full of intensity. "I'm talking about those big gunships we had in Vietnam — a UH-1D. Get on your pipeline to the National Guard, Burleigh. They've got Huey's in Billings."

The chief gazed up at the ceiling fan, back at Nate. "That wind can tear the hide off you. Any kind of helicopter could get busted to pieces."

Chambers shrugged. "Call and ask. It's worth a phone call, Burr."

The chief sat down heavily and reached for the phone.

Chambers turned to the fire chief. "Spud, you can help with supplies and equipment. You probably have everything I need right here. Let's get a checklist."

"For how many men?" Berlinsky asked.

Chambers looked at him. "Just me. I won't take responsibility for anyone else and won't need 'em anyway." He hesitated. "I need a pilot. That's all."

Berlinsky's eyes widened. "It's crazy, Nate! Take a minute and think about this."

Chambers kept his voice steady. "Believe me, Spud, I've been thinking about nothing else all morning. Don't sweat it. There's plenty of time to fly up there before the storm and locate Russell's Bronco on that flat plateau. We'll land, I'll talk to him. The chopper will bring us back. A piece of cake!"

Driscoll slammed down the phone. He said, "I don't believe it."

"What?"

"The Guard. They said *okay*. They got a pilot who needs the hours, and he's got nothin' better to do this afternoon."

"There we go," said Chambers.

Chapter 40: Separate Ways

SOOT-COLORED CLOUDS rolled over the Beartooths as the National Guard helicopter attacked the wind.

Shafts of sunlight slanted through gaps in the overcast, spotlighting patches of snowy landscape. But more clouds came pouring in, like huge blimps in ever-changing formations. One by one they snuffed out the rays of daylight.

Nathan Chambers concentrated on the craggy terrain while the huge rotor blades whacked overhead. The pilot, a Billings reservist named Bill Coody, normally spent his afternoons erecting prefab steel buildings. He tried to be nonchalant as he chewed a tobacco plug and wrestled the controls.

"We can't keep this up forever," Coody said, his voice crackling over the crew intercom. "Haven't you spotted anything yet?"

Chambers shook his head. "The wind must've wiped out his tracks."

The plateau was barren of trees, spotted with snow-swept arctic tundra — no cover for anything the size of a vehicle.

"Maybe he drove into one of those canyons," Coody suggested.

"No way. A bighorn sheep couldn't get down those walls."

The pilot chewed his tobacco and scanned the ground. "The winds get much worse... I don't know if I could land."

"You're the boss on that," Chambers said.

The pilot stopped chewing. "You ever had an aircraft come apart in your hands?"

Chambers didn't answer right away. Then he said, "Almost. Small arms fire nearly took the stabilizers off."

"Oh yeah?" The pilot looked at him with sudden respect. "Vietnam? The Air Force?"

"The Navy. Radar officer on the F-4 Phantom. Had the fun of watching carrier landings from the back seat."

"Shit." Bill Coody resumed chewing. "After that, I suppose this flight's a piece of cake."

A gust slammed the helicopter hard enough to tilt it sideways, sending Coody into a frantic chain of recovery motions. He cursed all the way through.

"It's no piece of cake," Chambers said, perspiring in his arctic clothing.

Confronted with the reality of this wind-rammed thrust into the teeth of the storm, he had second thoughts about the search.

In the relative comfort of Jackpine's sheltered valley, it was easy to underestimate the impact of high-country storms. Coody had flown the craft less than twenty-five miles from the Jackpine airport; yet the change in weather and terrain was so immense they might have crossed continents. Chambers remembered reading how the climatic change from the floor of Elk Basin to the top of the Beartooth Plateau was roughly equivalent to traveling from northern New Mexico to the Arctic Circle — a distance of some two thousand miles compressed into less than one and a half miles of elevation.

But few people gave due respect to the severity of high mountain weather. At least once each year, search and rescue teams had to seek out endangered mountain climbers, snowmobilers, or cross-country skiers. And still the outdoorsmen kept challenging the plateau in utter ignorance or indifference.

Like Chambers and Coody were doing now.

Chambers felt lucky that Valerie was among the ignorant in regard to the actual dangers. Her one snowmobile trip over the pass had been under ideal conditions, with fourteen machines traveling to Yellowstone during a balmy week in March. It had been a wonderful trip — not at all like this.

If Valerie had known or imagined what this was like, she would have fought twice as hard to stop Nathan. She had been tough enough anyway, first on the phone when he told her, later when she sped to the airport in Nathan's Jeep. Now — that whole scene belonged to a different, faraway world.

Nathan's last sight of Valerie stuck in his mind — her figure diminishing as the thrashing helicopter lifted him abruptly skyward, then swung dizzily over the dice-like buildings of Jackpine before arrowing south toward the rugged mountains and white surf of clouds...

***

Watching the clumsy aircraft struggle skyward, its rotor wind whipping her hair, Valerie Chambers couldn't believe she had let Nathan go. She waved frantically at the diminishing olive-drab contraption until it flapped out over the town and then skidded southward.

Burdened by a sudden stirring of her baby, Valerie staggered to the Jeep and climbed inside.

The infant kicked again, seemingly disturbed as she was. The thought struck her that the baby was protesting too late. Had Valerie been able to grab her husband's hand, make him feel the life inside her womb, she might have convinced Nathan to stay home.

Instead, Valerie discovered she had little influence over Nathan's decisions once he had made up his mind. In crucial matters, she felt less than equal. She had become a childbearing squaw... he the zealous warrior. It was infuriating.

The confrontation had been awkward, neither of them wanting to become emotional but both facing emotional issues.

"Nathan," Valerie had said, "you promised me. I thought you meant it."

Nathan had turned his face away, watched the black bug approaching from the northern sky. "I don't have time to sit down and debate this. I'll be back in a couple of hours. I'm not going far — maybe thirty miles."

They had been strolling aimlessly on the asphalt ramp. Valerie stopped. "We've got police and forest rangers. Search and rescue teams. They're equipped and trained for this sort of thing. So why do *you* have to play the *hero?*"

The helicopter became faintly audible, and it stepped up Nathan's pulse. He said, "You can stop trying to make me feel like a jerk. This isn't heroics. It's a sensible response to a serious matter affecting our entire community. We all agreed to it — our police and fire chiefs, the Forest Service, the local press, even the National Guard!" Nathan spread his arms wide. "We *all* gave it plenty of thought and we planned for *everything!*"

"Except *me!* I'm your wife, and you ignored *me!* Now you're flying without me. You're flying into a storm. You *promised* me you would never *do* that."

"I sure's hell can't take you along in your condition!"

"You sure's hell can stay home!"

Nathan turned and looked in the direction of the helicopter's loud staccato bark. The craft formed a waspish-looking silhouette against the gray clouds.

"Valerie," he said, "let's not have a fight over this." He wrapped his arms around her. "Nothing's going to happen."

Valerie glared and pushed him away. "Easy for *you* to say, macho man. *You're* not carrying a baby. *I'm* carrying it, and I'm aware of it every second. I'm worried about you and worried about the baby if anything happens to you. *God*, I wish you'd think of that!"

The helicopter settled toward the ground, blowing dust. The rotor wind sent Valerie's hair streaming across her face. She squinted to keep dust out of her eyes, and that dust stuck to her tears. She turned away.

The police car rolled up, and Driscoll and Berlinsky got out, hauling supplies from the trunk. Chambers went to help load the helicopter.

Valerie stood shivering, keeping her back to them, alone in her grief...

***

And now the helicopter was gone. Valerie felt no more movements from her child. She no longer felt anything. She reached for the Jeep's ignition key and barely noticed when the engine stuttered to life. She bounced the vehicle onto the highway heading west, toward her father's ranch. Her father was partly to blame for this, and Valerie intended to let him know it.

In minutes she was driving like an automaton around the unbanked turns and across the dips and swells of the county road. Her mind ignored the potholes even when the Jeep hit them hard enough to rattle the doors.

An image flashed in her mind — a strange one, of the tiny red smear on Nathan's cheek. Valerie knew its source, without question. Of the women Nathan knew in Jackpine, only Lana French wore that bright shade of lipstick.

During the commotion at the airport, Valerie had wiped the smear with her fingers. Nathan had shown no awareness of this. It seemed to establish a kind of innocence for him, and she put the tiny suspicion out of her mind. She knew all about Lana French, her past longings for Nathan and her current romance with Bancroft. There were no secrets in a small town. And she felt a pity for Lana because of this — a pity for *all* women, herself included, who were subordinated in a town ruled by stubborn men.

The other women accepted their fates and filled their days with card parties or group yoga lessons. Valerie scorned that and was scorned in return. Even as wife of the mayor, she never received social invitations from other women.

She understood Lana French perfectly — a desperate woman cast aside by too many men, never accepted by other women.

It was strange how Valerie realized all this now. It led to other thoughts about the strained relationships of men and women. Her mother, for instance. The strong-willed Geneva Ensign had waged a daily power struggle with Valerie's father for as long as Valerie could remember. Geneva knew her husband's weakness — that without the power and authority of the United States Army, without his uniform and insignia of rank, Arnold Ensign was a helpless man. Geneva could manipulate him, either stripping his rank or promoting him with her choices of words and manner.

Nathan wasn't like that. Nathan's power was inside him. Valerie couldn't get to his source. He was independent and self-assured to the point where he didn't mind announcing his own mistakes. His major problem was being the worst kind of chauvinist — the kind who honestly is unaware of his chauvinism.

And Valerie's father, with all his good intentions, was busily paving a road to Hell.

Valerie intended to deal with her father now, with the advantage of being almost hysterically angry. She steered with one hand, reached for the wiper switch as she saw moisture streaking the windshield. The right front tire caught another pothole. The engine emitted a loud snap, a clanging rattle, and died. Without engine vacuum, the power steering failed. Valerie tensed, tried to guide the flying Jeep through the curve manually but lacked the strength. Momentum carried the vehicle at a slant toward the ditch.

Valerie felt her infant kick as the Jeep plunged. "Dear God," she breathed. The front end plowed through weeds and branches. "God, please save my baby..."

The Jeep slammed into unyielding earthwork and stones and froze at a crazy angle in the ditch, its hot metal hood pinging with large raindrops, its wiper blades arrested half-way through their arcs.

Later, the rain turned to sleet.

Chapter 42: The Beartooth Plateau

SLIVERS OF SNOW pelted the empty Ford Bronco. Overhead, the National Guard helicopter hovered into the wind, its tail boom wagging, rotors flashing.

Slammed by gusts, the aircraft began to settle, its landing skids feeling tentatively for the rock-strewn plateau. Bobbing, listing, it resembled a schooner in violent seas — and then its skids sank into tundra and its massive weight compressed the spring-like tubular steel of its struts.

It landed about twenty yards from the Bronco. Dropping from its shivering metal body, Nathan Chambers hit the ground and immediately was felled by the wind. Snow stung his cheeks like salt sprayed from a hose. He pulled down his helmet visor and crept forward in a low crouch. With another gust, his snowmobile boots skidded on loose rock and he fell again.

Reaching the vehicle, Chambers gripped its door handle to steady himself but felt, instead of solidity, a distinct wobble. The Bronco sat with two blown tires on a slanted ledge of sharp rock. He peered inside. The keys were in the ignition, the rifle was in the gun rack, and there was a hump of canvas in back and a five-gallon gasoline can. Chambers turned to the helicopter, saw its slowly revolving blades lifting and falling in the wind. He shrugged at Coody.

In response, Coody signaled with his hands. His intentions were clear. He wanted to go up for a quick look around while Chambers searched the Bronco.

The craft began lifting enough to release the compression on the landing skids while the rotors beat faster. Straining, its olive-drab skin rippling, the machine lunged skyward. Chambers watched, fascinated, as it wriggled into the shrieking elements, its tail boom swinging like a saloon door. Through the lower front Plexiglass, he could clearly see Coody's feet working the pedals, his left hand on the collective pitch control, his right hand maneuvering the cyclic stick. It was a full-bodied effort trying to maintain a hover at 10,000 feet — nearly three thousand feet above the UH-1D's rated hover ceiling.

Chambers was about to turn back to his inspection of the Bronco when he noticed something odd.

Rushing toward him across the plateau from the west was a broad white cloud. Miles wide and rolling like an ocean breaker, it came with ominous speed. Apparently Coody had seen it also, because he began maneuvering the helicopter toward the ground.

Too late. The stampeding air mass knocked Chambers over, kicked the teetering Bronco onto its side within inches of his legs, and sent the helicopter reeling earthward in a fearsome cant.

Chambers tried to observe the events, but a filthy gray veil obscured his vision. Above the wind roar he heard a tremendous clattering din, like pots and pans dumped down an elevator shaft. Deep in the cloud he saw a burst of sparks.

As quickly as it had come, the noisy violence ended — a thundering locomotive gone in the night, leaving behind only the whistle of wind. Chambers scrambled to his feet and stumbled toward the impact area. He arrived in time to see the pilot squeezing through a partially open cargo door.

Chambers helped Coody to the ground. "Thank God," he said. "I thought you'd bought it."

"Run like hell!" Coody shouted. "There's fuel all over the frickin' place!"

They reached the shelter of the overturned Bronco and flattened their backs against the grimy underside. Heads flung back, they gulped bites of air out of the wind.

The explosion produced less violence than Chambers had expected. The Huey did not disintegrate all at once, but went piecemeal, with dull pops drowning in the wind roar. Oily black smoke shot away in shredding puffs. Some flames flashed and died. Then more flames caught and spread, until the helicopter became a rumbling blowtorch blasting downwind.

Chambers watched silently as the main rotor mast collapsed, its control links and rod bending and snapping. A pop at his side startled him until he realized it was the pilot, slapping his gloved hands together.

"Sonofabitch," Coody blurted. "What'n hell was *that*, some kind of goddamn white tornado?" He spat tobacco juice that sailed ten feet before skimming the ground. "And not a ham sandwich between us."

They listened to the blowtorch consuming the supplies and survival gear and the radio. Both were stunned by the enormity of the wind that had grounded them.

"Didn't even have a chance to holler mayday," Coody said. "Sonofabitch. Stinking son-of-a-strawberry-bitch!"

The wind, as if suddenly apologetic, quieted as the pilot smacked his gloves, kicked at rocks, cursed some more.

Chapter 43: Family Emergencies

IN CHICAGO, Rebecca Chambers trembled as she put down the office phone. The things she had said to calm her mother were of no help in calming herself. She fumbled with a cigarette, inhaled it twice, snuffed it out. She picked up the phone again and dialed Evan Black's extension, thankful he was working late.

Rebecca drummed her fingers on the desk, waiting. Her computer printer kept clacking out square-foot cost updates on building materials...

"Yes." Evan answered, sounding tired.

"Thank God you're still there," she said.

"What is it?" Suddenly wary.

"I'm going home — to Montana. Nathan is missing, Evan. He was in a helicopter, in a storm... "

"Nathan, your brother? Good Lord... "

"God, this is awful," Rebecca said. "I need to pack, get a flight, reservations... Help me, Evan."

There was silence, then a sound like a pencil cracking. Evan said, "What do you need, Reb?"

"Come with me," she said.

"I can't. You know I can't do that. Christ."

"At least take me to O'Hare. Please?"

"Christ." Evan was breathing hard on the phone. "I have four sets of detail sections on the university project due at nine in the morning... "

"This is an emergency, Evan!"

"And Nancy's coming," Evan said. "She's bringing some legal papers, and we were going to eat downstairs. Christ, Reb, this stinks, I know — but can I get you a limo?"

Rebecca didn't answer. She brushed away the long hair from her forehead and the tears from her eyes.

Then she said, "Screw you both."

Rebecca slammed the phone, switched off the printer and shut down her PC terminal. She tripped against her chair as she grabbed her personal items and hurried out, not knowing whether she'd be coming back.

***

In Jackpine, Arnold Ensign walked like a deep sea diver, buffeted by the current of nurses and candy-stripers who swept past him in the hospital corridor. He shuffled to the alcove where Woody Chambers sat staring at a tattered copy of *Field and Stream.*

Woody glanced up, saw Arnold's lean frame outlined against the white corridor. "How's she doing, Arnie?"

The colonel waved his arms and sat. The two men gazed at each other across a vase of yellow daisies on a coffee table.

"I told her," Arnold said softly. "I meant no harm. That resort stock was intended for a surprise. For when the baby was born. I meant no harm, Woody."

"What in the world are you talking about?"

Arnold wagged his head. "Oh, I made arrangements to trade some of my land for shares of the ski project. I didn't tell the kids, on account of I wanted it to be a surprise. You know? Now they found out and Val's all upset, like I somehow ruined everything for Nate, got him into this mess. She's sick over it."

Woody looked curiously at Arnold.

"Look, Woody. Your boy was all tickled pink about that ski hill. How was I supposed to know they'd get in trouble with me takin' a small part in it? I was only thinking of the child."

"Arnie," Woodrow said, "I don't give a damn about that now. What's *Valerie's* condition?"

Arnold's expression went numb. "Doc Fuller says they ought to prepare to deliver the infant tonight. Otherwise, he says Val should be fine, just fine."

"Tonight? You mean an induced labor?"

"No. She's already in labor. But she don't want it, not yet. She wants Doc to give her somethin', slow it down until Nate gets here."

Woodrow dropped the magazine on the table. "That's foolish. We don't know when Nate will get back... " He sorted possibilities, then said firmly, "She needs to be told what's happened."

"Uh, I don't know, Woody. Could make things worse for her... "

"It's now or later. Later might be too late. If Valerie endangers herself or the baby... "

"Couldn't you wait maybe a couple of hours? We might hear somethin' definite."

Woodrow shook his head emphatically. "It could be days, Arnie. Even a week. That's big country up there."

Geneva Ensign approached down the gleaming corridor with heels clicking. She stopped abruptly in front of Arnold, then wiggled her hands and looked at Woodrow. "Woody," she said. "You're the one. You go see if you can talk some sense into her. She won't listen to me."

"Where's Jessica?" Woodrow asked.

"She's with Val. She's waitin' for you. Go see 'em both."

Woodrow stood. "If you see Doc Fuller, tell him I'd like a talk." He turned and stepped off down the hall, broad shoulders rocking in rhythm with brisk steps. From behind him, he could hear Geneva Ensign scolding her husband.

***

On the high plateau, the darkness was total.

It was so black Nathan couldn't tell when his eyes were open or shut. Huddled with Coody in a snow cave, he listened to the screaming wind attacking their crude shelter.

"I'm not sorry I quit," Nathan said, "But this is one of those times a cigarette would be mighty fine."

Coody's response sounded scratchy and far away, yet the pilot's face was within inches. "The smoke would choke us to death in here. I got a plug, though. You want one?"

The thought of chewing tobacco wasn't bad; it seemed a downright luxurious idea. "Hell yes," Nathan said.

Nathan jerked off a glove with his teeth, felt barehanded for the pilot's hand, found the plug, jammed it into his cheeks. The hot bitterness revitalized his senses. "This is the best damn stuff I ever tasted," he said.

"You ever been camped out like this before?" Coody asked.

"Holed up in a snow cave? Yup. I was, matter of fact. Long time ago."

A lull in the wind produced a silence etched only by their heavy breathing. Then Coody whispered, "Didja get out alive?"

"That long ago... I don't remember," Nathan said.

Chapter 44: Waiting

WOODY CHAMBERS parted his lips from Valerie's flushed forehead and regarded her with an easy smile. His whisper reached into all corners of the private room. "How are you feeling?"

Valerie answered faintly. "Stupid. Really stupid." Her hazel eyes were filmy, her pale lips dry. "Where's Nathan?"

Woodrow's eyes uncontrollably flicked away.

Valerie said, "I know something's wrong, Woody. Tell me — please."

Woodrow opened his mouth to speak, was unable to muster appropriate words.

Jessica came alongside. "Dear," she said to Valerie, "don't you worry about anything except yourself right now. You might be delivering soon. Get some rest."

"I want Nathan here. *God*, I want him here!"

Jessica leaned down to hug her. Woodrow turned and stared at the door, muttered, "Where'n hell's that *doctor?*"

"Woody... " Jessica, clinging to Valerie, looked up pleadingly. "She somehow *knows*. You must explain it to her."

Woodrow felt at a loss. They all trusted him to handle delicate situations with calmness and reassurance. He never felt adequate. He had to force himself. He said, "Valerie, honey... Everything's going to be fine. I know that — just as I knew Nathan was coming back from Vietnam. He'll be back with you very soon — but not tonight."

***

The blackness gave way to a whiteness of equal intensity. Nathan, head and shoulders thrust above the snow, could not make out any form or substance. *"Whoo-ee!"* he said. "It's like looking at a blank movie screen. We can't move anywhere in this mess."

A grunt emerged from the invisible pilot two feet to his left. "Is this one of those white-outs you hear about? First time I ever saw it — or *didn't* see it! Holy shit."

Nathan turned in the direction of the voice. For an instant, Coody's face appeared — black bristles tipped with white frost against purpled cheeks — and then the white curtain came down again.

"Let's get down out of the wind," Nathan said. "There's nothing to do but stay holed up until this blows over."

They squirmed under the snow like worms, into the semi-dark of the cave where body heat had turned the snow into glistening ice. The humidity was high and climbing.

Until their eyes adjusted to the change, they looked gray to each other, like grainy black-and-white television images; but gradually solid colors emerged. Nathan made out the olive-drab of Coody's parka, the faint blue of his eyes, the pale orange of a knit cap showing under the fur-lined hood.

Coody's mouth opened. "How long do you think it's likely to continue blowing like this?"

"It could last days. Or quit any second. No way to tell."

Coody tugged at the front zipper of his parka and reached inside. He withdrew a pair of dark goggles.

"Where you going?" Nathan asked.

"Out."

"What for?"

Coody shrugged. "Figured I'd grab that gasoline can in the Bronco. We might need it."

"Wait awhile," Nathan said.

"Shoot, man. It's getting colder by the minute. I can feel it creeping into my shorts."

Nathan grabbed the pilot's arm. "Bill, we've been through that. Forget it."

They had argued about the gasoline since yesterday. Coody wanted to start a fire, using the fuel to ignite the seat cushions from the Bronco. Nathan insisted most of the gasoline would evaporate in the wind; or if they succeeded in starting a fire, it would burn out in minutes. He had pointed to the cold wreckage of the helicopter as an example. Better to save the precious fuel until after the hard wind abated and the bitter cold settled in.

They had argued also about trying to upright the Bronco, Coody believing they could start the engine and drive away — or at least keep warm with the heater.

Nathan had known the task was hopeless but agreed to try it, simply because the exercise would do them both good. So they struggled for two hours ripping parts from the helicopter to use as levers and wedges when they really needed a winch or a crane.

At least they had kept busy.

"Come on," Coody insisted now, shaking loose from Nathan's grip. "What's wrong with getting the fuel — just to
have it handy?"

"What's wrong? You might get lost trying to find it.
That's what's wrong."

"You're crackers, buddy. The Bronco's not more than
fifty feet away. How could I get lost?"

"You saw what it's like out there."

"Sure. Like being blindfolded," Coody said. "That's no
big deal. You just make a lot of noise, so I can hear you and
find my way back. I've got my bearings, see. The way we're
planted here, we're aimed right at that vehicle. And if I can't
navigate a line for fifty feet with my eyes shut, I got no
business being a pilot."

Nathan gave up. "You win. But we'll both go."

"Why both? You should stay here," Coody said.

"Take my word for it," Chambers said. "We need to stick
together like chuckwagon beans. If we lose this cave, we can
dig another. But we can't afford getting separated. You hear?"

Coody shrugged.

Nathan looked at his watch. It was 6:08 Friday morning,
the first day of November, less than eighteen hours since
their take-off from Jackpine and less than thirty miles distant. And yet, the life he had been living seemed so long
ago and far away...

Chapter 45: Activity

IN THE DIMMED corridor, Dr. Roscoe Fuller motioned for Woody Chambers to follow. Woody got up from his chair, leaving Arnold and Jessica dozing. Geneva Ensign had left an hour ago to find a bathroom and had not returned.

"In here," Doc Fuller said. He pulled Woody into a small medical library. "Listen up," Doc said. "Valerie's in Delivery, getting prepped. Couple of minutes, then I'll be with her."

"I see," Woody said. "Have you seen her mother?"

"Twenty minutes ago," Doc said. "Gave her a sedative. She's snoring like a lion in one of the vacant beds. Best place for her. You oughta leave her alone."

"Okay." Woodrow nodded.

"I'm going to tell you straight," Doc said. He indicated a chair. "Sit."

Woodrow glanced at the chair. "No thanks, Doc. I've been sitting long enough."

"Suit yourself." Doc stripped off his jacket and began unbuttoning his shirt. "She came in with cramping and bleeding — signs that her accident could've caused a premature separation of the placenta. So we treated her with an

I.V. and transfusions, and we gave nothing to slow down her labor. That woulda been the worst thing in spite of her demands. I hope you understand, Woody. A separation of the placenta is nothing to fool with. It could cut off oxygen and nutrients to the fetus — kill it right there. Got me?"

"I understand, and I agree, Doc. Go on."

"Few minutes ago, it all started happening. Membranes ruptured, bleeding stops, various other nasty clues." He tossed his shirt on the chair, grabbed his gown. "No more waitin', Woody. I'm draggin' that critter out of her. Now."

The shock of it hit Woodrow a few minutes later, after Doc Fuller had gone scrambling down the corridor.

***

"What'cha got, Janice?" Doc Fuller stared at the nurse.

"The baby's heart tone is slowing," Janice answered anxiously. "Down to seventy from one-thirty."

Doc turned to the anesthetist. "The mother?"

"She's ready when you are, Doctor."

Valerie moaned, and her feet squirmed in the shock blocks, but she was unaware of what was happening. *Dammit to hell,* Doc thought. She and Nathan had been looking forward to participating in this delivery, Valerie with a caudal anesthetic, he with a shot of bourbon under his belt. Now Valerie lay there flat out under Demerol, Seconal, and scopolamine, dreaming of some other place.

"Forceps," Doc said.

Reaching, he almost missed and dropped them. But he sucked a breath, steadied himself — then inserted the instrument with proper speed and precision. He found the head right away, well down in the birth canal. "Gotcha!"

Slowly, reluctantly, it came — and with it, blood.

"Oh hell," Doc said. "The infant is cyanotic." He glared at its blueness. "And the mother has a pool of blood in her the size of Jenny Lake. We ready with a transfusion?"

The nurse's eyes widened above her sterile mask. "The blood," she said. "It's not up here. I'll call the lab."

"Oh for Christ's sake, Janice, get those people off their fannies!" Doc Fuller was having a difficult time resuscitating the infant and was dangerously irritable. "Set up the plasma. Get me some ergotrate. That uterus isn't clamping down. This gal could bleed to death. Let's get moving, moving, MOVING!"

The anesthetist looked up. "Doctor? Her pulse is weaker and rapid. She's short of breath… "

"Hemorrhaging into the wall," Doc said. By now he should be doing the episiotomy repair and they were still waiting for blood. "Janice? What's the hold-up on the blood!"

Janice dropped the intercom. "It hasn't arrived," she said, her face pale.

"Hasn't arrived? What the hell… "

"The Blood Service van — it got stuck in the storm. The lab thought we had supplies up here. Her mother donated some… "

"Well, do we have any more blood or not? Dammit, what's the status?"

"Mrs. Chambers took all of it earlier. We gave her so much… "

"Jesus God. Get her mom back in here. Why can't people find out these things before it gets too late!"

Doc Fuller cradled the infant, staring at it. He couldn't concern himself any further. "Take it," he said to the nurse. "Do the best you can." His first concern was with the mother.

From what he could see, her uterus still hadn't clamped down, and the plasma wasn't going to keep up. Mrs. Ensign's donor capabilities were sketchy, and for the first time in all of his years of doubling in O.B. work, he actually feared that he'd lose both the child and its mother.

Chapter 46: Denver Doldrums

THE DENVER SKYLINE was curtained with smog, making the Front Range invisible from Stapleton Field. Rebecca Chambers paced until her legs ached, unable to sit on the plastic chairs in the Frontier Airlines lounge.

She had chartered a fast little Beechcraft to carry her in hops from Chicago to Jackpine, intent on beating the scheduled Northwest Airlines flight. But the storm in the Rockies had made a Jackpine landing impossible, and Billings Logan was open to commercial flights only. Faced with sitting out the storm east of Miles City or connecting with a commercial flight to Billings, Rebecca picked the second option; so the Beechcraft pilot had adjusted his heading to Cheyenne, only to be rerouted farther south, to Denver.

And now Rebecca waited for her twice-delayed boarding call, and she paced in her short brown skirt and suede jacket, avoiding the advances of wandering servicemen on leave. She probed the gift shop and scanned magazine racks, finally went into the bar.

Had she been less anxious, Rebecca could have taken Northwest to Billings and been there. That thought kept irritating her, but it wasn't the only problem. The other was Evan Black. Something had destroyed a years-old relationship. And it didn't seem to matter. What mattered was getting home. She couldn't figure it out. It seemed to nullify the years she had spent in Chicago.

Rebecca ordered a martini and perched at the bar. She raised a trembling hand to her straight hair and pulled it back from her forehead, sighed, and gazed at the dismal sky-line of the Mile-High City. It seemed the loneliest place in the world to be waiting — almost as lonely, she realized, as her apartment.

Venturing westward in the small plane, Rebecca had felt a sensation in the pit of her stomach, a sensation she hadn't experienced in a long time. It had something to do with Jackpine and her family there. In Chicago, she had felt nothing like that. In Chicago, she had been part of the swarm, caught in the whirlpool of commerce and industry.

The television announcer in the set over the bar had been talking about a "killer storm" taking toll of livestock in Montana and Wyoming, with severe wind-chill factors across the entire Northwest. The announcer had said some-thing about persons stranded in a storm at 11,000 feet.

It hadn't dawned on Rebecca — until suddenly — that the announcer was talking about her brother.

"Oh God! Everyone shut up! Please be quiet!"

People around the bar stared at her. The TV announcer took up another topic. The bartender rushed to her aid. "Miss, are you all right?"

"I'm sorry. I'm sorry!" She buried her face in her hands.

"Can I get you something?"

"You can just get the hell away from me." Rebecca opened her handbag and removed tissues and pills. "Please. Go away."

The bartender drifted off, arranged bottles, went to a customer at the far end.

Everyone else went back to quiet drinking and quiet conversation.

The bartender hooked a thumb at the girl in the suede jacket and confided with his regular customer. "We get all kinds in here. This airport's a hub now. We get crazies from all over the world."

Chapter 47: The 'Sherman Tank'

SPARED FROM THE WIND, Jackpine acquired a heavy but gentle fallout of snow, swirling down like feathers, pillow-deep on rooftops and pavement. As two snowplows worked along the clogged streets, the townspeople entered a new season and forgot the old.

Shallow tracks remained where trick-or-treaters had scampered the previous night, past wax smears on windows and frozen shards of pumpkins.

The rodeo, the riot, demonstrations, the fire — all of it had faded into history.

A wrinkled widow in a plaid woolen jacket raised her gloved fist at the orange plow which rolled past like a surfacing whale, trailing a wake that buried her little green Volkswagen up to its door handle.

Along the mainstreet, the Gambles Department Store had set out two shiny snowblowers with hand-scrawled signs offering easy credit.

At the Night Rider Saloon, Ivan Bezdicek wiped a rag against an obscene word written in wax on the new plate glass window, failed to budge it, and hurried inside. The word would remain there for several months before he'd remember it and remove it.

The pharmacist at the Rexall store stood aside for the twentieth or thirtieth time to allow pedestrians to pass, then bent down again to scrape at the sidewalk with his shovel. He hadn't ever been able to understand why so many people insisted on walking through town during a storm, packing down the snow before he could shovel it aside. It made his task that much harder. He straightened again as another stroller approached, greeting the pharmacist with yet another stale comment on the storm.

At the *Spectator* office, Benjamin Bayliss wrapped a woolen scarf around his long neck and tugged down the earflaps on his cap. Then he walked south along the sidewalk, stepped gingerly around the pharmacist's shovel, and continued to the next block.

At a small door next to the auto parts shop, Bayliss turned into a narrow hallway and stamped his galoshes on a rubber mat. He mounted the creaky wooden stairs to the second-floor office of Webster Forsythe.

Inside, Forsythe and Burleigh Driscoll, and a third man, looked up as Bayliss entered and brushed snow from his coat. The third man spoke first. "Here's that rabble-rouser now! Hullo, Ben."

"Sherman Armstrong! You old coot! Where the hell you been hiding out?"

"As far away from your blimey newspaper as I could get. Lucky for me, that rag don't get to Deaconess Hospital."

"You're looking okay," Bayliss said. "*Are* you okay?"

"Kickin'. Which surprises the hell out of me. Lucky I quit bein' mayor."

"Lucky for you," Web Forsythe said. "Not so lucky for Nathan Chambers."

"Ain't that the shits," Armstrong said.

Bayliss found a chair and sat. "Any word yet?"

"Nothin'," said Chief Driscoll. His eyes were bloodshot.

Forsythe, behind a worn wooden desk, peered over his eyeglasses at Bayliss, tapped his pipe on an ashtray. "Do you feel about the same as we do, Ben?"

"How's that?"

"Responsible."

Bayliss nodded. "Yeah, I feel about like that."

The attorney nipped at his pipestem and gazed at his law degree framed on the wall to his left. "Burr stayed up half the night," he told Bayliss. "He worked with the sheriff, trying to organize a search party. They might get started in the morning, if the weather clears."

Bayliss pressed thumbs against his temples. "Two nights," he said. "In that storm... Incredible."

"Maybe longer," Chief Driscoll said. "There ain't much chance we'd find those fellas on the first day."

"Not even with a helicopter?"

Driscoll lifted his shoulders. There was a ring of sweat around his neck. "No more helicopters. Not from the Guard."

Bayliss, dismayed, asked: "Why not?"

The chief shifted his bloodshot eyes to the newsman. "After what happened to the first chopper, I can't blame 'em. The Guard commander got his ass chewed to grits, from up in Great Falls. They're callin' it a boondoggle."

"But after the storm quits... "

"Makes no difference." Driscoll gazed at the carpet. "This time of year, weather conditions up there are changing by the minute. It's too risky."

Bayliss turned to Forsythe. "Well, it didn't seem too risky when we let Nate Chambers go up there. Me and my bright ideas."

"I'm equally to blame, probably more so," Forsythe said. "If I hadn't let those bigshot corporate clients of mine get out of hand... "

Driscoll sighed. "And I'm the cop. I'm the one who shoulda known better."

Former Mayor Armstrong said, "Don't leave *me* out. I 'm the one who got him the job!"

All merely hung their heads until Bayliss asked, "What are the chances of finding him without a helicopter?"

"Not good," Driscoll said. "The Park Service agreed to send up a snowcoach from Yellowstone, but them things are slow. And that's mighty wide country up there. The Forest Service will chip in their snowmobiles, but that's only three. I managed to round up a few more volunteers last night, but... hell."

"That's not bad," Bayliss said. "That seems like a good start, Chief."

"No it isn't. It could be forty below up there by morning. The chill factor could be a hundred below. The snowmobiles could freeze up. I'd have to bunch 'em together, keep a tight search pattern, or we'd just end up with more people stranded. It's happened before."

Armstrong leaned forward. "Then what's the answer, Burr? There's gotta be an answer."

"I don't know. More snowmobiles, I suppose. Enough to fan out in groups, cover wide territory before dark. We'd need about forty. That's my guess."

Benjamin Bayliss folded his arms and wrinkled his brow. "I'll bet there's at least that many around. It's what — a matter of getting in touch with everybody. Right?"

Driscoll sagged against the chair arm. "I was callin' folks all night. A few was all I could get."

"Others refused?"

Driscoll nodded.

Forsythe hunched forward and pointed his pipe stem. "I think I know the problem. It's the boondoggle thing. If we look at all the things that have happened since Nate became mayor, it's been constant turmoil. Nate gets the guilt by association. That statement from my corporate clients didn't help, especially with Spears throwing in my name — without my knowledge or permission, I might add. Anyway, I'm afraid a lot of people believe those charges." The attorney raised a brow. "Do you see what I'm driving at?"

The others nodded.

"So," Forsythe said. "The reaction Burleigh is getting — just a few volunteers — it's an approximate measure of Nate's approval rating as mayor. The rest probably believe he's getting what's coming to him."

"But it isn't an election," Bayliss said. "It's a matter of life and death."

"They don't know that," Forsythe said. "They believe Nate and Bancroft are a couple of healthy young bucks, perfectly capable of finding their own way back. They think a few snowmobiles are plenty. They forget we're not looking along the usual roads and trails."

Driscoll shrugged. "There must be a way we can get more help by mornin'. Any more bright ideas, Ben?"

Bayliss said, "Maybe." He turned to Forsythe. "Web, how much can you tell me about Spears — like, what he's up to?"

Forsythe leaned back with his pipe, gazed at the transom above his door. "Well... ethically speaking, I can't say anything. It was an attorney-client relationship, strictly confidential."

"Come on, Web," Bayliss urged.

"I did quit them, by the way." The attorney chuckled. "Lost two jobs in two days. It looks like I'll have to move in with you, Sherman."

The former mayor grinned. "I hope you can cook. I ain't had a decent meal since Ethel died."

Forsythe turned to Bayliss. "What do you need, Ben?"

"Give me the lowdown on those guys. Then I can let our citizens understand what Nate's been up against. I'll whip out a special edition of the paper. If we get humping, I'll have it distributed by tonight."

"Golly, Ben," Forsythe said. "If you could do that, I'll contribute everything I can — maybe even stretch the ethics a bit." He smiled faintly. "It seems I already have, and for the wrong people. Well, I'm going out of business anyway. I might as well go down in flames. In the interests of justice, so to speak."

Driscoll looked back and forth between them. "Mind tellin' me what you gents hope to accomplish?"

"Chief," Bayliss said, "by this evening, folks around here are going to know damn well whose side they're on. If we get lucky, some will change their minds and agree to help. Or the power of the press is good for poop."

Sherman Armstrong sniffled, wiped his nose. "You fellas go ahead and do that. Meanwhile... " He reached over and thumped Driscoll's knee. "Burr, how's about you lend me that list of snowmobile registrations."

"What you got in mind, Sherman?"

"Well, if I ain't mistaken, ninety percent of those gents will owe me for one thing or another. I reckon it's time I got onto the phone and called in the chits."

"Now we're gettin' somewhere!" Driscoll boomed. "The *Sherman Tank* is rollin' out!"

Chapter 48: Delirium

NATHAN CHAMBERS felt firm ground beneath his boots — a dismal indicator. Gazing down through whiteness whirling swiftly around him, he glimpsed a patch of naked earth.

It seemed ridiculous — and frightening — to encounter bare ground after more than a day of screaming blizzard.

The wind had stolen his breath, blinded him, exhausted him; and now it cruelly blasted away the snow, sending it down into the canyons, leaving the burnished plateau drier than it had been before the storm.

Along with the snow went Nathan's chances for survival. There could be no snow cave to provide refuge from the descending cold. The plateau yielded no firewood. And the Bronco and its fuel were somewhere beyond the maddening white swirls.

Out there somewhere wandered a pilot; dead or alive, Nathan Chambers did not know.

"Not a ham sandwich between us," Coody had said. And no shelter, no heat, no radio, no water, no visibility, no sense of bearings, no strength.

And no Bill Coody.

They had strutted side by side from the snow cave that morning, unknown hours ago, grasping each other's mitts like school children, taking what they had thought was a beeline to the Bronco. After twenty trudging paces in deep snow, they had stopped.

"We musta come fifty feet," Coody had shouted in the wind. "We should be right on top of it! You check left, I'll head right. If you find it, yell!"

Chambers had consented, adding, "Just a couple of paces, though. Let's stay in earshot."

To maintain his bearings, Chambers had taken lateral steps without turning his body. He had found nothing. He had returned an equal distance and called, "Find anything?"

No answer.

"Hey," Chambers had shouted. *"Hey!"*

Momentarily, Chambers had thought he'd heard an answer, a faint yip in the cries of the wind. Muttering, he had taken a few more plunging steps. Nothing. More steps, still nothing. He had shouted and shouted; heard nothing and nothing.

Logic had told him to stay riveted, but impatience and near panic had forced him through the snow, trying to cover a grid. It had been useless. Each step had twisted ever so slightly, until his directions had become totally confused.

There came a weird floating sensation — weightlessness and dizziness, like being blindfolded and liquored up at a party, trying to pin a cardboard tail on a cardboard jackass.

How long he had wandered he couldn't tell. His electric watch had stopped, battery frozen. He knew, dropping to the ground, that something else was happening to him. Hypothermia, probably. Potentially fatal hypothermia.

Night? So soon?

The question filled his mind like an audible voice as the earth became darker and the swirling brightness faded.

***

Dimly awake, Valerie felt so old and faded, she wondered if she'd slept a lifetime. She raised a hand and examined it, expecting wrinkles. It appeared smooth, normal, still tan from summer.

She became aware of someone else in the room.

"Nathan?" Her mouth was dry, voice feeble.

The person approached out of the shadows and bent over. "It's me. Woody." Woodrow's face came into the dim light near the bed.

"Oh... Hi." Valerie tried licking her lips. "Is there some water?"

"Yes." Woodrow fidgeted at the table, brought forth a glass with a plastic straw. "Can you hold it?"

"I think so... "

"That's it. Fine. How're you feeling?"

Valerie sipped. "Tired... Numb all over." She sipped more, lips pressed to plastic straw. "It's better. Thanks."

Woodrow took the glass before she dropped it and placed it on the night table. "Your folks went for some food," he explained.

"My father... how is he?"

"He'll be okay. None of us are over the shock, but... "

Valerie, raising herself in bed, winced with pain. Woody hurried to help her, arranging a pillow behind her back. He was surprised at how light and frail she felt.

"I was mean to him," Valerie said. "I blamed him for everything. Poor Dad... "

It began to dawn on Woody that Valerie had forgotten the entire day, that her mind was on the night before. Before she had gone into delivery.

Valerie suddenly noticed her abdomen, diminished in size. "What happened to... Where's my... Good Lord, my *baby!* Where *is* he?"

Woody sat quickly on the edge of the bed and took her hands in a firm grip. "You were in delivery this morning. Can you remember?"

Valerie's eyes darted wildly. She trembled. "Why must I scream? Why do I have this feeling of horror? Woody?"

Woody pulled her into his embrace, stroked her damp hair with his large soothing hand. "It's all right, Val. Cry it all out. Let yourself go."

"My baby is dead!"

"I know," Woody said. "Couldn't be helped. It's no one's fault... "

"Oh my God, my God! Why? *Why?*"

"An accident," Woody insisted. "The Bronco threw a damned piston rod. A damned freak accident that was nobody's fault." He held her tightly, stroking her, doing his best, knowing he was a poor substitute for his son.

After an eternity, Valerie settled back against the pillow. "I can't go back to our *house*," she said, knuckling her eyes. "I can't look into the nursery — the room I had painted and fixed up with giraffes and zebras and... I just *can't* go back there, Woody."

He nodded grimly.

"For eight months," Valerie said, "eight long months, I carried the baby and suffered with him and got so mad, so many times. And now... now I'll *never*... *see* him. Oh, dear God!" She wailed and shook, and Woody went back to her, and he was crying, too, tears dribbling down his unshaven cheeks and into the stubble of his chin.

And suddenly Valerie stopped. She pulled back to look at Woody with wild eyes. "Where is *Nathan*, Woody?"

Woodrow opened his mouth and closed his eyes.

***

From out of the fog loomed a shape; then it disappeared behind gray sheets of snow.

Chambers stared, lips frozen shut.

He raised his helmet visor and peered into the dark swirls. Exposed to the wind, his nose and cheeks went instantly numb.

He thought about Eskimos, with flattened noses better able to withstand arctic cold. His own nose protruded far from his body's heat. This seemed very interesting.

I'm fantasizing, Chambers thought. Hypothermia?

And then — *there!* That *shape* again.

Hallucination, it had to be. Visions of many sorts had appeared before his partially blinded eyes — sometimes dark shadowy things, often bright specks. But this monstrous shape beyond the gray swirls looked, somehow, *real*.

A monstrous *eye?*

The image was oval and glossy, dark in the center and rimmed by white. It was huge — and hypnotizing. It seemed to have a gap beneath it, to each side — dark gaps like the mouth of a shark, filled with long white strands like teeth...

It beckoned Chambers closer.

Nathan urged his body forward, glancing down to make sure his thighs responded to his will. Strange that he needed visual confirmation to know when he was walking...

His thighs, mere stumps above the churning gray, moved forward, first one, then the other.

It grew darker again. Chambers did not want to look up to see the eye, for fear it would be there; or worse, that it would not.

His head struck something hard. It clanged against his helmet.

Slowly, he urged his arms upward and pressed forward with mittened hands. They met firm resistance.

Then he *saw*.

Fire-blackened metal with crinkled seams and popped rivetheads, strands of melted Plexiglass dangling in the burnt-out window openings.

The great eye in his vision had been the frosted nose of the wrecked helicopter.

Chapter 49: Awakenings

ONLY FOUR PAGES and no advertising, but it wasn't a bad little edition. Bayliss was proud of it.

He sat with his feet on the rolltop, the edition propped against his knees. He clutched a coffee cup and surveyed his work.

He had finished the special edition by early afternoon. He had delivered bundles of copies to the Jackpine schools, for children to take home to their families.

Chief Driscoll had sent Buck Chism out with more bundles, for the stores, bars, gas stations, and the post office. Bayliss envisioned his paper riding on school buses, trailing behind county plows, reaching most of the outlying ranches. At this hour, he felt distribution was complete.

The lead story covered the missing helicopter, with Driscoll's frustration in finding help, and Armstrong adding his personal appeal. Below that was a box with the unedited text of the Spears statement and, beside it, a point-by-point refutation from Web Forsythe.

The second page reviewed the events which had occurred too late for Thursday's regular edition, including Wednesday's emergency meeting in the gymnasium. Set off in another box was the full text of Bancroft's confession — a confession that ought to win a few sympathizers.

All in all, Bayliss felt his straightforward presentation of facts would shatter the falsehoods that had been flowing from mouth to mouth like a flu virus.

The third page was devoted to the issues — the coal and recreation developments and their expected impacts on Jackpine. Bayliss had obtained enlightening figures from an organization known as the Environmental Information Center in Helena. He also had made effective use of his own files of reports from the state-sponsored Environmental Quality Council, the Montana Department of Fish and Game, the state Land Board, the rancher-oriented Northern Plains Resource Council, and various other public and private agencies concerned with the state's future life quality.

In fact, Bayliss was pleasantly surprised to discover the extent of Montana's initial preparations for dealing with these matters.

Finally came his editorial, to which he devoted the entire fourth page in large type. Bayliss believed he had proposed reasonable answers for the knotty questions, and he closed it with a simple appeal to local residents: help the community in its crisis; help Russell Bancroft and Nathan Chambers in theirs.

Folding up the paper, then standing and stretching, Ben Bayliss looked out the front window at the weather-beaten storefronts. And gradually his expression of self-satisfaction changed to grim concern.

His words had appealed to Jackpine's sense of justice and civic pride. Yet, what he saw through the window was litter flying in the wind; burned-out streetlights never repaired; beer cans planted in the snowbanks; obscene words scrawled in wax on store windows; and a dozen other indications that — nice folks or not — Jackpine's residents had long ago stopped giving a damn.

***

Aware of a glow on his face, Nathan Chambers snapped open his eyes. In front of him, intruding on his sleep, a pale crescent gradually took focus.

The moon!

And there were stars, billions of them, bright pinpoints seeded across the black void. The pale lights of the universe shown down on the plateau and whitewashed the torn and jumbled interior of the helicopter.

The wind had stopped, and in the hush Nathan heard the slow thumping of his heart and the faint flows of his breath. It was a relief to see again and hear again.

Nathan lifted his arms, slowly at first, exerting willpower. He couldn't feel his legs, but by staring at them in the moonlight and concentrating, he made each one move.

Like a rusted suit of armor, squirted with lubricants of hope, Nathan's body obeyed his commands until his arms beat his thighs, and brief stings penetrated his numb flesh. The stings at first dissipated quickly; but as he kept beating, urgently willing his blood to flow, the stings lasted longer.

Following a long session of this flagellation, Nathan risked jerking off a glove. He slapped his bare fingers against his thighs until he could feel his fingertips, then grasped his jacket zipper and yanked at it. He couldn't hold it, but he tried again. And using both hands, he got the zipper parted.

Furiously now, Nathan tugged the zipper and felt the strain in his face, the blood returning there. He rubbed hands against bearded cheeks and lead-hard nose, thrust the hands inside his jacket and under his armpits.

With the wind no longer blowing, the chill factor had subsided. But it remained below zero inside the helicopter cabin, where melted Plexiglass hung like spider webs from ragged openings. And Nathan realized his life probably had been saved — or at least prolonged — by a simple thing from beyond the earth that had awakened him:

Moonglow.

Looking out, he saw the Bronco on its side, its metallic surface reflecting needle points of stellar light. He noticed something else — a heap on the ground — about midway between the two felled machines.

The pilot? Bill Coody?

Chambers hoisted himself. A pressure in his loins overcame him, and he forced down his leggings and urinated on the charred floor. He found it supremely encouraging to feel his body functioning still, all systems normal and running. He pulled up his shorts, thermal long-johns, jeans, waterproof nylon leggings, and carefully zipped and snapped everything in place.

At the cargo door, he squeezed through the same slit the pilot had used after the crash and jumped to the ground. Pain stabbed his feet and legs. Brittle as glass they were, but nothing broke. He pushed forward.

Reaching the sprawled figure, Chambers bent down and shoved at it. He dropped to his knees and tugged, finally managed to roll it over.

It was not the pilot, not Bill Coody.

It was Russell Bancroft.

Chapter 50: End Games

STRETCHED ACROSS his rumpled orange bedspread, Ernest Lucius Spears stared at his yellow socks and said, "You know, I'm getting plain goddamn sick of this place."

Joseph Bartz sat in one of the tweed chairs, caving in the cushion. Having come from a hot shower, he wore a white bath towel around his layered stomach. He held a drink in one hand, a half-smoked cigar in the other.

In the other chair sat Hal Dexter, his skeletal limbs dangling while he studied the four-page newspaper. Unlike the others, he wasn't content to lay about in the morning, drinking and smoking. He was fully dressed and ready — but had nowhere to go.

The television hummed with off-key color images of a morning news and variety show.

"Try the channels," Spears ordered. "Get me a weather report."

Setting down his drink, Bartz obeyed. The next channel offered a game show. He continued clicking around the dial, back to the original program. "Only two channels," Bartz declared.

"Then turn it off." Spears aimed his narrowed eyes at Dexter. "You through with that? Let me have that paper again." He snatched it from Dexter's fingers.

Dexter stood, tightened his necktie, reached for his coat. "I'll try to catch a ride down to mainstreet." He felt bitter at the loss of Forsythe's chauffeuring service.

Spears shot a glance at him. "What for?"

"The stores will open soon. I'll buy us some overshoes or something. We didn't come prepared for this weather."

Spears grumbled, returned his attention to the paper.

Dexter hesitated at the door. "I'll try to learn if anyone's going to clear the runway. Maybe we can leave today."

Spears did not answer, and Joseph Bartz drank more scotch. Hal Dexter turned up his collar and went out.

Silence hung in the room until Spears broke it. "Did you see these figures?"

Bartz glanced around his cigar.

Spears tapped the newspaper. "This article claims *our* ski project would cause a five hundred percent growth in energy consumption over the next five years — burn some thirty thousand kilowatts. It says that's the equivalent of the combined peak loads of three medium-sized Montana cities."

Spears looked back at the tabloid, continued reading silently. Then as Bartz stood to scratch himself, Spears said, "Then it claims local taxpayers would get stuck paying for improvements to access roads and highways, enlarging the airport, and paying higher utility rates to compensate for powerlines and substations to deliver the increased electrical load."

Bartz stopped scratching.

"Then there's *this* editorial," Spears said, folding the back page over. He quoted:

"The ski resort is conceived as a super playground for the rich, but its developers expect our taxpayers to foot the bill for ancillary improvements. On top of this, they would lay waste to eastern Montana, even our own county, to mine coal for the energy needed just to keep their playground operating."

Bartz winced. "Seems they figured out the connection between those mines and the ski project."

"Here's the worst of it, Joseph. This paper wants the county commissioners to declare a moratorium on all local subdivision and land development for at least a year, until the state legislature convenes to deal with all these so-called *threats* to Montana's rural lifestyle. How about that, huh?"

Bartz picked up another towel and wiped perspiration from under his arms.

Spears folded the paper and dropped it to the carpet. "Well? Would you say you did your job out here?"

Bartz sat down and picked his cigar out of an ashtray. "It's talk, Mr. Spears, just talk." He waved the cigar and stuck it into his pursed mouth.

Spears narrowed his eyes at the fat man. "Joe," he asked quietly, "how much you got invested so far? Personally?"

"Fifty... sixty grand." Bartz said it as if the amount were insignificant.

"You know how much I've spent?"

Bartz shook his head, shrugged. The cigar twirled in his mouth.

"I'll tell you, Joe. From my pockets, less than four grand."

Bartz grinned around the glowing butt. He seemed satisfied that the risk was small indeed for a multi-millionaire.

"How much *more*," Spears asked, "will it cost me to complete the project? Under these circumstances?"

"It depends, Mr. Spears. It all depends."

"For Christ's sake, Joe. Depends on what?"

"On who," Bartz said. "Of your three principal opponents — and I'm speaking of the newspaper, the mayor, and the game warden — none are popular. And of course, two are lost in the mountains. In this grand storm!"

Bartz became excited, waving his fleshy arms. "They're outa touch now — what? Forty hours? There's a chance they've *expired* by now! A *good* chance!"

Spears watched in grim silence as Bartz continued, rising from his chair and orating like a towel-draped Caesar.

"Thus far, I have sold stock in the corporation to a dozen local merchants. *They* don't want to lose out. And that rancher, the guy with the land-trade. He stands to collect twenty thousand shares — a *fortune* to him. The Forest Service, they find nothing wrong with our master plan — nothing serious, anyway. And when we bring in those new architectural renderings, the promotional film, and start showing the condos, tennis courts, all that other great stuff... Hell, they'll all follow us around like puppy dogs."

Bartz paused for dramatic effect, sat, straightened his towel, and added:

"Against all that, what does that feeble opposition have? Words. Just *words*, and a foolish stunt that already jeopardized three more lives. *Hah*."

Bartz proudly patted his bare stomach, unaware of the cigar ashes that had dribbled into his navel.

"I wouldn't sweat it," Bartz said, sweating.

Spears had allowed the speech to go uninterrupted. Now he silently glanced at the newspaper on the carpet, then back at Bartz. He said:

"You think we'll win, Joe — if the opposition croaks."

"We'll win in any case. But yes, it would be helpful if the opposition croaks. And it looks to me like they have."

Chapter 51: Clear Skies

THE PLATEAU EMERGED as an island above a foamy sea of clouds. To Nathan Chambers, it seemed he stood at the top of the world.

That rolling white ocean spread across the distant plains for more than eighty miles. Fleecy tides swept into the inlet valleys and canyons and lapped at the plateau's fringes.

Overhead, a purple sky spilled down the invisible deep cold from outer space. The sun, an ultraviolet flare, glanced its harsh rays on unprotected granite and sparkled on the pitted surface of Nathan's visor. His eyes squinted in this glare; his throat and nostrils were parched by the bitter cold.

But Nathan's blood was circulating — more than could be said for Bancroft, whose stiff body remained as Nathan had found it, glazed with frost.

Bill Coody had been lucky. During the storm he had stumbled into the Bronco and, following his original intentions, he had made a smoldering fire with the gasoline and seat cushions. It hadn't burned long, but it kept him alive until the brunt of the storm had passed.

Now the pilot stamped and jogged while Chambers scanned the pink horizon and wondered about Bancroft.

Nathan had tried being philosophical; tried, but he was shaken.

Bancroft could have survived. He had known the techniques better than anyone. He had supplies stashed somewhere — supplies missing from the Bronco. His death had to be the result of indifference to the dangers he had faced.

It was very possible Bancroft had witnessed the helicopter crash from wherever he had taken shelter; then he would have come to help, ignoring his own exposure to the storm. It made some sense that way, especially if Bancroft had no intention of ever returning to Jackpine.

The game warden had known the law. He knew the penalty for his conviction might be death or imprisonment up to one hundred years. For Bancroft, an outdoorsman, imprisonment for any length of time was worse than hanging. Given the choice, he would have preferred to die on a wilderness trail.

Bancroft's departure from Jackpine, probably, had not been impelled by any particular escape plan, but rather by a notion of choosing his own circumstances for dying.

Now there could be no direct answers. Bancroft, a corpse abandoned in the ebbtide of the storm, had left behind a mystery and, maybe someday, a legend.

Chambers stamped the ground and went to help the sagging pilot stay on his feet.

***

At 10:45 A.M., the fog-like cloud cover began dissipating over Jackpine. City and county plows worked in tandem teams on the airport runway, clearing a path a thousand feet long while impatient pilots warmed the engines of the Piper, the Cessna, and one of the yellow Stearman biplanes. Four men worked with shovels around the buried landing gears, while spinning propellers fanned the snow into silvery clouds.

After thirty minutes, the first plane — the Stearman — lifted from the runway with a window-rattling roar and climbed steeply above the remaining wisps of clouds, scattered like sheep grazing the mountainsides. The Cessna wobbled into the air seven minutes later, closely followed by the Piper. They all aimed toward the Beartooth Plateau, now clearly visible in yellow sunlight.

The Learjet remained cold and idle, its landing gear sunk in deep snow. No one was available to shovel around it, and the plows only contributed more heaps in front of it.

Hal Dexter hadn't been successful in his attempts to hire men with shovels. His last offer, a fifty, had no takers.

Chapter 52: The Montana Solution

WHEN HAL DEXTER returned to the Parkway Motor Court, he found Webster Forsythe in the room with Ernest Lucius Spears and Joe Bartz.

"Get in here, Hal," Spears said. "This you've got to hear."

Dexter draped his coat over a chair and sat, watching as Forsythe flipped through pages of a yellow legal pad. Spears remained sprawled on his rumpled bed. He hadn't strayed more than thirty feet from it in three days.

"I'm representing Arnold Ensign now," Forsythe explained to Dexter, glancing up from the pad. "But before going into that aspect, I brought several items from our local officials."

Dexter made himself comfortable in the chair. "Items?"

"Yes." Forsythe found the page he was looking for. "First, a Forest Service letter that arrived this morning. I put the original in your safety deposit box. But I thought you might be interested in a summary, before you leave."

"Fine," Dexter said patiently, flipping his hands.

"The letter claims that your environmental impact statement is incomplete, specifically on migrations of the Wapiti Mountain elk herd. It says your permit cannot be processed until you provide the requested studies."

Joseph Bartz, shifting in his chair, said, "That's complete nonsense. We gave them data on that. This is bureaucratic nit-picking."

"Nonetheless," Forsythe said, "the questions are specific. You'll need to give them specific answers."

Bartz looked at the tycoon. "Don't worry about it, Mr. Spears. I know a guy, we can get a waiver on that."

Spears grunted.

Forsythe glanced over the top of his eyeglasses. "Shall I go on to the other matters?"

"By all means," Spears said.

Forsythe shuffled documents and said, "The Board of County Commissioners voted this morning. They decided by two-to-one to declare a moratorium on new development of county lands for one year, or until a master zoning plan is prepared and adopted, whichever comes first."

Bartz rose to his feet, snapping his fingers. "Now that — it's not legal! Two slow-witted road commissioners can't stop us from developing our own land!"

"Mmm, perhaps not," Forsythe said. "But again, perhaps yes. This state has a law enabling them to do just that. It hasn't been tested in the courts; but if you wish to be the test case, I imagine it will take no more than four years to decide."

"It's a bunch of crap!" Bartz insisted.

"Not really," Forsythe said. "What it does, you see, it gives counties a one-year grace period to produce a master plan without pressure from on-going development. And because you haven't yet filed your certificate of survey... "

"That's enough," Spears grumbled from his bed. "For-sythe, I had my fill of your legal ramblings when you were on payroll."

"There's one more item," Forsythe said without rancor.

"Make it brief," Spears grunted.

"It concerns Colonel Arnold Ensign... " Forsythe stashed the legal pad in his briefcase and withdrew a folded white document. "I have here a photocopy of the buy-sell agree-ment you and he negotiated on the, uh... yes, one hundred and sixty acres at the base of Wapiti Mountain... "

Spears said, "Bartz handled that, not me."

"No matter. The agreement is subject to several condi-tions. For one, the exchange is contingent on Forest Service approval of your permit within twelve months. That was to protect you, of course, in event the permit didn't come through, and you'd have no use for the land without it. Let's see... Other conditions involve easements, water rights... But the permit is the main thing. Well, it appears now that you won't meet the twelve-month provision."

Bartz, seated again, took the cigar from his mouth and crossed his arms like a Sumo wrestler. He was indignant. "So. I suppose the man isn't content with our *arrangement*. He'd like a larger slice of the action, eh? Wants to renegoti-ate something better for himself, before renewing? Well, you can tell that man, Mr. Forsythe, that he can... "

"He isn't interested," Forsythe said.

"Interested in what?"

"Renewing. Colonel Ensign has requested that I notify you that he won't renew this agreement, under any condi-tions and, furthermore, even if you succeed in obtaining the permit, which seems most unlikely, he will not meet any of the other conditions you require of *him* — such as easements, water rights, and so forth and so forth."

Forsythe, satisfied with the exchange of looks among the others, rocked back on his heels and felt a little young again.

Bartz fumed. "This is idiocy. Who does that man think he is? If this is his goddamn notion of horse-trading... "

"He means it," Forsythe said calmly. "You cannot have his land. Not now, not next year, not ever. Not at any price."

Spears glared at Bartz. "Joseph? You claimed you had that rancher in your hip pocket!"

"I do! Don't you see? It's all a bluff! He... "

"Forsythe?" Spears looked hard at the attorney. "*You* tell me. Why wouldn't that rancher want to complete the deal?"

Webster Forsythe, perfectly comfortable in this group for the first time, divulged the answer slowly and with much relish. "I believe you would find that his attitude has something to do with your shoddy treatment of his son-in-law."

"His *what?*" Spears turned scarlet. "We don't even *know* his goddamn sonofabitch son-in-law!"

"You most certainly do," Forsythe said. He paused for effect. "He happens to be Nathan Chambers. You know — the mayor."

Spears turned to Bartz. "*Joseph...* "

"How should *I* have known that?" Bartz whined. He scooted in a circle, waving his arms. "I can't look up everyone's family tree!"

The thought crossed Hal Dexter's mind, how the mayor's wife, during dinner that night, had mentioned her father was a retired military man — as was Arnold Ensign.

But it had not occurred to him to pursue it. *Lots* of ranchers were retired military men — were they not?

"Looking up family trees in a small town is *basic,*" Spears said to Bartz with monumental disgust.

Bartz sat and hunched forward, the slabs of his stomach reaching halfway to his knees. "Look, suppose we push for the permits. We can get that done before the agreement expires. Then we hit this Ensign guy with everything we've got. We'll put together a legal team and scare the shit outa him... "

Spears blinked. "Joseph? *Cool* it! You outsmarted yourself with that conditional buy-sell agreement. Now you're reamed out like a pig on a spit. Without that land, your whole scheme isn't worth a jigger of piss!"

Bartz dribbled cigar ashes from trembling fingers. He looked at Forsythe, at Dexter, back at Spears. He said in huge desperation, "You *can't* quit now, Mr. Spears! I got sixty thousand invested!"

"You asshole, don't you tell me what I can't do! If you want to dump good money after bad, that's up to you. But it sure as hell won't be any of *my* money! Joseph, you're an imbecile."

Spears cast his angry glare at Forsythe. "Mr. Attorney, how soon can we get the hell out of here?"

Forsythe looked at his watch. "The plows are still clearing the north end of the runway, but I imagine you'll be able to take off within the hour." He looked at them without giving any outward sign of his personal pleasure. "I'll be glad to arrange clearance and drive you to the airport."

Spears swung his legs over the bedside and plunged his yellow socks into his sneakers. "Beats hell out of walking."

Hal Dexter stood, face set hard, but feeling inwardly relieved. He'd never been sold on this project, and he certainly knew which side his bread was buttered on. "Joseph," he said, "you'd better get hustling. We'll have to make restitution on the stock you've sold — unless you want to battle with the Securities and Exchange Commission."

Bartz raised himself slowly and shambled up to Forsythe. He said, "Why did you never inform us that Colonel Ensign was the mayor's father-in-law?"

"You never asked," Forsythe said.

Spears laughed.

"Tell me something else," Bartz said. "What's so terrible about our project? What's wrong with these people? Don't they like prosperity? Do they want to live all their lives on the edge of poverty? What the hell's wrong with them?"

Forsythe thought about it, chewing his pipestem. Then he said, "Maybe it's their pride."

Bartz studied the attorney's face, then flung his short arms sideways. "Bah!" he said.

"Bah to you," Forsythe said.

***

Nathan Chambers forced himself to move. He tugged feebly at Coody, barely more than a corpse with whitened brows, shoulders hunched under tons of cold. "Let's walk," Nathan said.

"Walk, shit. You only want to go in circles."

"Like I said. We need to stay by the wreckage. It's our best chance of being found."

"Hell, they're not looking," Coody said. He toppled over.

Nathan dropped beside him. He lay on his back, staring into the deep purple. The sky was immense, filling his whole vision. He could see Valerie again, face coming down to him from way up there, like an angel, her slender arms extended toward his reaching hands... But as before, she was too far from him. They were both reaching, but they couldn't... quite... touch.

This time she was smiling, though — a dimpled, flashing smile. A flash...

A real flash was up there — a glint of sunlight about thirty degrees above the northern horizon.

Another bright flicker, higher and closer, merged with a faint engine drone.

An airplane? Chambers considered the possibility with a melancholy state of mind.

He sat upright.

"Hey. An airplane." He slapped at the pilot. "You hear me? It's a plane, heading this way."

Coody swiveled his head toward the sound, loud enough now to be unmistakable.

In seconds, the yellow Stearman biplane swelled to life-size, its blunt piston-clogged nose aimed directly at them, its pilot's white face peering through sun-smeared Plexiglass. It thundered overhead in a gush of wind, its wings waggling.

"He saw us!" Coody said.

"Yes he did," Nathan said. "Yes he did."

The open-cockpit Stearman climbed steeply, its double spread of yellow wings whirling in sunlight. It peeled over like a banana skin and swiped at the trembling tundra with a monstrous roar.

"Pete Hawkins!" Nathan Chambers shouted. "You old son-of-a-bitch! Quit showing off and get down here! Come on down, you old bastard!"

Chambers and Coody were both on their feet, flinging tired arms while the biplane completed a dazzling barrel roll.

From the north came other metallic reflections, these on the ground, strung in a wide line at the edges of a thin sheet of snow. Chambers could faintly hear the snarl — of snowmobile engines.

"Hey," Chambers yelled, slugging Coody on the shoulder. "We're having a big old party!"

Coody fell against Chambers, wrapping weighted arms around Nathan's shoulders and thumping his back. Grappling with each other like punchdrunk prizefighters, the two men hopped and stumbled on the hard ground, gurgled out breathless grunts that substituted for laughter, shed watery tears that dribbled across purpled cheeks and froze in the fringes of their beards.

"Hope they brought girls!" Coody hooted.

And still the Stearman rolled and looped while men with hand-held radios flashed messages back and forth, rounding up all the scattered elements of their search team and announcing the electrifying news of discovery —

— While the frosted remains of Russell Bancroft rippled faintly in the wind from each pass of the Stearman's mighty propeller...

Chapter 53: Epilogue

Back to the Present

TEETERING ON CRUTCHES, Doc Fuller managed a crash-dive into his leather chair. The cast on his leg had nicks and cracks from many collisions. Even so, Doc smiled at his quiet guest, the young ski patrolman with his laptop computer. This fellow had said he was actually 34 years old, but anybody that young was just a boy to Doc Fuller.

Doc said, "None of us knew Russell Bancroft had conceived a son. In fact, I wonder if Russell knew."

The ski patrolman nodded. "He didn't. My mom didn't know until a month after Russell died. That's when she decided to name me Russell Bancroft-French."

Doc's face showed some concern. "How is your mom?"

"Actually, not bad. She's okay being a single parent now that I'm a real adult. Her years of hard work have paid off. She also owns a souvenir shop in Seattle."

"That's good to hear," Doc said. "Lana skipped out the day after they found your father..." He took a breath. "And we haven't heard from her since."

"Well, I think she was mad at everybody here, especially Nathan Chambers. She blamed him for my father's death. That's why I came here, to settle things concerning him."

"I see." Doc inhaled and grabbed a handful of papers he had brought to the table beside his chair. "Then you oughta show her this old stuff."

Russell accepted the papers. "What is all this?"

"What you asked for. They're copies I kept of the *Spectator* newspaper clips about Nathan, including his mayoral speech at the 1974 Chamber of Commerce Christmas banquet. Ben Bayliss helped Nate with that speech; so the clips are pretty accurate. But there's one part where Nate ignored the script and mentioned... uh, pardon me, that's the wrong word. He *eulogized* your father. I was there, you see..."

***

That December evening in 1974 contained the chilly dampness that often precedes a storm from the Pacific.

Montana had not received any fresh snow since mid-November. Except for some old dirty snow in pockets hidden from the sun, Jackpine was dry and brown. The Christmas wreaths wired to lampposts looked forlorn against a muddy sky.

On the hills to the east, what appeared from a distance to be a huge and brightly lighted Christmas tree was only a core drilling rig leased by Consolidated Energy. Up close, under its intense lights, it was a clanking metal monster coated with rust and grease. It sometimes bloodied the hands of the crewmen who worked it around-the-clock in ankle-deep mud. They had extracted a few truckloads of coal samples, but mostly they were bringing up water. The geologists were not happy.

In the log-raftered dining room of the Pine Ridge Supper Club, Nathan and Valerie Chambers sat at the head banquet table, arranged perpendicular to four other long tables occupied by Chamber members. Festive holly and wreaths dangled from ceiling fixtures, and red candles burned on the tables.

Nathan sat sideways, fidgeting with his napkin, watching his wife. Valerie sat contentedly at the finish of her meal, her complexion golden in the candlelight. Nathan watched her profile, so perfectly presented in the flickering highlights and shadows, until Valerie felt his eyes and turned.

"Nervous?" she whispered.

Chambers nodded. He had made speeches for his high school debating team, but that had been long ago. Now he faced the mayor's annual stint to address the Chamber's Christmas banquet — as the first *new* mayor in many years.

Pharmacist Jack Monroe, the organization's retiring president, stood at the rostrum introducing new officers and directors. Nathan paid no attention. He preferred to study his wife's profile.

There were at least three times when Valerie's beauty had affected Nathan profoundly, the first time being when they had met, obviously.

The second time, Nathan had barged into Valerie's hospital room after coming off the plateau. His sister Rebecca had been there, and for a moment neither woman had recognized Nathan. His face had been copper-colored and whiskered, his lips purpled and swollen. Then Valerie had inhaled a storm of breath and rushed at him, coming up from her bed in pain, her face contorted, landing barefoot on the tops of his dirty boots, clutching at him through the thickness of his damp parka. Despite all that, despite the news he'd received that they had lost their son, Nathan had found Valerie to be beautiful beyond belief.

The third time was right now, in candlelight. Valerie, for whatever reason, wore a shorter and higher hair style that exposed her graceful neck. This displayed a fresh and mature aspect of her beauty that Nathan hadn't noticed before. In fact, Nathan saw many facets to Valerie that he hadn't noticed until recently.

"... Mayor Nathan Chambers," said Monroe's voice.

Hearing his name on the restaurant's public address system, Chambers surveyed the hundred expectant faces in the audience. Monroe, having finished the introduction, stood aside from the rostrum.

Chambers went to make his speech.

***

Doc Fuller pointed to a few highlighted paragraphs in the clippings. "You asked me about those small pine trees up on the mountain. Remember?"

"I do," Russell French said. "Everyone asks about them."

Doc said, "Well, going back to 1974, here's where Nathan introduces them."

***

Nathan stared at his audience. He said, "Does anyone still want a ski development, coal mining, or any other new industry in Jackpine?"

The question, as promised by Bayliss, grabbed the audience's attention.

"Well, despite all that's happened in this incredible year, from President Nixon's impeachment nightmares to our own tribulations, a future lies ahead — and a ski project remains feasible.

"Some men from Billings recently came to me with a proposal. They had heard about our problems and came up with an idea. They had taken a look at Aero Mountain, where the steel companies tore everything apart for chromium during World War Two. It's an ugly mountain, barren and eroded. But in winter, covered with snow, it looks okay. And they said packing that snow for ski runs would hold the moisture longer. The runoff would be less severe. Grass and trees could grow again, and we could plant windbreak trees cheaper than cutting and transporting thick stands of non-lumber trees, just to clear ski runs on healthier mountains."

Nathan swallowed some water, then said, "That makes sense. We'd fix a mountain instead of ruining one. We could tackle just one piece at a time. After all, the mountain's not going anywhere.

"And that notion appealed to me so much, I've decided on something better to do than work in my Pop's store. I'm going to apply some engineering, finally, and work on plans to fix that miserable mountain. And every chance I get, I'm going up there to plant trees..."

***

Russell French sat upright, astonished. "You mean, *he* planted all those trees? Like Johnny Appleseed?"

For the second time in a single day, Doc managed a smile. He said, "No, he didn't. Remember, this was more than thirty-some years ago. He got things started, though.

He rounded up investors, volunteer workers, forestry experts, scout troops, whatever. Nathan's ski project picked up momentum, much like when this community built its own hospital and schools. Federal programs were out there, but nobody here wanted to deal with the bureaucracies."

Doc settled back. He concluded his assessment with a semi-serious frown. "So, after thirty-odd years of hard work and private financing, we've got a decent ski area. Except it attracts too damn many people in my opinion."

Wriggling forward in his easy chair, Doc pointed to another marked series of paragraphs. "Now look here. This is where Nathan talks about your father."

***

Nathan Chambers sipped more water and looked up from the rostrum. Seeing mild boredom, he said, "I want to say something about Russell Bancroft."

The listeners set down their wine glasses and raised their faces. The room became still.

"Russell was my lifelong friend, and I never found satisfaction with local attitudes about his death. Whatever you think, his death was not an insult to this town.

"I don't deny he made tragic mistakes. But you people should try to understand, like I've tried, over and over..."

Chambers lowered his head.

"You see... " He leaned across the rostrum and spread his right arm. "This great land around us, it was endangered. None of us felt like we could do much. After all, those were rich and powerful strangers mounting a real huge invasion against us. But Russ was willing to try. He was, in fact, determined to try."

Chambers straightened up. "Well, it didn't turn out the way he wanted. Erwin Wooster got killed. That hit Russ hard in the gut, because he... well, because this town wasn't his target. And he sure's hell didn't want to hurt anyone, especially an old coal miner who had worked with his father. So Russell went up on that plateau and died there. And I don't think his death was entirely an accident."

Chambers gazed out to an audience of frozen faces.

"Because Russ died on the plateau, the people of this town were spared the cost and trauma of a public trial. I'm sure that's exactly how Russ wanted it to end, with no further embarrassment to our citizens."

He hesitated a moment.

"Don't get me wrong. I'm not saying Russ committed deliberate suicide. But I think he took a deliberate gamble. I think he put himself in a situation where his chances for survival were no better than fifty-fifty. And then... well, he left himself in the hands of God."

Chambers drank more water, set down the glass. "So don't you folks dare feel ashamed of him. I sure don't."

Dead silence filled the room.

"Our land is our inheritance, and only fools will squander it. Have you ever noticed the kind of feeling you get when you see the beauty of this land? It's like evidence of a grand design, isn't it? I think I can actually see that an intricate and perfect order, not chaos, controls the universe. That helps me when I face my own problems or think about my own destiny.

"It's in nature's examples of perfection and diversity that we discover our purposes. The word for that is 'inspiration,' and I just don't find it in places of steel and concrete the way I find it on a mountain or by a lake, among birds and animals and insects and fish and every other living thing.

"I suspect the highest human achievements have been inspired by observations of natural wonders. But in diminishing the wonders which God created for us, don't we separate ourselves farther from God?"

Chambers had never spoken such thoughts to anyone — not to his father or mother; not to his wife or sister.

"Yeah, I know. Some highly educated men don't believe in God. But they haven't produced any better explanation for this universe, or for miracles. But I'm off track."

Nathan shrugged and returned to his speech.

"With so much at stake, we can't rely on others to build our regional society based on needs or wants from elsewhere. We can't expect others to appreciate the power of this land when we're only beginning to realize it ourselves...

"I don't know what Consolidated Energy will finally do with its coal rights. I have no idea what other kinds of schemes are being hatched by developers with sights set on Montana. But I do know that I don't want to *depend* on them for my future prosperity or the prosperity of my future children. I don't want extremists from *any* viewpoint deciding the fate of my family.

"There is a founding document that set this nation free, by declaring our independence. We fought wars for that principle. Yet, as a nation we've committed the folly of dependence on foreign oil, and as a state we've enslaved ourselves to the federal government. And while free enterprise is a wondrous thing, it is not a license to steal.

"We should *never* surrender our independence as a community. You won't ever get things done your way, meeting your individual needs, by letting others do it for you — or to you. You have to take charge yourself.

"And if that's all I learned in the past six months, then it was worth it. I repeat: for that one lesson, that whole mess and all its personal sacrifices... was *worth* it."

Nathan turned away from the rostrum, reached out for Valerie's hand, and quickly led her toward the exit.

Some clapping and, gradually, a standing ovation followed them out.

***

Russell put down the news clippings. After a minute, he said, "This changes things. I had come here to express my mother's ill feelings to Mr. Chambers, about Dad's death."

Doc nodded. "And now?"

"Now, I can't wait to tell my mother we've been wrong. She'll be much happier. Me, too. Doc, how can I thank you?"

"Why don't you go talk to Nate. I don't think he knows about you. He will be excited to meet you."

"Okay. Last question: Where can I find him?"

"They've got a guest lodge on the old Ensign ranch, west of town. Old Arnold quit the cattle business before he died, left the place to Val and Nate. Guess what. It's on the edge of the Absaroka-Beartooth Wilderness, which the United States Congress okayed in 1975, just like your dad wanted. He should have gotten some credit for it, but... he didn't."

"Well. He would have been proud anyway," Russell said.

"I suppose he would," Doc agreed. "It also turned out to be better for Arnold's grandchildren than a ski area. Nowadays, Nate and Valerie get visitors from all over the world, and their kids help guide the visitors along wilderness trails to lakes and streams full of trout and sightings of wildlife. It keeps everyone in good shape, that hiking and cross-country skiing. And as you know, I'm kinda into skiing myself, for the same reason — stayin' young at ninety." His third smile.

"In fact, when you're up there, be sure and look at Val's collection of wildlife photographs. Some of them have been in National Geographic. And now there's one more thing."

Doc Fuller sat up and checked his watch. Struggling to his feet, he arranged the crutches under his armpits and said, "I wanna show you somethin' outside. Follow me."

On the front porch, Doc looked at his watch again and searched the stars until he located the blinking lights of a westbound jetliner on its nightly run.

"Look up there... You see that plane?"

Russell found it and asked, "How'd you know it's there?"

"I've been watching it for years, before going to bed," Doc said. "It's a ritual. Once, I looked up the schedule. That thing for five nights a week is full of your Seattle folks, and probably some movers and shakers from Chicago or New York City. And you know what?"

Russell shrugged. "I don't know. What?"

"I am absolutely positive, young man, not one of them passengers ever heard of Jackpine, Montana. Do your best to keep it that way."

(!)

THE AUTHOR:

DAVID HENDERSON began his journalism career in 1960s magazines, when he wrote personal interviews with Henry Fonda, Barbra Streisand, Robert Preston, Charlton Heston, and other luminaries, along with a wide range of news and features. As editor for a Chicago suburban newspaper chain owned by Time, Inc., he managed the content of several papers including *The Evanston Review*, chosen by a national newspaper publishers' association as First in the Nation for General Excellence. Later, as editor and publisher of a Montana weekly newspaper, he won the press association's top statewide awards for editorial writing, column writing, feature stories, and news reports. In California, he created national print and video marketing programs for San Francisco Bay Area daily newspapers, including those owned by Gannett, The Tribune Company, Media News Group, and The New York Times. He now owns a small-market publishing enterprise in Northern California, where he is lovingly partnered with his wife of 50 years. For a change of pace, Henderson also wrote *Escape!* (formerly *Deadly Dividends*), a cross-continent chase thriller based on his interests in architecture, road travel and "good old-style" romantic mysteries.

Henderson may be contacted via www.pinetreearts.com.

17090587R00189